THE SECRETS OF

STAR WARS

SHADOWS OF THE EMPIRE

THE SECRETS OF

STAR WARS

SHADOWS OF THE EMPIRE

MARK COTTA VAZ

A DEL REY® BOOK

BALLANTINE BOOKS • NEW YORK

A Del Rey® Book
Published by Ballantine Books

http://www.randomhouse.com

Library of Congress Cataloging-in-
Publication Data
Vaz, Mark Cotta.
    The secrets of Star Wars : Shadows of
the empire / Mark Cotta Vaz.
       p.   cm.
    "A Del Rey book".
    ISBN 0-345-40236-7
       1. Star Wars films—Miscellanea.
    2. Perry, Steve. Shadows of the empire.
    3. Merchandising.
    PN1995.9.S695V42   1996
    791.43'75—dc20   96-3602
                                      CIP

Cover art by Jon Knoles for LucasArts

Manufactured in the United States of
America
First Edition: May 1996
10 9 8 7 6 5 4 3 2 1

To my Father, the Sage; my Mother, the Sustainer;
and those young Jedi Knights: Daniel, Johnny,
Matthew, Michael, Katelin, and Joseph

"Do. Or do not. There is no try."
—Yoda

TABLE OF CONTENTS

CONTENTS

ACKNOWLEDGMENTS

Special thanks to all the Lucasfilm folks, especially Lucy Autrey Wilson for giving me a ticket to blast off into the *Star Wars* universe, to Howard Roffman for his time and interest, to Sue Rostoni for fact-checking assistance and various courtesies (plus the invaluable *Shadows* glossary), and to Julia Russo for her *Shadows* contributions. My special appreciation to Allan Kausch, editor on the Lucasfilm side, for keeping me in the *Shadows* loop and passing along all the varied works in progress (as well as behind-the-scenes correspondence), making sure I was in touch with all the creative principles, editing the text and captions, and generally being the day-to-day go-to guy.

Thanks to all the creative individuals who gave of their time and insights, particularly Steve Perry and Tom Dupree for their novel ideas; Jon Knoles and Mark Haigh-Hutchinson at LucasArts for introducing me to the mysteries of interactive, 3-D gaming; Ryder Windham and Peet Janes for the Dark Horse action; Bob Woods and Jean Scrocco for ushering me into the wonderful world of the Hildebrandt brothers; Robert Townson for helping me know the score; and editor Steve Saffel for leading the charge on the Del Rey Books side.

Star Wars *original theatrical release poster; art by Tommy Jung.*

INTRODUCTION:
AMERICAN
POP

IT WAS A SWELTERING SUMMER evening in Lahore, Pakistan, a city variously described as "the Gateway to Hell" or "the Garden City." The year was 1979, and a Mr. Mukhtar was escorting this writer around during a brief stopover on an overland journey from London to Nepal. Early in the day there was a prayerful stop in the cool interior of a mosque where he whispered of devotion, of the will of Allah, and of the day when waters would once again cover the earth. By twilight we were strolling through a flowering park where, out of the lush foliage, another temple rose and where flowing fountain water allowed supplicants to wash off the sweat of the day in preparation for the evening prayer. When darkness fell, we hurried off to the local cinema for the evening's exhibition of *Star Wars*.

At the theater the well-heeled higher castes could reserve their seats in the upper balconies while the lower castes, many dressed in rags, had to line up at a side door and file into a separate floor level. There was much laughter and good-natured jostling as that separate line snaked in under the stern eyes of burly, shirt-sleeved policemen. Inside, the place was comfortably cool from the manufactured breezes of electric fans lining the walls. Up in the upper balcony uniformed attendants sold sodas and cigarettes until the house lights dimmed.

The mood was expectant and raucous, even through a half-hour program of commercials for everything from cigarettes to air-conditioning units. Then the image of Muhammad Ali Jinnah, the young nation's first governor-general, flashed across the screen to the applause of the assembled. All rose to attention as the flag followed and the national anthem played. Then it was full blast into *Star Wars*, with the crowd cheering every space battle and murmuring in awe at the visions of deep space.

Since that first film circled theaters around the globe, the resulting *Star Wars* trilogy has taken in more than $1.3 billion in worldwide box office and an additional $2.5 billion in merchandising sales. Some twenty years later *Star Wars*–themed conventions and fan activity from Australia to the United Kingdom celebrate the original trilogy and anticipate the preparation and release of new chapters in the unfolding saga.

The global impact of *Star Wars* is emblematic of the march of American popular culture around the globe. This cultural exchange has appeared in forms as innocent as G.I. Joes giving American comic books to kids in occupied Japan, or as economically significant as the fact that in 1993, one of the most financially successful years in movie history, Hollywood's overseas returns exceeded domestic box office returns fifty-two percent to forty-eight percent.

The great American dream machine has been a century in the making, and flourishes thanks to the mass media that have produced a pantheon of heroic characters and fantastic story lines. Some characters born in a particular medium have crossed over into other venues, in the process becoming modern folklore figures. Other pop creations have had only a fleeting hold on the public's imagination and have been lost in time (perhaps buried in a stack of old comics disintegrating in someone's attic or fading away on some forgotten reel of rotting celluloid).

To see where *Star Wars* fits in the time line of America's pop culture, let's take a little time-traveling trip through some of the highpoints of fantasy and imagination.

• • •

In 1900 author Lyman Frank Baum's *The Wonderful Wizard of Oz* was published to great acclaim. Baum had written that "the time has come for a series of newer 'wonder-tales,' " and there was such widespread agreement that a stage play based on his book opened on Broadway in New York in 1903 and ran for nearly a decade, a 1908 screen version was produced by Baum's own Fairylogue and Radio-Plays company, and more than forty additional Oz books were published (with the series continued after Baum's death by Ruth Plumly Thompson). And, of course, the classic 1939 MGM *Oz* film continues to entertain new generations even as we approach the millennium.

On the cheap, wood-fiber-flecked pages of the pulp magazines, a medium whose golden age began in the 1920s (and that began faltering, and ultimately expired, in the 1950s), appeared some classic characters and genres. There was Edgar Rice Burroughs's *Tarzan of the Apes*, the lord of the jungle who generated numerous books, movies, and a TV series, and there were Lester Dent's globe-traveling adventures of that bronze-skinned marvel of muscularity and mental magnetism, Doc Savage. The hard-boiled detective genre was created in the pulps with two leading avatars: Dashiell Hammett, whose Continental Op and detective Sam Spade worked the dangerous, fog-shrouded San Francisco streets, and Raymond Chandler, whose two-fisted pulp tales led to his 1939 novel *The Big Sleep*, which introduced detective Philip Marlowe. (Both Hammett's famed *Black Mask* magazine story "The Maltese Falcon" and Chandler's *The Big Sleep* would be made into classic Hollywood films starring quintessential tough guy Humphrey Bogart.)

The powerful medium of radio produced the Shadow, the mysterious host narrator of pulp publisher Street & Smith's Thursday night *Detective Story Magazine* radio mystery, who closed each episode with the cackling note "The Shadow knows." That disembodied voice, floating over the airwaves, so beguiled audiences that a Shadow character was created to star in his *own* radio adventures and pulp magazine series.

The writer of the pulp novels was Walter Gibson, previously a ghost-writer for magicians such as Houdini and Blackstone, and he crafted that eerie voice into the hypnotic, hook-nosed man with the slouch hat and swirling cloak who prowled the underworld armed with his twin .45 automatics.

The newspaper comic strips ushered in heroes such as Buck Rogers, Flash Gordon, the Phantom, Prince Valiant, and Dick Tracy. The comic book medium was born out of the instinct to put newspaper funny pages between the covers of a tabloid magazine. The first superhero comic book appeared in 1938 when Superman sprang from the imagination of a teenager named Jerry Siegel one hot, sleepless night in 1932 when Siegel had a revelatory, waking dream image of a superhero combining the strength of Samson and Hercules. "The Man of Steel" was followed on the comics racks by the likes of Batman, Wonder Woman, Captain America, and literally hundreds of lesser lights. (In that "golden age" of comics any cartoon character who could fill out his or her tights was pressed into service against all manner of evildoers.)

The arrival of television in the fifties began to change the landscape of popular culture. Radio thrillers, the Saturday matinee serials, adventure comic strips, and comic books couldn't compete with the allure of those visual transmissions received by the cathode tubes in millions of home TV sets.

Perhaps the most successful TV adventure program in terms of enduring fan appeal and multimedia popularity took form in the *Star Trek* adventures of the crew of the starship *Enterprise*, which debuted in 1966 with the mission "to boldly go where no man has gone before."

That same year a real-life *Gemini 8* spaceship, after accomplishing the first docking with another orbiting space vehicle, had to abort *its* mission because of misfiring thruster rockets. *Gemini* astronaut Neil Armstrong and fellow crew member David Scott used all their piloting skill to achieve, and survive, an emergency Pacific splashdown. (Armstrong would ultimately help pilot the *Apollo 11* lunar module to a safe touchdown on the Sea of Tranquility and become the first human to set foot on the moon.)

Star Wars arrived at a dramatic confluence of mass media, new technological wonders (which made the likes of Buck Rogers and Flash Gordon—even Tracy with that two-way wrist radio—seem prescient), and quantum leap advancements in feature film visual effects. From that very first film, positioned as episode IV and set "a long time ago in a galaxy far, far away," it was clear that this saga would be unfolding for a long time to come.

Creator George Lucas had always envisioned a sprawling nine-part series, with the original trilogy focusing on the period of civil war between the evil rulers of the Galactic Empire and the freedom fighters of the Alliance who sought to restore the Republic. In this new universe hyperdrive technology could lock a starship into the transdimensional flow of hyperspace and allow space voyagers—from bounty hunters and smugglers to Imperial and Rebel fighting forces—to almost instantly traverse any place in the known galaxy. The hardships of such travel were reflected in the dirtied and dented spaceships and hardware representing what Lucas and his Industrial Light & Magic (ILM) visual effects artists would call a "used universe" approach (a revelation, given the polished spaceships and utopian cities of the science fiction films that had gone before). In addition to evoking the sense of a real time and place, the entire trilogy would be filled with allusions to a war between the Old Republic and the Empire, a golden age of Jedi Knights, and an ages-old struggle between the light and dark sides of a supernatural power known as the Force.

The virtually endless storytelling possibilities inherent in this boundless universe have proved irresistible. Thus, even though Lucas wrote and executive-produced the final installment of the original trilogy in 1983, that galaxy of long ago and far away did not, like a dream, dissipate. Ongoing explorations into the *Star Wars* universe (apart from the cinematic jurisdictions—which Lucas would reserve for himself) would be conducted in a variety of different media, including a series of popular novels, comic books, role-playing games, toys, and interactive computer games, in the process enlarging the vision of an expanding universe.

In 1995 these creative explorations took a bold new direction with the development of the original story line, *Shadows of the Empire*. Unlike previous tales, which had been set in the past or future relative to the trilogy (or, if set in the time period of the movies, were kept wholly apart from the events of the films), *Shadows* would be seamlessly woven *into* the fabric of the original trilogy, picking up the threads left dangling at the end of *The Empire Strikes Back*.

In another unique move, Lucasfilm decided not only to explore *Shadows* through all the traditional licensing venues that today accompany blockbuster movie releases but also to extend the original story through various media *simultaneously*, including a Bantam Books novel, a six-part Dark Horse Comics series, a real-time 3-D interactive game produced by Lucas's own LucasArts division (which would be one of the first games produced for the breakthrough Nintendo 64 game sys-

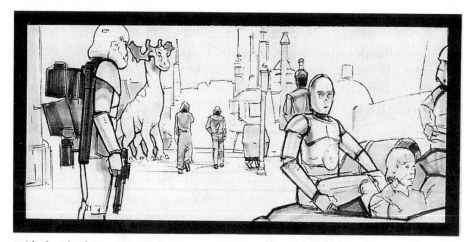

With the Shadows *story line encompassing a variety of media—from a novel and comics series to a computer game and toy figures—continuity was vital, and Lucasfilm's voluminous* Star Wars *archives were an invaluable resource. A Mos Eisley storyboard sequence, prepared by Industrial Light & Magic for the expanded version of the original* Star Wars *(set for release on the film's twentieth anniversary), also provided a valuable reference for computer gamers and comics creators.*
ILM Mos Eisley storyboard by TyRuben Ellingson.

With Han Solo frozen in carbonite and a prisoner of bounty hunter Boba Fett during the Shadows *action, other hands must man the controls of the fabled Millennium Falcon. In this scene Lando Calrissian (back in command of the ship he lost to Han in a sabacc card game), Chewbacca, Princess Leia, and C-3PO follow the lead of Luke Skywalker and the Rogue Squadron en route to a daring attempt to rescue Han.*

   Shadows Dark Horse Comic, *issue 2, page 6; unedited pencils by Kilian Plunkett.*

7

tem), a Topps card set, and even a recording produced by sound track specialists Varese Sarabande Records. As numerous creative participants voiced as one: "*Shadows of the Empire* is like a movie project without the movie."

The seeds of the *Shadows* project had been planted several years earlier during a dinner meeting between Lucasfilm publishing director Lucy Autrey Wilson and Lou Aronica of Bantam, the house that had been publishing the *Star Wars* novelizations. "He suggested that because of Lucasfilm's licensing arrangements—which cover everything from books and comics to toys and other merchandising as well as LucasArts Entertainment, our own interactive games company—we were perfectly positioned to do a multimedia event, with one story line going through different product categories," recalls Wilson, a Lucasfilm employee since being hired by Lucas after the release of *American Graffiti.*

"*Star Wars* seemed the best property to do such a project," Wilson continues. "A couple of years later the idea just seemed right. We could see down the road and realized 1996 was the perfect year, since there were no other major *Star Wars* projects, such as a movie launch. The idea was to allow two years to plan everything out. We wanted to have our key licensees involved, taking into account each medium and its particular requirements. But the project couldn't be a free-for-all; it had to be a directed, creative collaboration with a time line and a basic story premise. We had our initial planning meeting in the summer of 1994, and after that everything began to happen quickly."

The significance of the *Shadows* story would be found in its revelations of the political connection between the Empire and a galactic-wide criminal underworld. Waiting in the *Shadows* would be a plot revolving around the power struggle between Darth Vader and a new character named Xizor—reptilian overlord of the underworld. At stake would be dominion over the galaxy, with Luke Skywalker and Princess Leia caught in the deadly web of intrigue.

PART 1

THE EXPANDING UNIVERSE

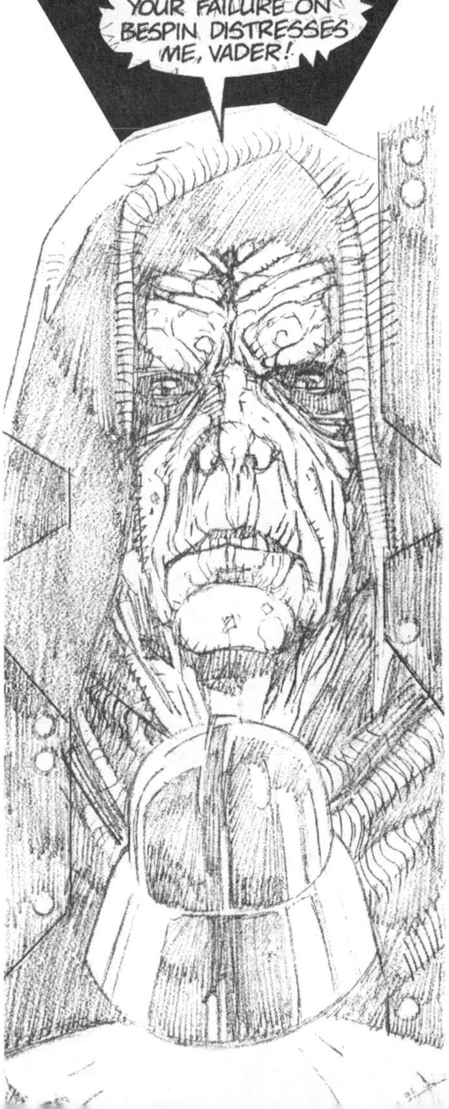

With Shadows of the Empire *set in the time of the original movie trilogy, Darth Vader remains a force to be reckoned with.*

  Shadows *Dark Horse Comic, issue 1, page 10; unedited pencils by Kilian Plunkett.*

I.
THE *SHADOWS* TALE

"When a renegade hero became a friend in desperate need and a dark villain faced his greatest challenge . . . When the Empire turned more and more to the forces of the underworld . . . the underworld moved in to crush the Empire and the Rebellion in a single stroke . . . After *The Empire Strikes Back* and before *Return of the Jedi*, there was a time when heroes and villains alike lived in the *Shadows of the Empire*."
(Voice-over narration excerpt from Lucasfilm promotional trailer)

IN ACTION-FILLED ADVENTURE MOVies the good guys are supposed to be in a high-fiving, victorious mood by the time the final credits roll. So it had been at the conclusion of *Star Wars*: the Empire's Death Star destroyed, Luke Skywalker seemingly growing in confidence and command of the Force, Princess Leia restored to freedom with the heroes Skywalker, Han Solo, and Chewbacca, and the droids R2-D2 and C-3PO honored by an Alliance assembly in a resplendent Rebel base throne room.

But when the much-anticipated sequel was released in 1980, the story would take an ominous turn. The title said it all: *The Empire Strikes Back*. From the opening battle on the ice planet of Hoth where Imperial forces routed a Rebel encampment to the final dramatic showdown on the Cloud City of Bespin, the dark side of the Force was in ascendance. By the time the final credits crawled, Han Solo had been frozen alive in carbonite and delivered into the hands of the bounty hunter Boba Fett for delivery to the crime lord Jabba the Hutt, while Luke Skywalker, who had seen his right hand severed and had nearly been killed in a lightsaber battle won by Darth Vader, was being comforted by Leia and the droids in the medical bay of an escaping Rebel cruiser.

Although *Empire* had its share of horrors and evil triumphant, it also introduced the sage Jedi Master Yoda, who revealed more about the mysterious Force. The darker tone of the second installment also allowed for a sharpening of the conflicts driving both the individuals and an entire galaxy in the grip of civil war. The film provided a galactic tour of fantastic new worlds: the icy wastelands of Hoth, Yoda's dark swamp world of Dagobah, and the mining post and trading station of Cloud City floating high in the atmosphere above the gaseous planet Bespin.

On the production side, the success of the saga's fifth chapter helped showcase the breakthrough work of Lucas's ILM effects division and solidified Lucas's growing entertainment enterprises, which had settled across the Golden Gate Bridge from San Francisco, in Marin County.

For Howard Roffman, Lucasfilm's vice president in charge of licensing and one of the architects of the *Shadows of the Empire* story line, *The Empire Strikes Back* remains a significant personal and professional experience. "I had been recruited by Lucasfilm out of a law firm in Washington, D.C., and was hired about two weeks before *Empire* was released," Roffman explains. "I was into corporate law and essentially had no business going to an entertainment company, but they were looking for young talent regardless of entertainment experience. I was a little nervous when I attended the premiere, because all my friends

Bounty hunter Boba Fett, bound in his Slave I *to deliver Han Solo to Jabba the Hutt, gloats in the presence of his frozen victim. But others lurk in space to try to claim the prize.*

Shadows *Dark Horse Comic, issue 1, page 17; unedited pencils by Kilian Plunkett.*

had been saying things like 'You're crazy for taking that job; *Star Wars* was just a fluke.' Because of that talk I didn't go in with high expectations, but I was totally blown away. The film was not only exciting and full of dazzling visual effects, but the whole Zen master dimension of Yoda and the Force really turned my head."

Sixteen years later the conclusion of *Empire* would provide the jumping-off point for the special *Shadows* adventure. Originally, however, *Shadows* had been planned for positioning between *Star Wars* and *Empire*. Early project discussions between Lucasfilm principals Howard Roffman and Lucy Wilson and the LucasArts games division had piqued the imagination of artist and game designer Jon Knoles, a font of *Star Wars* lore who had previously worked on LucasArts computer games such as TIE Fighter and Dark Forces. In a memo to Lucasfilm, Knoles broached the idea of setting *Shadows* between the second and third films instead. In Knoles's view, that time period provided more cliff-hanging, dramatic possibilities, and Lucasfilm agreed.

"The period between *Empire* and *Return of the Jedi* is a very dramatic time, filled with tension," Roffman notes. "Since we wanted to set

Shadows in the time period of the original trilogy, it seemed the perfect place for a bridge story. It's in the midst of the Rebellion, and Luke Skywalker, who's very vulnerable because he hasn't finished his Jedi training, is now diverted because he wants to rescue Han Solo, who's encased in carbonite and in the biggest peril he's ever been in. On the Imperial front you have the Emperor embarking on his plans to build a second Death Star while Vader is obsessed with finding his son and turning him to the dark side. So *Shadows* basically works off all these threads, adding the dimension of

Jon Knoles, LucasArts' lead artist and game designer. It was Knoles who suggested to Lucasfilm that the Shadows *story line be staged in the previously unexplored time period between* The Empire Strikes Back *and* Return of the Jedi. *Photo by Heather Sutton.*

the Empire and its relationship to the underworld, because we know that organized crime exists in the *Star Wars* universe."

It was in the first film, in a smoky cantina in Mos Eisley, the frontierlike spaceport city on Luke Skywalker's home planet of Tatooine, that audiences got their first real look at the gritty underbelly of the *Star Wars* universe. In this spaceport dive bounty hunters, smugglers, and other mercenary characters from across the universe met to intoxicate themselves, exchange gossip and schemes, and generally unwind from the hard life of roaming the spaceways. In his original *Star Wars* script George Lucas describes this den of thieves as "filled with a startling array of weird and exotic alien creatures and monsters at the long metallic bar. At first the sight is horrifying. One-eyed, thousand-eyed, slimy, furry, scaly, tentacled, and clawed creatures huddle over drinks."

That fabled bar would be the setting for some important events in the saga. It was there that Luke and the Jedi Master Obi-Wan Kenobi, while looking for an enterprising aerial ace, met and hired rogue pilot Han Solo for an off-world flight. But before Han left the cantina to join Skywalker and Kenobi, he'd have a fateful encounter with Greedo, a Rodian bounty hunter and an agent of the fearsome crime lord

Luke Skywalker; preliminary character sketch by Kilian Plunkett.

HOW 70s
? Pattern? IS TOO 70s?

- Pockets?

Gun
or
no
Gun?

Tatooine
Costume
- Back
to Basics? -

Kinda like
Luke's gear
in New Hope
but older looking
+ Mature + other stuff (?)

15

Jabba the Hutt. In the resulting scene, the audience learned that Han had dropped a smuggling shipment meant for Jabba, who in retribution had placed a bounty on Solo's head. Greedo had come to collect the dues, but the fire from Solo's blaster took him out first.

By the time of *Empire* the mysterious masked bounty hunter Boba Fett would, at the behest of both Jabba and Darth Vader, successfully track Han Solo and the *Millennium Falcon* to Bespin's Cloud City. Captured and carbonited, Solo's frozen-alive form would, by *Jedi*, be on display in the inner sanctum of Jabba's cavernous palace on Tatooine, a stronghold for space pirates, smugglers, bounty hunters, and killer droids, all of whom would do Jabba's bidding.

Lucas's original *Star Wars* script described Jabba as a gross, scarred-face killer, "a fat, sluglike creature with eyes on extended feelers and a huge ugly mouth." For the film, a scene had been shot in which Han, after leaving the cantina, would be confronted by Jabba at a Tatooine docking bay (with the production department planning to add the gruesome crime lord to the live-action footage as an optically composited effect). The key scene was cut, however, because of the limits of time and the visual effects technology that would be required to bring Jabba to life. Although the plot line of the bounty on Solo would thread through the trilogy, the Jabba scene was easily excised as Lucas, despite his dreams of a multichapter movie series, had no studio assurances that there would be further episodes if his space opera bombed at the box office.

With success, time, and technology in hand, Jabba would be successfully produced as a giant cable-puppeteered foam latex creature for *Jedi*. (The original docking bay footage would be resurrected by Lucas and cut into a twentieth-anniversary special edition *Star Wars* rerelease, with ILM digitally compositing a three-dimensional computer graphic Jabba into the scene.)

In the trilogy Jabba was presented as the all-powerful crime lord, although not in the same power league as the omnipotent Lord Vader. But in *Shadows* the balance of power in the underworld would shift from the gross, sluglike Hutt to the elegant, deadly "Dark Prince" Xizor (pronounced "Shee-zor"), the head of a galactic crime syndicate known as Black Sun and the third most powerful figure in the Empire, behind Darth Vader and Emperor Palpatine. Content to scheme from the anonymity of the shadows, Xizor maintains a public front as a shipping magnate commanding a fleet of freighters, hauling vessels, and escort ships. Both his Xizor Transport Systems (XTS) offices and his fortress-like palace and skyhook (a personal space station tethered to a planet's surface) are conveniently headquartered in the Imperial City, the Empire's capital city on the Imperial home planet of Coruscant.

The *Shadows* tale revolves around a deadly power struggle between Xizor and Vader for the ultimate confidence of the Emperor. With the tentacles of his Black Sun reaching into every dark corner of the universe, Xizor sees his influence with Palpatine growing, while Vader, sensing the ultimate danger to the Empire, warns the Emperor against this dark communion with the underworld. While Vader unleashes the Imperial Starfleet in a quest to locate his son, Xizor senses a paternal weakness in the once-impenetrable armor of the Dark Lord of the Sith. Xizor plots to find Skywalker first, assassinate the young Jedi, and displace

Xizor; early concept art by Paul Topolos, LucasArts.

Vader in the power structure by convincing the Emperor that Vader's emotional attachment to his progeny has put Imperial interests at risk.

The complex connection between Vader and Luke was another narrative thread picked up from *Empire*. In that film Vader would haunt Luke even as he began his Jedi training with Yoda on the swampy world of Dagobah. Full of youthful, indomitable spirit, Luke decided to leave Dagobah and help his friends defeat the Imperial powers. A frustrated Yoda could only warn that with his fledgling grasp of the Force

Emperor Palpatine commands the services of Xizor's shipping operations in preparation for the construction of a new Death Star, much to the consternation of Vader. (Of course, the wily Palpatine secretly delights in the power struggle that rages around him.)

Emperor and Imperial City throne room; concept art by Paul Topolos, LucasArts.

and his raw anger, Luke would be defeated if he rushed into battle against Vader. During one of their last training sessions together a resigned Yoda sat back as Luke entered a dark cave where he encountered the form of Vader and, in a dreamlike lightsaber battle, severed the Dark Lord's helmeted head, which, as was revealed when the dark mask shattered open, wore Luke Skywalker's countenance.

That hallucinatory encounter in the cave had been a grim foreshadowing. In the actual confrontation between Vader and Skywalker, staged on a gantry bridging a reactor shaft in the core of the Cloud City, Yoda's worst fears would be realized. Although Luke would display a relentless fighting spirit, Vader's dark side ferocity would end the battle, with a stroke of his lightsaber blade cleanly severing Luke's right hand, leaving him in shock, clinging to a narrow platform above a sheer drop. Vader announced that he was Luke's father, and rather than accept Vader's entreaties to join the Imperial cause, Luke relinquished his hold, went into free fall, and was sucked down to an exhaust port on the underside of the floating city. Dangling from an antennalike device, young Skywalker would be miraculously rescued by the passing *Millennium Falcon*, piloted by Princess Leia.

In the time between *Empire* and *Jedi*, one could imagine Luke's confusion on discovering that he wasn't an orphan but that his father lived—and was his hated enemy. The young, vulnerable Jedi would also be feeling the siren call of the dark side.

Part of the fun in conjuring up the plot situations and new characters for *Shadows of the Empire* lay in answering all these dramatic questions and possibilities. "In *Shadows* we go into and explain a lot of things only alluded to in the movies," Roffman observes, "such as, how did Leia get that Boushh bounty hunter disguise she's wearing when we first see her in *Jedi*? In *Jedi* there's also a briefing session where Rebel leader Mon Mothma explains that many Bothans died to obtain plans for the Empire's new Death Star. Although it wasn't important for George to have a such a scene in the movies, it obviously happened and was such an important event that we decided to include that in the *Shadows* story line."

A gallery of new characters would also be created for *Shadows*: Xizor, the dark star of the proceedings, followed by Dash Rendar, a rogue smuggler and an ace pilot cut from the Han Solo mold. The new cast members would include Guri, a female human replica droid who serves Xizor as a trusted aide and fearsome assassin, and LE-BO2D9 (Leebo), Dash's loyal droid and copilot.

The *Shadows* world would have to be outfitted with a host of new hardware, notably Xizor's personal ship, the *Virago*; Dash Rendar's battle-ready *Outrider*; and the swoop bikes favored by some particularly nasty biker gangs. New environments would range from the labyrinthine complex of Xizor's palace fortress on Coruscant to the moons of Gall and Kile orbiting Zhar, a giant planet with a deadly, gaseous atmosphere out in the same galactic system that includes Luke's home planet of Tatooine.

Of course, it is to Tatooine, and Jabba's desert palace, that Boba Fett is bound at the end of *Empire*. Then, in *Shadows*, Fett is beset by fellow bounty hunters eager to appropriate Han Solo's carbonite form and claim Jabba's reward. One of those on Boba's tail is the battle droid IG-88, another bit player in the films who first appeared in *Empire* as one of the group of bounty hunters hired by Vader to track down the *Millennium Falcon*.

Although IG-88 is defeated by Boba Fett in space combat, Fett's ship, the *Slave I*, is damaged, and the bounty hunter must land on Gall for emergency repairs. When Fett's ship is sighted, Princess Leia decides to hire Dash Rendar to lead a rescue of Han Solo, taking a team to Fett's location. The omnipotent Empire, of course, maintains an Imperial presence on Gall, and any rescue attempt will have to brave the collected might of two Star Destroyers and a host of TIE fighters.

The pursuit of Boba Fett by both Han's friends and greedy bounty hunters eager to snatch away the carbonited prize would provide an important subplot for the Dark Horse Comics *Shadows* story line. The other media would have their own parallel story lines and specific requirements, such as LucasArts' emphasis on action elements and player/character Dash Rendar's journey through the *Shadows* universe. In the domain of the written word tensions and conflicts between characters would be featured, from the Xizor-Vader intrigues to Luke Skywalker's personal struggle with both his Jedi training and the knowledge that his father is Darth Vader. Adding to the complexity of the project, each medium would feature both new *and* classic characters and environments.

Continuity has been the supreme commandment at Lucasfilm for *Shadows* and all its *Star Wars* projects. The company had made the decision not only to keep expanding its mythic universe but to have it unfold as a seamless chronicle. Whether a new star system is explored in a novel or a scene from ancient Jedi days is set in a comics series, nothing can contradict the history or logic of what has gone before.

To keep it all straight there is "the Canon," a time line of major events and the life span of characters prepared by the continuity editors at Lucasfilm and considered the in-house bible of the *Star Wars* universe. When further reference is needed, there are also stacks of binders listing everything from starship blueprints to the biographies of characters. Archival resources include all the painstakingly preserved movie props, models, costumes, and production art. All of it—from the bible to the treasures of the Lucasfilm archives—is located on the grounds of the famed Skywalker Ranch.

George Lucas had always envisioned the Ranch as a place that would provide the optimum environment in which creative people could do their best work. It was at the Ranch that *Shadows* was conceived by Lucasfilm creative personnel, where many of the project participants assembled for the meeting that finalized the key elements of the story, and from which the multimedia effort was guided.

The Main House at Skywalker Ranch.

II.
GALACTIC
LORE

ON THE PASTORAL GROUNDS OF Skywalker Ranch in Marin County, next to a horse corral, stands the barnlike structure that houses the treasures of Lucasfilm: the props, models, costumes, and art used in the making of Lucas's movies. In an auditorium-sized main room are *Star Wars* wonders such as Luke Skywalker's landspeeder, scale models for the Empire's All Terrain Armored Transports (the fearsome "walkers"), stormtrooper helmets, lightsabers, and even the life-sized slab of Han Solo's frozen carbonite form.

Another building on the grounds holds *Star Wars* storyboards, production illustrations, and costume designs. Lucas's original *Star Wars* story notes, written in longhand on legal tablets, are also preserved, locked away in a safe in the Victorian-style walls of the Main House. A time capsule containing *Star Wars* memorabilia—including the letter from Lucas's then-attorney confirming a green light from 20th Century-Fox for his space opera—was buried in the ground when the foundation for the Main House was poured in 1981.

This eye toward history and the instinct for preservation have been matched by the intellectual effort at maintaining continuity for a mythic saga that annually grows beyond the perimeters of the original movie trilogy. "The premise of all the comic books, novels, games, and other spin-off works is that they all work chronologically, that the continuity forms one unbroken story," explains Lucasfilm continuity editor Allan Kausch, who, along with production editor Sue Rostoni, is the steward of the history of the expanding *Star Wars* universe. "There are other properties in which spin-off works are consistent with the main characters but are all over the map as far as overall continuity.

"Since our movies have their own internal continuity, we maintain that in the spin-off works," Kausch explains. "Technically, George Lucas has been doing continuity all along by mapping out the nine films. But it wasn't until 1991, when Timothy Zahn wrote the novel *Heir to the Empire*, the first *Star Wars* best-seller, which was the beginning of what we call the *Star Wars* renaissance, that continuity became an issue."

Although licensed products tied to major movie releases have by the mid-1990s become customary (it almost wouldn't be a major release if there wasn't fashion wear or a fast-food mug attached to it), before the *Star Wars* phenomenon premarketing and merchandising tie-ins were virtually unheard of.

"*Star Wars* was absolutely the first major movie license that actually worked; it created the licensing industry," observes writer Steve Sansweet, a Los Angeles bureau chief of the *Wall Street Journal* and a leading collector of *Star Wars* memorabilia. "The only prior exception had been Walt Disney, who had been successful since the mid-1930s in licensing his characters. Disney was a visionary who realized that not only did licensed merchandise provide revenue, it helped make Disney characters a part of growing up, a part of the family.

"There were other licenses that came and went very quickly. Buck Rogers was real popular in the thirties; there was Flash Gordon, some stuff from the 1939 *Wizard of Oz* movie, but not a lot in the way of toys. But there wasn't the mass merchandise we see today until *Star Wars* broke through. When *Star Wars* was released in 1977, worldwide licensed products generated about $6 billion a year—by 1990 licensing revenue became about $60 billion. I can't think of a licensed line that's been as successful that came purely out of the movie medium."

As a case in point, Sansweet cites 20th Century-Fox's attempt to license through Mattel a line of toys for its release of *Doctor Dolittle*, a hugely expensive 1967 musical that starred Rex Harrison as the man who could "talk to the animals." Sansweet notes: "It bombed, and the toys went nowhere. That's why there was such reluctance in the beginning for any licenses on *Star Wars*. Even Kenner, the first *Star Wars* toy licensee, expected the movie would come and go. But the film had such a cool group of characters and vehicles, Kenner thought kids would just accept it as a space toy line."

Although merchandising had been an afterthought for Lucas and was anathema to the studio, the enterprising filmmaker managed to retain, in legendary style, the rights to any licensed products. In addition to Kenner, the first *Star Wars* licenses included a novelization of the film for Del Rey Books and a Marvel Comics series.

A notable source for early continuity glitches was the Marvel Comics series, which enjoyed a 107-issue run from 1977 through 1986. In those fledgling licensing days there was less creative control or direction for what often resembled an "alternative universe" to Lucas's saga. Campy creations emerged from the pages of those comics, such as Jaxxon, a pistol-packing six-foot green rabbit who teamed with Han Solo. The comics adventures generally had the Rebels on the run from Imperial forces,

Will Luke Skywalker save the galaxy—or destroy it? So asks the cover blurb on the debut issue of Marvel's Star Wars *series.*
Art by Howard Chaykin.

with stories revolving around the strange worlds and alien creatures encountered by the Alliance in its never-ending search for a safe haven.

Sometimes even the main heroes seemed out of character. On the cover of issue 2, a rather vigorous Ben Kenobi and a husky Luke Skywalker are alternately slicing and blowing away some mean-looking aliens in some dead-end cantina. "Swing that lightsabre [sic], Ben," Luke shouts, "or we're finished!"

Of course, the entire *Star Wars* universe was in flux during the period from 1975 through 1983, when the trilogy was being produced. In the first original *Star Wars* novel, *Splinter of the Mind's Eye* (written by Alan Dean Foster and published by Del Rey Books in 1978), a romance be-

CHARACTER SIZE CHART

CHEWBACCA	7'6"	LUKE SKYWALKER	5'8"
DARTH VADER	6'8"	SEE-THREEPIO	5'6"
STORMTROOPER	6'	PRINCESS LEIA	5'
BOBA FETT	6'	ARTOO-DETOO	3'2"
HAN SOLO	6'	YODA	2'2"
BEN KENOBI	5'9"		

Star Wars is a work in progress, with novels, comics, games, and other media constantly introducing new characters, places, and things. Continuity is the key, and to keep track of their expanding universe, Lucasfilm continuity editors have

tween Luke and Leia was alluded to, even though by the release of *Jedi* it would be revealed that they were brother and sister and that their mutual feelings were wholly familial.

By the end of *Jedi*, with the Rebels finally defeating the Imperial forces in the Battle of Endor and with the deaths of both Vader and Emperor Palpatine, the core trilogy of Lucas's dreams had fully entered the popular imagination. Utilizing the first *Star Wars* as year zero, the various spin-off novels, comics, games, and other media could be placed in a pre- and post-trilogy time line. The original films had a myriad of characters to keep track of: a core group of heroes including Luke, Leia, Han, Chewbacca, and the droids C-3PO and R2-D2; the Force-full presence of Obi-Wan and Yoda; Imperial villains such as Vader and the

WAMPA	11'	ZUCKUSS (bounty hunter)	5'8"
TAUNTAUN	8'	BOSSK (bounty hunter)	5'8"
IG-88 (bounty hunter)	6'5"	LOBOT (Lando's aide)	5'7"
DENGAR (bounty hunter)	6'	PROBOT	5'4"
LANDO CALRISSIAN	5'10"	UGNAUGHTS	3'4"
FX-7	5'9"		

a library of reference material covering everything from blueprints of the Millennium Falcon *to the character size chart pictured here.*

Emperor; and a galaxyful of alien creatures ranging from the Tusken Raiders of Tatooine to the furry Ewoks of Endor.

Lucas had staked out territory in the emerging time line to provide ground for his next *Star Wars* films, particularly the last years of the Republic and the young Jedi days of Obi-Wan Kenobi and Anakin Skywalker (aka Darth Vader), which would form the first three chapters in future films. Although spin-off stories were generally relegated to the period after *Jedi*, there were a few exceptions set in the time period of the original trilogy but distinct from the story lines of the films (such as

Darth Vader assembles some of the Galaxy's baddest bounty hunters to track down the Millennium Falcon *and her crew in this scene from* The Empire Strikes Back. *From left to right, these underworld mercenaries are: Dengar, IG-88, Boba Fett and Bossk.*

a 1995 Dark Horse Comics *Jabba the Hutt* series). Generally, the growing line of original comics and novels was pushing the historical chronology several post-trilogy decades into the future and four thousand years back into an ancient past of Jedi Knights and the occult masters known as the Dark Lords of the Sith. In the process new characters, historical events, and alien environments were embellishing and expanding what was being hailed as a modern mythology.

To keep track of the history of the universe, in 1992 Sue Rostoni began preparing a written chronology of events, from famous battles to the life spans of characters (which, as long as the universe keeps expanding, is an ongoing process). By 1994 Allan Kausch had begun translating the chronology into a visual reference, a taped-together scroll of 11 by 17-inch pieces of paper that unrolled to three feet in length and was marked with a horizontal time line drawn across and inscribed underneath with historic events.

"We have what we call Canon, which is the screenplays, novelizations, and other core works that are directly tied into the continuity, and then there are a lot of marginal things, like the old Marvel Comics series, that we don't really try to work into the continuity when we're planning new projects," Kausch explains. "Even the LucasArts interactive games have a premise, a backstory with player characters that we're trying to tie into the overall continuity. It is sort of a godlike undertaking. We are creating this universe as we go along, but somebody has to keep his finger on everything that came before."

To appreciate the breadth of the *Star Wars* universe, consider that more than four hundred major and minor characters are listed in *A Guide to the Star Wars Universe* (Bill Slavicsek, Del Rey Books: New York, 1994). "I have an on-line service, and someone E-mailed me a compendium of 112 single-spaced pages just on the planets," marvels Steve Perry, the science fiction and fantasy writer enlisted to author the Bantam Books novelization of *Shadows of the Empire*. "When I was hired on to the *Shadows* project, one of the first questions I asked Allan

Kausch was if someone had made a map of all the planets in the *Star Wars* universe. He just laughed. There's no way; there's too many planets. One of the things is, when a new writer comes on board, you have to do a lot of research if you're setting action in an established planet like Tatooine or Coruscant. It's very tempting to just create a new planet to serve the interests of a story."

Shadows of the Empire would mark the first time a significant spin-off story had been set directly *within* the dramatic flow of the core trilogy. The decision to have the main *Shadows* narrative reverberate through a novelization, a comic book series, and an interactive game posed major continuity challenges. "Part of the idea of using three different media was not to simply retell the same story but to look at the events from different perspectives," Roffman explains. "The novel looks at things from the overall Rebel-Imperial situation, the comics have more of a bent for Boba Fett and the bounty hunter side of the story, and the game focuses on the action sequences. Basically, it was a case of looking at which aspect of the story best fit each medium."

Shadows began as a two-page outline of the basic premise and main characters prepared by Roffman and Lucy Wilson (with George Lucas approving the project's setting within the flow of the original trilogy). With the story line set between the cliff-hanging action of *Empire* and *Jedi*, certain story points had coalesced, such as the idea of having an assassination plot threaten Luke, with a bodyguard type guarding the young Jedi Knight. Some particulars also had to be worked out, such as the name of the overlord of the underworld. "I came up with the name Xizor based on a cool Portuguese sound," Lucy Wilson recalls. "I had an old Portuguese boyfriend named Xico, with the 'x' sound pronounced 'sh.' I'd always liked that 'sh' sound, and I just combined it with the 'zor' ending of 'razor' to get a name that had an exotic and dangerous connotation to it."

After some fine-tuning of the plot elements during meetings between Lucasfilm and LucasArts, creative discussions began in earnest at Skywalker Ranch, with a key November 1994 meeting between Lucasfilm executives and many of the licensees, including LucasArts representatives and author Steve Perry on behalf of Bantam Books. Perry had come to the meeting with a list of characters, several of which would be incorporated into the crossover saga, including Guri, Xizor's trusted female replica assassin droid, and Koth Melan, head of the Bothan spy ring. Perry also introduced Dash Rendar, who would become the bodyguard character Roffman and Wilson had initially envisioned foiling the assassination plots against Luke Skywalker.

Since the meeting would be a somewhat freewheeling creative discussion, Perry performed secretarial duties, taking the notes that would inspire the basic *Shadows* story line. "I've written for television, which is a very collaborative universe, so at that initial meeting I was trying to get a sense of what everyone needed to have," Perry explains. "It was back and forth, all of us trying to decide what worked best for each medium. For example, having two swoop bike chase sequences was discussed, but it was decided that although that might work well in the LucasArts computer game, there only needed to be one in the novel.

"And right away, the games people wanted to use Dash Rendar as the player/character for their game. Ultimately, the outline I wrote from those notes became the template from which everything was to be constructed, and the book itself was the foundation, with parallel story lines running in the various media."

The movie-without-a-movie project would prove to be an enormous undertaking. Adding to the challenge was the need for all the designs and characterizations to be consistent throughout the various narrative media, whether the internal mindscape of the written word, the static images printed on a comics page, or the three-dimensional, interactive environment available when the *Shadows* cartridge game was plugged into a home TV set. "Every creator had his or her own input, and each medium its own demands," Wilson explains. "It's more fun than developing individual projects, but it's also loads more work. It was hard on Allan Kausch and Sue Rostoni to keep track of it all, because you're juggling so many things, it's a fluid creative process. If one thing changes in one area, it has to change in all the other areas as well."

In late November 1994 Steve Perry kicked off matters with a twenty-five-page outline that began circulating between Lucasfilm offices at Skywalker Ranch and Bantam editor Tom Dupree's office in New York. Perry, in a cover letter to Dupree that accompanied the outline, observed: "I tried to put in all the stuff the gang at the Ranch meeting wanted and maintain a dramatic line. Mostly I was trying to get the action beats down, and I don't know how much of the darkness came through, but they want it Godfatherish, and I plan to punch that up in the manuscript."

The central plot would be the power struggle between Xizor and Vader, with Luke Skywalker as the pawn in Xizor's deadly game to discredit Vader. Other plot points would be put into play: the rescue attempt of Han Solo on Gall; Princess Leia's bold attempt to uncover who was behind the assassination plot against Luke, leading to her infiltration of the Black Sun operations on Coruscant and a face-to-face meeting with the evil Xizor (who attempts to seduce the daring Princess); Luke's meditations on the Force while in hiding at Obi-Wan's old digs in the arid wasteland of Tatooine's Western Dune Sea—and his challenge of surviving a swoop bike battle against a biker gang sent to kill him; the full details behind the fateful Alliance raid on the Imperial freighter holding the secret plans to the new Death Star; and a climactic space battle in the skies above Coruscant.

Response to the outline was swift and enthusiastic but was accompanied by several long memos of suggested changes and additions to be incorporated into the preparation of the manuscript. As Christmas 1994 neared, the final, premanuscript missive from Dupree to Perry ended with a hopeful note: "We'll sit back now and let you do the heavy lifting."

CONJURING

Plot points and character descriptions from the Steve Perry novel inspired the concept art developed by the various Shadows *toy licensees, such as these sketches of Xizor (above) and Dash Rendar (preceding page) prepared by Applause for its line of collector's dolls.*

Applause concept art sketches by Dave Williams.

I.
NOVEL IDEAS

IN THE GLORY DAYS OF THE PULPS writers could pound out fantasy on their typewriter keys with a machine-gun rhythm: The *Shadow* writer Walter Gibson one year cranked out twenty-four stories and 1,440,000 words on his trusty Corona. In this rush of work, stories could be shorn of pretensions and a gritty clarity could be achieved. For *Shadows of the Empire* novelist Steve Perry would be prolific in the grand tradition, producing a four-hundred-page first draft within four months.

"I consider myself a pulp writer more than a slick writer," Perry observes. "The pulp style is heavy into plot and action. I've also particularly liked the sense of wonder that came with the science fiction genre. They say the golden age of science fiction is when you're age twelve, which was my age when I started reading it. All the stuff that's happening today was all science fiction when I was a kid. I can remember getting my first electronic computer, and it was as big as a suitcase and all it could do was add, subtract, multiply, and divide. Now you can buy one at K-Mart and it's a wristwatch. I laugh about this with some of the writers I know: 'Isn't it great to be living here in the future?!' "

The release of *Star Wars* was a revelation for Perry. The film, coming only eight years after human beings first walked on the moon, was flush with the hope and breathless spirit of real space travel. Lucas had infused his script with mythic flourishes that had universal appeal. "*Star Wars* is space opera with a galactic sweep," Perry notes. "The idea of space opera is that one person can make a difference in the way the whole galaxy works. The characters are also so archetypal. You have Luke, the young kid coming of age, the wise old man in Obi-Wan, evil incarnate in the Emperor, and Vader as his cat's-paw. In fiction there are three basic kinds of conflict—man against man, man against himself, and man against the universe—and you've got all that in the *Star Wars* stories. These characters are in conflict with themselves and others, you've got this hostile universe, and by the end of any *Star Wars* movie or novel the characters have changed."

For Perry the chance to personally explore the *Star Wars* universe was the proverbial dream come true. "Nobody's really sure how much time really elapses between the end of *Empire* and the beginning of *Jedi*, but it's some months, maybe even up to a year. This universe is so big, there's so much in it, you can hardly do anything without checking the time line to make sure you don't have Luke meet an alien he's not supposed to meet until four books later. Actually, it was a little easier for me than for other writers because the novels, except for direct novelizations of the movies, take place after the third film. Since this novel is set between the second and third films, we can't use Han Solo because he's essentially on ice that whole period, but we got to use all the other major characters. Darth Vader is still alive, so I got to use him as a viewpoint character, which was a lot of fun."

Perry had come to his *Shadows* novel assignment by a circuitous route. Around the time of the first *Star Wars* release he was in his late twenties, a physician's assistant in Louisiana who was stricken with the writing bug. With a now-or-never attitude, Perry pulled up stakes, moved to the Pacific Northwest, and began carving out a niche, specializing in his beloved space operas and fantasy tales. A lifelong practitioner and enthusiast of various forms of martial arts, he brought a knowledge of fighting forms to his character the Matador, about whom he wrote some eight novels for Ace Books. His other books include *Spindoc* and *The Forever Drug*, the movie adaptation of Conan the Barbarian, and an *Alien* movie novelization, but it was a Bantam adaptation of the 1994 hit film *The Mask* (an original property of Dark Horse Comics) that helped win him the assignment to write *Shadows of the Empire*.

Steve Perry, Shadows of the Empire *novelist. The project provided Perry the unique opportunity to write a* Star Wars *novel featuring the saga's classic characters.*
Photo by Mÿk Olsen.

"What happened was Tom Dupree, my editor at Bantam, had called me about doing the movie novelization for *The Mask*," Perry explains. "It was one of those hurry-up deals with little money and no royalties, but would I be interested? Well, okay, it sounded like fun. So, because I did Tom that favor, he presented me to Lucasfilm as a potential writer for *Shadows*."

Perry's *Shadows* would feature some surprising twists involving Vader's character. Rather than presenting an almighty incarnation of evil, Perry would reveal a powerful man who, for all his dark side allegiances, could still feel the smoldering spirit of his past as Anakin Skywalker, that noble Jedi Knight and Clone Wars hero. The Vader of *Shadows* would also be a man driven by fatherly urges, willing to scour the universe to find Luke and bring him to his side. This is also a Vader clearly uncomfortable, and at times frustrated, with having to restrain his iron hand and bide his time as Xizor plays his cunning games of intrigue.

And Perry would take readers into the "hyperbaric medical chamber" where a physically vulnerable Vader could sit naked and breathe without the aid of his mask or the protection of his heavy armor, struggling to heal the burned flesh ravaged by a fateful fall into a molten pit during a duel with Obi-Wan Kenobi (as recounted in the 1983 *Return of the Jedi* novelization by James Kahn). The following is an excerpt from Perry's novel chronicling both a hyperbaric chamber session and the Dark Lord's effort to will himself to health, unencumbered by the machinery of healing:

Vader waved his hand over the motion-sensitive controls in his chamber. The spherical chamber opened and the lid lifted with a hydraulic hiss and escape of pressurized air. He sat exposed to the surrounding room, unprotected by the super-medicated and oxygenated field inside the chamber.

He concentrated on the injustice of his condition, on his hatred of Obi-Wan who had made him so. With the anger and hatred, the dark side of the Force permeated Vader.

For a moment, his ruined tissues altered, his scarred lungs and dead alveoli and constricted passages smoothed out and became whole.

For a moment, he could breathe as normal beings breathed.

His sense of relief, his triumph, his *joy* at being able to do so drove the dark side from him as surely as a light chases away shadow. The dark side eagerly consumed anger but it was poisoned by happiness. It left him and when it did, he could breathe no longer.

Vader waved his hand and the half-dome lowered and sealed him into the chamber once again.

He had achieved it briefly, as he had done several times before. The trick was to maintain it. He must not allow himself to feel relief, but must somehow cling to his rage even as he healed.

It was difficult. He had not purged all of Anakin Skywalker, that blemished and frail man from whom he had been born. Until he did, he could never give himself over totally to the dark side. It was his greatest weakness, his most terrible flaw. A single spot of light amid the dark that he had been unable to eradicate over all the years, no matter how hard he had tried.

"A good intricate villain has a lot of layers you can peel away to show the reason why they're doing what they do," Perry explains. "I truly enjoyed playing with Vader and Xizor and all the characters, because when I write, I'm very visual. So, when I had Vader come out on stage, I would see him and hear his voice. I'd sit and repeat the dialogue so I could write it and make sure it'd sound as if Vader had spoken it."

Although Perry had a rare chance to dance with some of the fabled *Star Wars* characters, there would be the requisite creative input from Lucasfilm and collaborative overtures involving the other *Shadows* principals. For Perry, who had also scripted numerous television programs, including Saturday morning fare such as *Ghostbusters* and Disney's *Gargoyles*, the collaborative demands of *Shadows* were business as usual.

"When you write for TV, you may have thirty people who can lay hands on your script and make comments or changes, so you learn very quickly that what you've written is not set in stone but usually written in sand," Perry says, laughing. "So the Lucasfilm people all had their say-so. Although one thing I can say about the people out at the Ranch is they were easy to get along with, helpful, and not 'suits' that are going to give you a lot of corporate flack. But that's why I wrote such a detailed outline that everybody signed off on. If you write for television, that's the first thing you learn—stick to the outline. Once the first draft went in, there was some fine-tuning, but nothing major because I managed to stick to my outline, which had all the major beats, action sequences, and character tone. Once the outline was accepted, that became sort of the bible around which everything revolved.

"It was an interesting process. For example, Boba Fett doesn't show up in my book at all; his ship just appears in a fight sequence. But in the comics he's a central character. At one point I was on the phone two or three times a week with Ryder Windham, the editor at Dark Horse Comics, to make sure we didn't cross wires on what I was writing and what they were writing. If I was going to have a scene with the swoop bike gang and they were going to have a similar scene in the comics, we wanted to make sure we had the same characters in the gang."

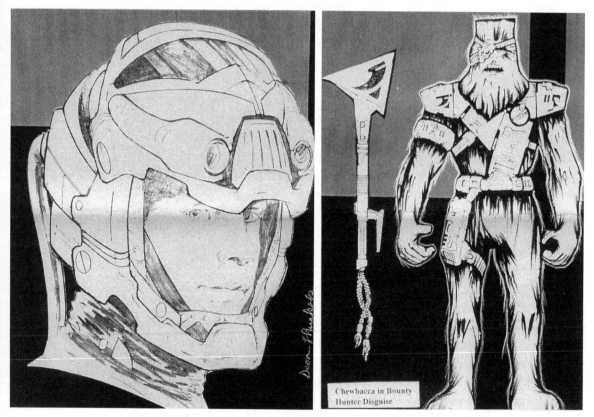

Kenner, the original Star Wars toy licensee, produced these design sketches inspired by the Perry novel:
Left: Luke Skywalker disguised as a guard.
Right: Chewbacca disguised as Snoova (a notorious Wookiee bounty hunter).

Rather than becoming an adaptation of the novel, Dark Horse's six-part *Shadows* series would explore aspects of the story line—from bounty hunter battles to swoop bike rumbles—suited to the unique textual and visual demands of the comics medium. The Oregon-based publisher had been the primary comics licensee with Lucasfilm since the popular *Star Wars: Dark Empire*, a six-part series published in 1991–1992. For *Shadows*, Ryder Windham, then Dark Horse's group editor for licensed titles, handpicked a creative team that included veteran comics writer John Wagner and newcomer artist Kilian Plunkett.

Wagner, a storied scriptor who had cocreated the British cult hero Judge Dredd, was known to Windham as a superb creator of both character and action. Windham had long admired Wagner's work, particularly a 1991 one-shot story published by DC Comics in which Wagner's grim Judge Dredd faced off against Batman (*Judgment on Gotham*, cowritten with Alan Grant). Before tackling *Shadows*, Wagner had already become acclimated to the *Star Wars* universe by scripting a separate Boba Fett comic for Dark Horse.

"Working on licensed properties requires, up front, somebody who knows what he's getting into," Windham observes. "There are so many writers who unintentionally fumble with the characters because they don't realize there are limits to what they can do. Then there are the horror stories about lying-deadline, egotistical writers and artists who work on a licensed character and threaten not to turn in their work until you agree to publish it their way, that kind of nightmare experience. But John Wagner is one of the best comic book format storytellers in the business and a total professional. We also wanted a really good action adventure for *Shadows*, and John is really good at action stories. He knows how to build suspense, setting up scenes so when you turn a page, there's a payoff. In my experience there's only a handful of writers who really consider things like that. It's more than just putting words in balloons; you have to visually direct a scene."

John Wagner, writer for the Dark Horse Comics Shadows *series. One of the best writers in the comics medium, Wagner's talent for scripting an action tale made him perfect for* Shadows.

II.
COMICS
SCRIPT

IN A TUDOR VILLAGE SOME HUN-
dred miles outside London, on a four-acre plot of land surrounded by
four walls, is an old house that served as a rectory when it was built in
1540, during the reign of Henry VIII. On the grounds are gardens, a
piece of an old graveyard, and a church adjacent to the main house
(with an extension added on in Victorian times). The main building's
oaken beams are said to have been cut from a tree planted circa A.D.
900, while the main house's thatched roof was replenished with eleven
tons of wheat straw in the 1960s. The walls themselves were built from
wooden frames, built up with sticks and dung, and plastered over.
Reportedly a stray ghost or two has haunted the place, but writer
John Wagner, who's been living there with his family for several years,
has never had the pleasure of a spectral haunt. With a wink and a
grin Wagner will talk about his beloved medieval rectory, about
the pleasures of isolation and working out of his "wee office" in a
cozy study outfitted with a stained glass window of fleur-de-lis and
Tudor rose.

"The place has so much history to it, it's a wonderful place to live,"
Wagner says. "What I'd like to do is write the house into a lot of stories

and get full pages drawn by all the artists I like, to put up on the walls. I'd love to have a picture of Batman sitting up on the roof of my house."

No doubt Wagner's own Judge Dredd, that supercop from the future (whom he cocreated with artist Carlos Ezquerra), could find a comfortable nook of the rectory to rest his battle-weary bones. Dredd had made his first appearance during 1977 in the second issue of *2000 A.D.*, the famed British tabloid comic magazine. That year, of course, also marked the beginning of the global *Star Wars* phenomenon that had helped fire up the success of *2000 A.D.*'s special brand of science fiction.

"When it comes to *Star Wars*, I think—clean lines," Wagner says with a cryptic laugh. "I don't know what that means exactly, except that when you're done with a *Star Wars* story, you know when it's right, whereas a lot of stories are fuzzy and you're not sure if you've done a good job. But with *Star Wars* the characters are already so well defined, you just know when you're using them properly. In the case of *Shadows of the Empire* everything had to be plotted out in advance, which is the kind of thing that usually worries me. I just like to have a vague idea of how the story is going to run, with a beginning and an end, and then I start writing it. If it's all been figured out, the story can get stale, and when it comes time to write it, there's nothing new going into it. That's one of the reasons I don't usually like working from a synopsis. But with all the changes we had to make during *Shadows* it did, in a way, grow. It changed and evolved. One of the reasons I didn't object to scripts coming back from Lucasfilm with changes is that you expect that from them; it's their property, they're looking after it, they're bringing the whole project together."

It helped that Lucasfilm and Dark Horse had already developed a creative dialogue from years of collaboration on both *Star Wars* and Indiana Jones comics. Unlike those rudderless days with Marvel, the Dark Horse *Star Wars* titles would be tied directly into the overall continuity of the expanding universe.

First up during the Dark Horse era had been 1992's *Dark Empire*, an original story scripted by Tom Veitch and illustrated by Cam Kennedy (another *2000 A.D.* veteran), which was set six years after the Battle of Endor, that victorious final battle in *Return of the Jedi* in which the Alliance seemingly ended Imperial rule. In the dramatic story line Emperor Palpatine, killed in *Jedi*, resurrected himself using his dark side powers and created a clone lab so that his dark spirit could enter a fresh young body. A grim Luke decided that the only way to overcome the Imperial forces again gripping the universe was to give himself to the dark side of the Force. Meanwhile, Han and Leia had married and started a family while Leia, after coming into possession of a Jedi Holocron (an ancient hologram record of Jedi history and teachings), had begun to assert her own status as one born of Jedi blood.

In the late 1994 release of *Dark Empire II* the Alliance and Imperial struggle would continue to rage, with Luke Skywalker, led on by the revelations of the Jedi Holocron, going deeper into a personal voyage of discovery that would take him to Ossus, an ancient Jedi planet laid to waste during the legendary Sith War some four thousand years in the past. In the ruins of ancient Jedi cities Luke would discover such artifacts as a book on Jedi battle meditation and even the struggling survivors who were possibly the last of the original Jedi.

Another 1994 Dark Horse release would do more than merely dig about in the ruins of Jedi culture; it would actually take readers back in time to that fourth millennium, to the golden age of the Galactic Republic. *Tales of the Jedi: Dark Lords of the Sith* not only would feature the samurai-like gallantry of Jedi Masters and students but delve into the occult side of those times, revealing secrets of the Sith, the dark side force that would one day feed the transformation of Anakin Skywalker into Darth Vader.

With *Shadows of the Empire* set squarely in the context of the original movie trilogy, Ryder Windham broached with Lucasfilm an approach geared to the visual dynamics of the comics medium, with the Wagner script following Boba Fett on a tumultuous journey to deliver the carbonite-encased Solo to Jabba the Hutt. Windham's imagination had been piqued by an unpublished *Star Wars* short story titled "A Barve Like That" (from a planned anthology *Tales from Jabba's Palace*) that also picked up at the moment Boba Fett left Cloud City in his ship, *Slave I*, to deliver Solo to Jabba. However, in that tale, before he can reach Tatooine, Boba Fett is engaged in a space battle by IG-88, the battle droid turned bounty hunter, who in *The Empire Strikes Back* had been among those originally commissioned by Darth Vader to hunt down the *Millennium Falcon* and its crew. Fett wins the battle and continues his otherwise uneventful voyage to Tatooine.

"We know in *Return of the Jedi* that Boba winds up delivering the goods," Windham notes, "but I brought up the idea of the comics story turning into a race across the galaxy. I said to Lucasfilm, 'What if we kept the opening bit basically as it was in the short story, up through where Fett has this battle with IG-88, but *Slave I* is so badly damaged in this battle that maybe he can't land on Tatooine?' Then he realizes that if IG-88 was trying to get Solo and collect the reward from Jabba, maybe other bounty hunters are down around Jabba's palace, waiting to kill him as well. He's also being chased by the Rebels, who want to rescue Han, and the Imperials, who want to get Solo because they know they can use him as a lure to trap Luke Skywalker. During this journey Boba has something of a dialogue with the frozen Han, certain terse one-liners like 'You're getting to be more trouble than you're worth, Solo.' "

For *Shadows*, Lucasfilm continuity editor Allan Kausch provided Dark Horse and other project players with a time line flowchart that included the project's characters and plot situations put into chronological order. Wagner had also gone through the Perry novel outline and highlighted areas of concern to his scripting work, breaking those plot elements into individual story arcs that could be contained in the six-issue series format.

"Getting together a story is a bit like rebuilding a car engine," Wagner observes. "You keep tinkering and moving things around and fine-tuning, and if there isn't room for something, out it goes. To write a

LUCASFILM LICENSING
PUBLISHING
LICENSOR'S PRODUCT APPROVAL FORM

LICENSEE Dark Horse   DATE RECEIVED 1/5/95

ATTENTION Ryder Windham   DATE CALLED

                                  DATE FAXED 1-12-95 3 PAGES

                                  FAX # (503) 654-9440

TITLE: STAR WARS: SHADOWS OF THE EMPIRE

DESCRIPTION: Script for Issue 1

WRITER: John Wagner
PENCILS: Kilian Plunkett
INK:
COVER ART:

_____ APPROVED

_XX__ APPROVED WITH CHANGES

_____ DISAPPROVED

COMMENTS:

The error is in quotes, followed by the correction.

1.   Page 2, panel 3: "NEED HANDS" NEED BOTH HANDS

2.   Page 3, panel 1: "TIE FIGHTERS" Since TIE fighters aren't
      equipped with hyperdrives, they couldn't be this far from a
      capital ship: add (then eliminate) a Strike Cruiser (a
      medium-sized cruiser capable of carrying the TIEs)to the
      battle. See WEG's *Imperial Sourcebook*, page 54 for
      reference on this ship.

3.   Page 3, panel 2: "READY PHOTON TORPODOES!" READY WEAPONS!

4.   Pages 4-5, panel 4: "BIG BROTHER" Delete.

5.   Pages 6-7, panel 4: "SHOOTING, TWO!" GOOD SHOOTING, TWO!

First page of Lucasfilm approval form, with comments by Allan Kausch, for Wagner's first draft script for Shadows 1.

STAR WARS:
SHADOWS OF THE EMPIRE
PART 1

John Wagner

*   INTRO PAGE (to come) brings the readers up to date re HAN and FETT and mentions
LANDO and CHEWIE heading for TATOOINE to wait for FETT.

PAGE 1

1.   Full page shot with pic 2 as an inset, bottom right.   The REBEL FLEET filling the
picture, streaking through space, central in pic the STAR CRUISER .

JAG: PRINCESS, WE'RE PICKING UP A SHIP APPROACHING RAPIDLY.
                        WE SUSPECT IT'S <u>HOSTILE</u>.

2.   LEIA and LUKE are in a dining area, ARTOO and THREEPIO there too.   Artoo is
tinkering with the electronics of a drink dispenser, Threepio could be serving Luke and Leia
at their table.   The face of the COMMANDER of the Star Cruiser is large on a screen
behind Leia, she's turning to speak to him.

LEIA: AN IMPERIAL SHIP?   HOW DID THEY FIND US?

CAPT(JAG):   JUST CHANCE.   WE MAKE A PRETTY BIG BLIP ON THE SCANNERS.

LINK: WE'RE DIVERTING TO <u>INTERCEPT</u>.

PAGE 2

1.   Luke starts for the exit and Leia is not pleased.

LUKE: C'MON, ARTOO - !

LEIA: <u>LUKE</u>!   WHERE ARE YOU GOING?

LUKE: I'M NEEDED, LEIA!

*A good comics script must not only tell a story but provide stage directions for the
artist to follow. In this first draft script, writer John Wagner provides a tense open-
er, with Wedge Antilles leading the Rogue Squadron into battle with Imperial TIE
fighters. Wagner also picks up on a story thread from* The Empire Strikes Back *as*

2.   Threepio stands in his way.   Luke stops, his robotic hand grasping the edge of the heavy aluminium table fixed to the floor.   Both turning their attention to the hand.

THREEPIO: MASTER LUKE, THIS IS MOST INADVISABLE! YOU'VE HARDLY
                       RECOVERED FROM YOUR INJURIES - AND BESIDES, IT WILL BE
                       SOME TIME BEFORE YOU'VE MASTERED THAT NEW PROSTHESIS...

LUKE: IF YOU MEAN MY HAND, IT'S FINE --

3. Now we turn our attention to the hand.   As Luke moves it we see he's been grasping the table so hard that indentations of his fingers are left in table.

THREEPIO: I BEG TO DIFFER!

LUKE: SO I NEED A LITTLE MORE PRACTICE.   I DON'T NEED BOTH
                       HANDS TO FLY AN X-WING ANYWAY.

4. Artoo steps in and Threepio looks smug.

FX(ARTOO):   Bleep Blee-Blee!   Bleeple!

THREEPIO: THERE YOU ARE!   ARTOO-DETOO SAYS YOUR X-WING IS IN
                       SERVICE BAY FOR A REFIT!   I TRUST THAT SETTLES THE MATTER!

5.   Luke isn't happy but we can see he's still pretty exhausted.   To emphasise the robotic hand it would be a good idea here in fg to have him opening its little hatch, making a small adjustment with a fancy little tool.   Leia has come up, sympathetic.

LEIA: THREEPIO'S RIGHT, LUKE.   YOU HAVE TO REST, REGAIN YOUR
                       STRENGTH.

PAGE 3

1.   External.   WEDGE and ROGUE SQUADRON peel away from the fleet, one of Rogue Squadron peeling away from the others.   Draw an inset headshot of Wedge at his controls, top left of pic.   The caption goes above this, all Wedge's dialogue comes from the inset.

CAPTION: "WEDGE ANTILLES AND ROGUE SQUADRON ARE WITH THE FLEET.
                       THEY CAN PROVIDE ALL THE BACK-UP WE NEED!"

JAG: WEDGE!   WE HAVE CONFIRMATION!   IT'S AN IMPERIAL STRIKE
                       CRUISER!   IT'S ESSENTIAL IT DOES NOT ESCAPE TO GIVE AWAY
                       OUR POSITION!

WEDGE: MY FRIEND, YOU'RE SINGING OUR SONG!

WEDGE(over main pic):   ROGUE FIVE, SWEEP WIDE!   THE REST OF YOU STICK
                           LIKE GLUE!

Luke contemplates the prosthetic hand that has replaced the one he lost in a brutal battle with Vader.
   Second draft Shadows *Dark Horse Comics script for issue 1, pages 1–2.*

This Shadows *comics art incorporates the instructions from Wagner's script.*
Shadows *Dark Horse Comic, issue 1, pages 2–3; unedited pencils by Kilian Plunkett.*

good comics script you need to know how to compress a story, to isolate essential scenes, knowing what's important to the story and what's superfluous. It's so easy to overexplain. Quite often you can reduce the amount of dialogue by a quarter of the script. Sometimes I'll purposely write a story four or five pages over length so that when I've tightened it up, there's no wasted panels, no two-page stretches of nothing but dialogue. When I'm writing I'll also see in my mind how one picture will flow into the next picture and how one scene will flow into another scene. Sometimes it's a shock when you get the art back and see that the artist is looking at a picture from a wholly different perspective than you were.

"Everything I have to say, any instruction, is in my script. But I like working with artists who can see whether my interpretation is working properly and, if not, how to improve it. Because the artists are the directors, they see how their picture, combined with my dialogue, is working. Maybe I have a scene with two people together, and instead of doing one picture, the artist will say, 'This'll work better if I divide it up into two separate head shots so you can get action from one character and reaction from the other.' There's more of a punch to it that way. Artists like Kilian Plunkett and Cam Kennedy and Carlos Ezquerra will change something if it's not working."

Although Wagner and Kilian Plunkett were teamed on *Shadows*, they would in fact have little contact during the creative process. The duo would not actually meet and converse until the special *Star Wars* day at the July 1995 San Diego Comics Convention. "This project has been kind of a thrill because John Wagner used to write so much of *Judge Dredd*," says Plunkett, born and raised in Ireland and a lifelong *2000 A.D.* comics fan. "Although I had his phone number, I didn't speak with him until the Con. I really didn't need to; his scripts were so well structured."

Plunkett's *Star Wars* work for Dark Horse before *Shadows* had included drawing covers for *Droids*, a series featuring the duo of See-Threepio and Artoo-Detoo, and for *Classic Star Wars*, an anthology of the famous newspaper strip series. Windham would rave that Plunkett was a natural, an artist who could draw from memory fully dimensional views of the *Millennium Falcon* or the droids, down to their last bolt and mechanical joint.

And then there was Plunkett's sample art, which had caught Windham's eye, especially that piece with the couple taking a nocturnal stroll in a garden and being surprised by the man with the exploding head . . .

Before his Shadows *work, comics artist Kilian Plunkett had rendered a few other* Star Wars *assignments, such as this Boba Fett cover for a series reprinting the original newspaper comic strips.*

Classic Star Wars: The Early Adventures *9, April 1995, Dark Horse Comics; cover art by Kilian Plunkett.*

III.
SHADOW
ART

WHEN DARK HORSE COMICS BEGAN publishing in 1986, it was as an "independent," which then meant an alternative to Marvel Comics and DC Comics, which between them controlled the lion's share of the comics market. In a bold departure from traditional publishing practices, independents such as Dark Horse put out titles in which the creators could hold the copyrights to their own characters.

As Dark Horse flourished, the company began branching out into the arena of licensed film property titles, beginning with a six-part original *Aliens* series in 1988. Other film-based miniseries titles followed, including *Predator* and *Terminator*, an original James Bond thriller, a miniseries based on the 1951 RKO sci-fi/horror classic *The Thing from Another World*, and a direct movie adaptation of Universal's 1994 release *The Shadow*. Dark Horse's very own *The Mask* would also become a hit New Line feature film release in 1994.

Although most of the movie titles were based on the basic themes from the original theatrical releases, the comics' story lines generally supplemented the properties with original characters and situations. Even for the direct movie tie-in of *The Shadow*, artist Michael Kaluta drew the characters without adhering to the likenesses of the actors in the film.

For the Lucasfilm titles continuity was a must—and it was a challenge for the artists. Any depictions of the cast from the trilogy had to maintain a resemblance to the actors, with the film's distinctive spacecraft similarly having to match the look of the models created by ILM.

"There are certain problems inherent in translating characters from one medium to another," artist Kilian Plunkett says. "In film work you have to take two-dimensional production designs and make them work three-dimensionally, but on a project like *Shadows*, all the concerns are backward. *Star Wars* characters like Darth Vader were really designed for the cinema screen. That's where they look their best; that's where they're most effective. They're not like the classic character designs for comics characters such as Superman and Batman. When you reduce a *Star Wars* character to a static image, they're not simple. There's all these weird, clunky shapes on them, so it's very hard to make them look particularly dynamic. Probably the most challenging character is Darth Vader. His helmet is a tough shape, and he's so reflective that he can look completely different from one scene to the next. With Vader you get the cape, which helps; you can sweep the cape around. But still, there are characters that don't lend themselves

"Vader is hard to draw," Plunkett writes on one of his many early sketches of the Dark Lord.

to doing what comics do best, which is extremely exaggerated physical action.

"And when you're working with established characters, there's the issue of likeness. Although I have stacks of photo references, when you go back and look at the *Star Wars* films, you see that the props change, so photo reference in this case is very dangerous. The *Millennium Falcon* doesn't look the same in every film, the droids don't, the actors are aging, everything gets upgraded all the time. There are Philips head screws all over R2-D2's torso in the first movie, but by the third movie they'd gotten rid of all that stuff and he looked like some otherworldly robot. And I didn't want to just do the same photos we've seen a billion times. I do think there's some room for interpretation, because no matter how faithful you try to be to a likeness, the style of your drawing sort of changes that person, anyway. With the established characters you have to make it look like something you haven't seen before."

Besides the problems inherent in adapting iconic characters and complex spacecraft to the paneled comics page, there were the normal concerns of visually telling the story. "The concern with doing comics is how to tell a story in nonmoving pictures," editor Ryder Windham notes. "There are considerations for the visual reading from left to right and for page layout. There are surprises: You might not want to show some climactic explosion on a right-hand page which faces a left-hand page if only because the suspense builds on that left-hand page and you can peripherally see the explosion on the right. So that gets into page design considerations."

Dark Horse editor Ryder Windham had been eager to have Plunkett illustrate one of his *Star Wars* projects. But Plunkett was keen on drawing the characters and spaceships from the movie trilogy, not the new characters and original story lines of titles such as the *Tales of the Jedi* series. With *Shadows* the old gang would be back (except poor Han, frozen in that block of car-

Drawing a classic character such as Vader proved a challenge because an artist's two-dimensional drawings must capture the dynamics of a live-action character originally designed for the movie medium.

bonite), and with some exciting new creations in the bargain. In particular, the project offered a rare opportunity to portray Darth Vader, who had not been available for titles set in the ancient time of Jedi Knights and dark Sith Masters or in the posttrilogy comics set after Vader's demise.

Plunkett had initially come to Windham's attention around 1992, when the editor was searching for an artist to do an *Alien* series. The project required an ability to render technical equipment and real people dressed in real clothing that went far beyond the generic look of the typically square-jawed, spandex-clad superhero. A Dark Horse submissions editor showed Windham art samples submitted by a twenty-one-year-old artist living in Dublin named Kilian Plunkett. "I couldn't believe that nobody had hired this guy," Windham recalls. "They remain the best amateur art samples I've ever seen. But he hadn't even left his phone number. I had to call Dublin, and I got his uncle, who gave me Kilian's phone number." Contact was achieved, and Plunkett got the job.

The samples had included familiar characters such as the Predator and Lobo, a DC Comics character. One of the most arresting original samples was a six-page black and white story with an accompanying copy also hand colored by Plunkett. The vignette showed a man and woman dressed in formal evening wear taking an evening walk through the garden of a sprawling estate, with a man crashing through brambles and bushes in pursuit.

"Then the running man emerges into this clearing in front of the man and woman,

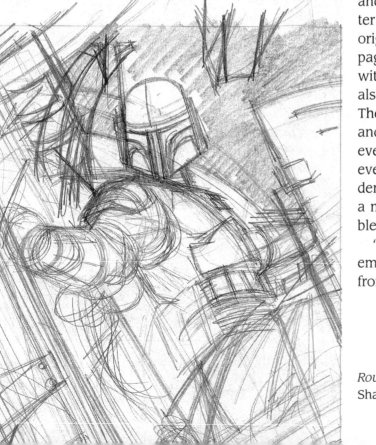

Rough Boba Fett sketch for Shadows; *art by Kilian Plunkett.*

Responding to a security alert, Boba Fett fires his wrist lasers into the hold of Slave I.

  Shadows *Dark Horse Comic, issue 1, page 18; unedited pencils by Kilian Plunkett.*

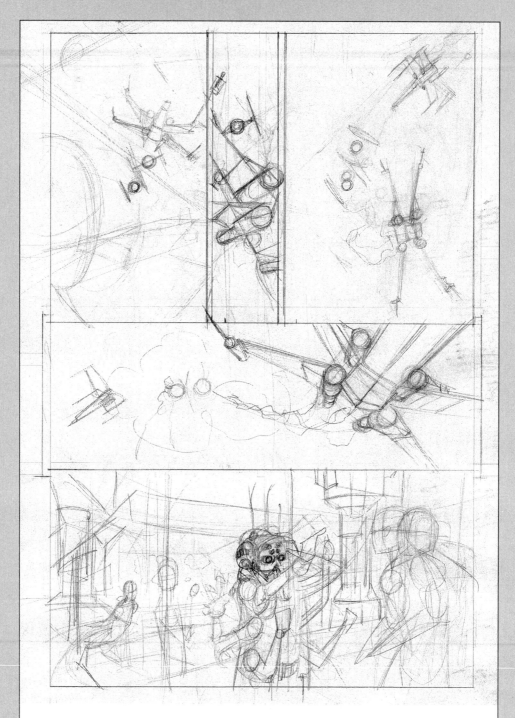

These Plunkett pencil breakdowns depict furious battle action between the Rogue Squadron and TIE fighters, the last panel showing Alliance freedom fighters who are following developments from the command deck of a nearby star cruiser.

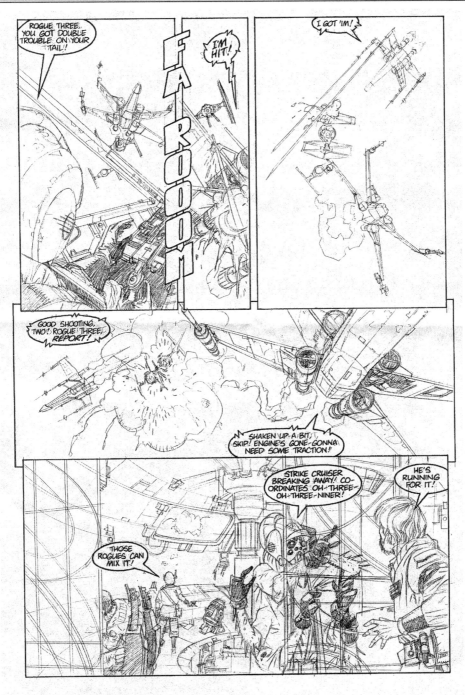

Final pencils; Shadows 1, *page 6.*

Plunkett produces pencils for a Shadows *page.*
Photo by Ryder Windham.

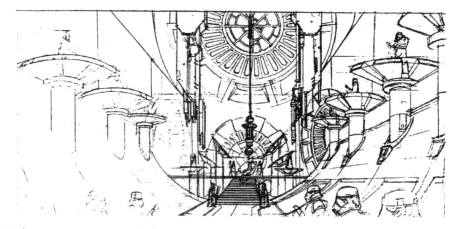

Project concept art extended to environments as well as characters and vehicles.
Considerable research and preliminary art went into conjuring up a rare view of
the Emperor's throne room in Imperial City, such as this preliminary Plunkett
sketch for the Shadows *comics.*

Plunkett provided Shadows *character and vehicle designs for consideration during the project's conceptual stage (such as this sketch of the* Stinger, *the ship flown by Guri, Xizor's trusted aide).*

and his head explodes in violent crimson colors," Windham explains. "The story ends with the man and woman looking at the exploding head, where it's revealed that the running man was this android, with a robot skull and wires hanging out. What Kilian demonstrated in that drawing was his ability to tell a story visually, to render figures and clothing as well as show a sense of pacing, color, and light."

When he was a kid, Plunkett's imagination had been stoked from such disparate sources as the weekly release of *2000 A.D.* and his personal explorations of the rolling green hills and forests where his family lived outside Dublin. When he was twelve years old he was caught up in the fantasy worlds created by J.R.R. Tolkien and by sword and sorcery illustrators, a period he wryly recalls as "sad, dwarf-induced days." But *Star Wars* had always had a particular impact, and Plunkett exercised his developing artistic abilities by drawing Darth Vader and the other classic characters and spacecraft.

"I went to see *Star Wars* for my seventh birthday," Plunkett recalls. "I don't want to say it changed my life, but it made a big impression on me. Actually, one of the things that slowed me down when I began work on *Shadows* was I got brainlock—this was *Star Wars*! There were so many cool things I wanted to do, and for a while I tried to do it all in one page, which makes no sense in a series that's almost 140 pages long. For example, in the second issue there was a swoop bike chase with Luke and the bikers, and I was trying to plot it out with all these different angles and cool explosions. Then I realized there were about twelve more pages of swoop bikes scripted and I didn't have to do it all at once. As with everything, there would be time to do whatever I wanted to do."

Relocated from Ireland to Oregon, Plunkett works out of a makeshift studio in his Portland apartment. In his normal work process he reads the script and prepares thumbnail sketches a few inches high, complete with matchstick figures. The resulting "very quick scribble comic" forms a sort of road map for working out page and panel compositions and allowing for editorial input.

Boba Fett's Slave I *emerges from hyperspace above the planet Tatooine.*
Shadows *Dark Horse Comic, issue 1, page 16; unedited pencils by Kilian Plunkett.*

For *Shadows*, concerns about rendering both familiar faces and new characters would be made problematic by the multimedia nature of the project. New creations in particular had to be designed to adapt to both illustrative and interactive visual media. "I'd underline in the script possible aircraft and characters that might have been designed by someone at LucasArts," Plunkett explains. "For example, there's the big scene on Gall where the Rogue Squadron attacks an Imperial cruiser during the Han Solo rescue attempt. So I'd check with Ryder to see how necessary it was to make the planet look as it appeared in the 3-D game. In this particular case it was quite important. I received all the reference for the planet Gall that LucasArts had already designed, so I could look at the scenario and figure out a way of staging the action to get the perspective right so I got the most dynamic look."

Although Plunkett would provide some character and hardware designs on his own, all this visual conjuring began with artists Mike Butkus, who would provide conceptual character designs, and Doug Chiang, who would design the main spaceships.

Butkus had been hired by Lucasfilm art director Troy Alders to create *Shadows* sketches and provide classic character drawings for both Del Rey's

Star Wars: The Essential Guide to Characters and an in-house style guide. Butkus had been in business for a decade, with his varied career ranging from movie poster art and production design work to developing licensed merchandising concepts and his client list including the likes of Disney and DreamWorks SKG.

Mike Butkus takes a break in his studio.
Photo by Troy Alders.

At the beginning of the Shadows *project, Lucasfilm hired artist Mike Butkus to provide concept art for the major players, leading to the first images of most of the new characters. Here Butkus's pencil and ink sketches capture the exotic physique and commanding presence of the Dark Prince, Xizor.*

67

All Butkus would have to go on for *Shadows* would be a sentence or two describing each character—which was how he liked it. "It's easy for me to make something out of nothing; I like to just take an idea and run," notes Butkus, who developed concepts during a roughly four-month period beginning in January 1995. "The more freedom I have, the better. I become more creative that way."

Butkus, who would work in a variety of artistic media (from oil painting to charcoal drawings), depending on the particular project, created pencil and ink sketches for his *Shadows* assignment. Dozens of preliminary sketches were required just for Xizor and Dash. "As the drawings developed, they stayed roughly close to my original design, with a lot of tweaking: different boots and armor, things like that," Butkus recalls. "I didn't mind Lucasfilm asking me to change things; it's part of the business to do things over. You're working with very creative people who have an idea of what they want, and you're bringing your talent to the process. Actually, in the initial stage there's a tendency to nitpick, but as deadlines get closer, people will go 'Fine, we'll run with it.'"

Although many artists employ live models and photographic references

Character sketch depicts starfighter pilot Wedge Antilles, leader of the famed Rogue Squadron.
Illustration by Mike Butkus.

when designing characters, Butkus likes to conjure his work from the wellsprings of his imagination. (A student of anatomy and physical motion, Butkus admits that he once considered going into genetic engineering, contemplating the possibilities of creating new life-forms.) Since he needed only a sketch pad and pencil for *Shadows*, Butkus did many of his designs during short camping trips to a lonely southern California beach, one of those pristine places of sun-drenched legend where an old man ran a venerable burger stand and surfers in the know would come to ride the waves. He'd set up a tent, build a campfire, and let loose his boxer dog to chase seagulls as he began drawing. On a good day he'd have some twenty sketches finished by the time the sun had set below the ocean horizon line. A compact disc changer in his car would provide musical inspiration while he worked. "Music is a part of the creative process when I sketch," Butkus notes. "For Xizor I had on some Danny Elfman *Batman* soundtrack music, while Dash was more Elvis, 1960s rock 'n' roll. Music helps give an attitude to your characters."

The gamemasters at LucasArts would play a major role in realizing *Shadows* designs as well, from the inscrutable look of Xizor to Dash Rendar's spaceworthy *Outrider*.

The LucasArts Entertainment Company had been forged in 1982, with early efforts ranging from an interactive multimedia American history teaching project aimed at middle school students (developed in concert with the National Geographic Society and the California State Department of Education) to a trilogy of World War II air combat simulation games that, company press releases noted, "strap the player into the pilot's seat of six classic American and Japanese war planes during four pivotal air battles in the Pacific Theater." (It had been historical footage from just such aerial dogfights that had originally inspired Lucas's design for the Rebel and Imperial space battles in the *Star Wars* movies.)

The *Star Wars* universe would be explored by LucasArts in a variety of best-selling titles that in many cases would introduce new characters to the saga. There was the 1993 release of X-Wing, a space combat game in which gamers could test their starfighter skills on missions ranging from deep space reconnaissance operations to an assault on the Death Star. The TIE Fighter game would mark the first time in the entire saga when matters would be seen from an Imperial perspective. (As a LucasArts winter 1994 catalogue noted: "The black cockpit wraps around you, snug like your flightsuit . . . Hatred of the Rebel Alliance courses through your veins.") In the 3-D Dark Forces game released in 1995, gamers could assume the identity of the player-controlled character Kyle Katarn, a mercenary hired by the Alliance to match wits with the evil Admiral Mohc (and, along the way, battle dark troopers, Boba Fett, kell dragons, and other dangers).

LucasArts' *Star Wars* games would prove so successful that in a July 14, 1995, *Entertainment Weekly* "Multimedia" section article highlighting the top-ten movers and shakers of the interactive world, George Lucas would be touted as a visionary force largely because "his interactive company is arguably the most successful publisher in the business, with seemingly every title it releases becoming a best-seller."

Shadows of the Empire would be one of the inaugural games designed for Nintendo's 64-bit Nintendo 64, the fifth platform system introduced by the company (joining the Nintendo Entertainment System, the Super Nintendo 16-bit machine, the portable Game Boy, and the Virtual Boy system). To produce a breakthrough new system, Nintendo entered into a partnership with Silicon Graphics (SGI), one of the leading developers of workstations in the entire computer industry and a technical power in the film industry. (SGI's superpowered workstations have provided the tools for many a breakthrough movie and have contributed to ILM's computer graphics work on successful films such as *Jurassic Park, The Mask,* and *Casper.*)

"The Nintendo 64 is a real leapfrog over most of the so-called next generation 32-bit systems," says Perrin Kaplan, Nintendo's corporate communications manager. "If you imagine a freeway clogged with slow traffic, what the Nintendo 64 does is widen the freeway and provide a lot of entrances and exits, which allows information to move on and off really quickly. Previously video games would be limited to movements popping from left to right, with one color range. Because the Nintendo 64 is so fast and powerful, we can provide different lighting for scenes, more fluid movements for characters, realistic environments, and real-time interactivity. It becomes a very immersive experience for the game player."

But in Perrin's words, "software is what sells the hardware." (And Nintendo had sold a lot of hardware, with an estimated forty percent of U.S. homes owning a Nintendo game system, according to Perrin.) To ensure that its breakthrough system would run with the best games possible, Nintendo assembled what the company dubbed a "dream team" of twelve different companies, of which LucasArts was a key player.

"Normally any game developer who has funds and talent can make a game for our systems," Perrin notes, "but the introduction of the Nintendo 64 was like a movie debut, and we wanted the absolutely best companies capable of producing blockbuster games. And Lucasfilm and LucasArts are very creative and high-tech. And I think Lucasfilm understands how games played on a system like the Nintendo 64 provide a creative venue for stories that might once have been considered just for the movie medium."

The gamemasters at LucasArts also understood that despite the rendering power of the system and its ability to allow for a virtual 3-D environment in which a player can maneuver the hero character Dash Rendar through a world of troubles, the platform was only a tool. "Megabytes don't equal quality," comments *Shadows* project leader Mark Haigh-Hutchinson. It would be up to the gamemasters themselves to take advantage of the machine and design and program the fantastic journey through the dark universe.

The LucasArts Shadows *teams assemble.*

(Back row, left to right) Steve Dauterman, Peter McConnell, Jon Knoles, Andy Holdun, Paul Topolos, Mr. B. Fett.

(Middle row, left to right): Jim Current, Matt Tateishi, Bill Stoneham, Brett Tosti, Ingar Shu, Tom Harper, Chris Hockabout.

(Front row, left to right): Garry Gaber, Mark Blattel, Eric Johnston, Mark Haigh-Hutchinson. Not shown: Paul Zinnes, Larry the O, Eric Ingerson, and Darren Johnson.

Photo by Heather Sutton.

IV.
GAME
MACHINE

IN THE EARLY *STAR WARS* DAYS, when computerized motion control visual effects photography was in its infancy, it was a mental stretch to imagine a time of interactive media, of compact discs and cartridge units that could be plugged into and played off TV sets or personal computers. The interactive industry had begun with the arcade games of the 1970s. Pong, one of the earliest, which featured two vertical bars batting a ball in a kind of video tennis match, seems positively Stone Age compared with the real-time interactive games issued by an industry that by 1995 was reportedly generating some $5 billion a year, with grosses expected to at least *double* by the year 2000.

Shadows of the Empire would be a cartridge game with a console designed to run off a television set. With the aid of a joystick, a player would be able to make his or her virtual surrogate respond in real time to all the game action as it played out in simulated three-dimensional worlds. Opponents, from the hulking Imperial walkers to Boba Fett, would be programmed with a kind of rudimentary artificial intelligence to be able to react to the actions of the player/character. It was to take advantage of such interactivity (and to stage real-time situations such as snowspeeders battling walkers on the ice planet Hoth) that Shadows was designed for the cartridge system and not a compact disc system.

CD-ROM games, because of their technological edge over cartridges in terms of memory and storage capacity, have traditionally been utilized to present "predrawn" or "prerendered" scenes. While the average cartridge can store several megabytes of information, with each megabyte equal to approximately 1 million bytes of computer memory, the typical CD can store more than 500 megabytes of information, allowing for superior computer graphics and the inclusion of music and dialogue. For example, while a compact disc can hold eighty minutes of recorded dialogue, just a few minutes of dialogue can fill an entire cartridge. Even the "cut scenes" that precede separate levels of game play can be presented in the CD format as sophisticated live-action video or prerendered scenes. (LucasArts' first game designed for the CD was the 1993 release Rebel Assault. That first-person game boasted attractions such as three-dimensional graphics, digitized *Star Wars* movie footage, and a sound track featuring the original musical score composed by John Williams.)

The CD medium, when accessed through the personal computer (PC), could boast the superior storage capabilities needed to accommodate high-end graphics. "CDs allow us to store predrawn scenes and then spool them off just like a video," Haigh-Hutchinson explains, "but the problem is that getting to the data is very, very slow. A cartridge doesn't have as much space but allows *immediate* access. CDs weren't originally designed for interactive game playing; they were designed for linear music playback. Now we're getting hardware facilities on the PC more amenable to game development. It's all about graphic usage. Most PCs don't yet have the accelerated drawing capabilities you get with a Nintendo, Sega, or Sony machine. Drawing a polygon on the screen, actually writing the pixel into screen memory, takes processing power. In the past the PCs had to do it all through the main central processing units."

On the downside, while a CD game such as Rebel Assault could boast wonderful graphics, the player was restricted to limited movement within preset path patterns. By utilizing an 8-megabyte cartridge for Shadows of the Empire, LucasArts hoped to provide players with both real-time interactivity and superior 3-D graphics. In the final analysis, the Shadows cartridge would provide a storage medium different from a CD-ROM but, lacking the storage space, would not be able to accommodate video sequences or prerendered 3-D scenes.

In Shadows, game players would be able to control the movements of the swashbuckling Dash Rendar through twelve separate missions, or "levels," in which a variety of threatening obstacles would have to be hurdled to accomplish the mission required for each level. Awaiting the player at the end of each level would be a "boss monster," game lingo for the level's final, supreme challenge, which could take the form of a fearsome killer droid or a death-dealing spaceship.

In the world of games, if the player/character is "killed," one can resurrect that character simply by starting over—becoming "restored," as they say. The only penalty is to find oneself knocked back within, or sometimes out of, the particular level. "In games main characters don't die," explains lead artist and game designer Jon Knoles. "In our Super Nintendo games, for example, we'll have an infinite number of IG-88 robots that you kill off but that come back and keep on attacking. In Dark Forces, maybe Boba Fett just got hurt and was lying down sleeping. Normally, when a player/character gets killed, you'll usually go back to the beginning of the level you died on."

Although most games concentrate on one form of game play, such as nonstop aerial action from the cockpit of a fighter plane or hand-to-hand battles in a running game format, various aspects of the Shadows story line would be explored with various game play genres. "In the past most games usually stuck to one genre or one graphic representation, but we've gone out of our way to make multiple genres the main element of the Shadows game," Haigh-Hutchinson states. "For example, Super Star Wars, the 1992 Super Nintendo game done by

LucasArts, is what they call a side-scroller, which represents the game from a two-dimensional, side point of view. Dark Forces and those games would pretty much stick to a first person point of view, so you could only look *ahead* while in that world.

"With Shadows the player can also run around in the first person, but we have other situations where it becomes the third person and the camera pulls out of the body so you can see your character moving around the 3-D world. In other sequences you're flying a snowspeeder in real-time battles with walkers on Hoth and riding swoop bikes in a canyon on Tatooine. There's also an asteroid phase where you're in a spaceship cockpit and you're a gunner."

Although the *Shadows* team would be working in earnest by January 1995, the delays in Nintendo's manufacture of the actual Nintendo 64 meant that LucasArts would not have a game machine on hand until late July. To get around the unavailability of the new machine needed to design its game, the *Shadows* team wrote development system software using high-powered Silicon Graphics Onyx systems to emulate the software capabilities of the Nintendo 64.

"It was a very interesting challenge developing a game for a machine

that didn't exist," project technical lead Eric Johnston notes. "That's unusual in the games industry. Usually you develop a game for a machine that's already in use. In the case of the Nintendo 64 we knew that the specifications of the machine would be impressive, so we wanted to develop one of the first real-time 3-D games for the system. The reason we used the Onyx, which is this big, heavy machine that looks like a file cabinet, is it's the only computer that could keep up with what the Nintendo 64 could do. Even our smaller Silicon Graphics machines don't come close."

Technical lead Eric Johnston. According to Johnston, delays in Nintendo's manufacture of the Nintendo 64 system forced the LucasArts team to design the game using special software and high-powered hardware systems that emulated the unavailable machine. Photo by Heather Sutton.

"The graphics and real-time rendering capabilities of the Nintendo 64 console machine are staggeringly powerful for its price (approximately $250 per unit); it's a breakthrough," Haigh-Hutchinson adds. "Why is it so powerful? First of all, SGI are very clever; they really know what they're doing. They're also always working with powerful machines, on the other end of the spectrum, so to speak. With this machine they've brought it down to a level that to us in games seems very powerful but to them isn't. You can't do absolute miracles, but they've come close. There are still limitations, but the Nintendo 64 excels in so many areas, we can concentrate on other aspects of the game production. For example, we've gained so much from the graphic side of things that we can concentrate more resources on artificial intelligence issues. And this is only the tip of the iceberg. If you look back five years to when Super Nintendo came out, nobody really knew how to exploit the hardware, so the games were very primitive in comparison to what you get these days. And while what we're doing now is really advanced, in a few years it'll also look a bit passé."

One of the graphics advantages with the Nintendo 64 was special electronic filtering hardware to deal with the problem of "aliasing," those jagged pixels that had traditionally been the nemesis of quality, low-resolution computer graphics images. With advanced antialiasing capabilities, once ragged pixels and even texture map effects could be smoothed out. Another traditional image problem of 3-D games, in which an annoying sparkling effect can occur, was addressed with advanced Nintendo 64 "Mip Mapping," which helped smooth out the three-dimensional graphics, allowing players to perceive finer details when coming close to an object.

According to Mark Haigh-Hutchinson, when he first started writing programs professionally in 1984 a programmer would typically do everything. By the late 1980s the age of specialization had begun. For Shadows, the work would require three programmers, three more level designers to build the 3-D worlds, several modelers defining the environments, background artists, texture mappers, motion capture work for the cut scenes, and a project leader with three leads dealing with technical, design, and art direction issues. Through the use of a process called "compiling," all the hundreds of files of project information on LucasArts' development computers would be folded down into a compact form for play on the game platform, with the end result being a cartridge five inches long and six inches wide.

The technological advances in computer games enabled the gamemasters at LucasArts to create ever more realistic computer-generated characters and 3-D environments. Most of the LucasArts Shadows team members hailed from backgrounds in which it was normal to push technological envelopes. Tech lead Eric Johnston, for example, had majored in electrical engineering and computer science at Berkeley and had graduated to the NASA Ames Research Center in Mountain View, California, where he had worked on graphics computers and robotic systems.

"At NASA Ames we were essentially designing and testing new uses for robots," Johnston notes. "I'd wear head-mounted displays and gloves that allowed me to control a robot's movement, and with the goggles on, I could see through the robot's eyes. This sort of technology is developed so you can control a robot to work in some place you can't go, such as deep under water or in a radiation-leaked area. From a programming standpoint there's no difference between controlling a real robot and writing a game like Shadows of the Empire where we're controlling a lot of imaginary robots. The big similarity is they're both real-time. In Shadows we're not playing a prerendered movie or video. We're actually moving objects around and controlling what they do all the time the player is playing the game."

This scene of the Falcon *and an X-wing rendezvousing on Tatooine was originally an ILM matte painting that had been cut from* Return of the Jedi, *but was digitized into LucasArts' computers for manipulation and inclusion into the finale of* Shadows of the Empire.

Tom Harper (left) and Eric Johnston (right) check out game animation data.

*Immediately after LucasArts'
battle of Hoth sequence, the
game action follows Dash's*
Outrider *on a daring escape
through an asteroid field. In
this cut scene storyboard
sequence by Paul Topolos,
Leebo informs Dash that Han
Solo's* Falcon *is escaping
from approaching Star
Destroyers by flying through
the asteroid field. "Captain
Solo is crazier than you,"
Leebo says. Fighting words to
Dash, who announces that if Solo can do it, so can he.*

*3-D artist Andrew Holdun builds the low polygon models that will represent
X-wings, Star Destroyers, and other Shadows ships.*

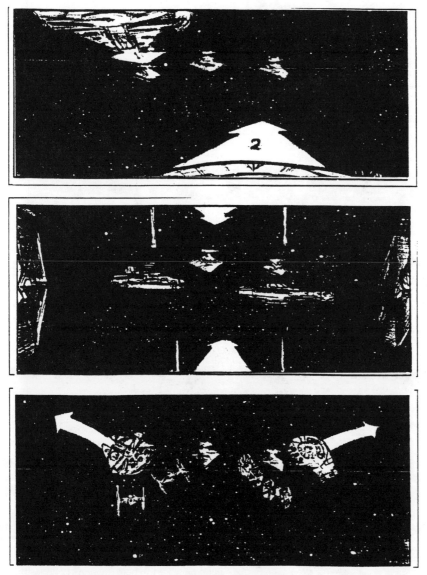

In another post-Hoth cut scene storyboard, the Falcon and the Outrider split up with TIE fighters in pursuit. The game action follows the Outrider into the 'asteroid chase' level, where players must take the gunnery controls to fire at attacking TIEs and blast away the floating asteroids.

Dash: "Han!Chewie!! I thought you two were still on Ord Mantell. Bounty hunter trouble?"

Han: "Yeah... I see you've still got the Outrider. Looks like you've made some expensive modifications.Running supplies for the Alliance couldn't have paid for all that..."

Dash: "Well, you know--smuggling ain't a clean living, but it pays well. I'd sure like to see some action with Skywalker's Rogue Squadron while I"m here, though. I'll show those guys how to really fly."

With Shadows, *the gamemasters at LucasArts saw a chance to stage some inter-active action during the fabled Battle of Hoth. In this storyboard for a preliminary cut scene flashback, Dash Rendar, running supplies to Echo Base, greets Han Solo just before jumping into a snowspeeder for some battle action against Imperial walkers. Text by Jon Knoles, art by Paul Topolos.*

V.
LEVELS OF
ADVENTURE

AT INDUSTRIAL LIGHT & MAGIC many magical screen images are created by digitally compositing various elements into one final image. Whether for the three-dimensional computer graphic dinosaurs of *Jurassic Park* or for the image-processing techniques used on a film such as *Forrest Gump*, enormous software and hardware resources are utilized in the creation of the final product.

In the world of LucasArts such image creations are referred to as "prerendered." In an interactive real-time game such as Shadows, technological limits preclude the use of these high-resolution video effects and of elaborate sound tracks. So the challenge in creating real-time 3-D environments is to push the existing limits.

"Some of the worlds get really complicated," observes lead artist and game designer Jon Knoles. "Everytime you build a world, you're storing geometry. In Shadows there are memory restrictions because of the space the cartridge can hold, but the characters, the vehicles, and the world itself are created as virtual objects existing in a 3-D world of their own. For example, we have a sequence where Dash battles walkers on Hoth, and when he leaves the planet, he has to fly through an asteroid field. In our real-time game environment there are actually hundreds of asteroids floating around in 3-D space, and no matter where you turn your head, you'll see them all. Also, once our characters and objects have been built, texture-mapped, and placed in the various levels, they have to be programmed with AI [artificial intelligence], which gives them something to do."

The AI programming must be based on the behavior of the particular character or machine, whether stormtrooper or Imperial walker. The programming was designed, of course, for maximum danger to player/character Dash Rendar, with lurking enemies designed to recognize the hero and attempt to terminate his progress. "We have a whole bunch of animations—walking, running, spinning around, standing still, get-hit-and-die animation—which all have to be triggered at some point by what the player does," Knoles says. "So when you walk into a room full of stormtroopers who don't know you're coming, an animation is triggered of the stormtroopers spinning around and acting surprised. Then they begin to shoot at you. And if you shoot a stormtrooper, the programmer will have arranged for that to trigger the get-hit-and-die animation. Even if the player/character is looking away when you happen to shoot at your stormtrooper and you don't see him get hit, he's going to die, anyway."

"In a game like Dark Forces the stormtroopers weren't particularly

intelligent; they didn't know too much about the world they inhabited," Mark Haigh-Hutchinson adds. "They did know where the player was in respect to them and could turn and face and home in on the player. In Shadows we programmed our troopers with more knowledge of the world, which in this real-time game became a question of balancing resources, because the limited computing power will always define how complex the world can be. We had to do things that take less processing power because we didn't have the luxury of doing

"It's quite scary, actually, how technology has progressed," says project leader Mark Haigh-Hutchinson, marveling at the current crop of computers that can reproduce, in real time, 120,000 polygons a second.
Photo by Heather Sutton.

something like a computer chess game, where you typically wait a few seconds for a computer to make a decision. In a real-time action game, things are happening thirty times a second and the player's reacting constantly. So you have to proportion out how much time you've allotted to each task."

Although the Nintendo 64 would be supplying breakthrough rendering power, the technological limits would mandate the use of simple shapes in creating objects, such as a triangle sufficing for a distant Imperial Destroyer. The game design stage involved referencing the Doug Chiang ship designs and the Mike Butkus character art.

"There were so many people involved in the *Shadows* project, and when you have a bunch of people with different deadlines working on their own versions of something, you have the potential of ending up with a real big mess," Knoles says. "Plus there were a lot of people art-directing the Chiang and Butkus drawings, which is difficult as well. But with the initial designs we were able to not veer too much. It helps to have something set in stone first. The main thing for the game was not to contradict the novel, even though we added a couple of levels that aren't in the story. The story itself went through some changes, but the good news for us was that since the game was a real-time adventure, we didn't have a lot of rerendering to worry about if something had changed.

"In designing a game we'll usually work off rough pencil sketches because you don't usually need highly detailed sketches for low-resolution work," Knoles adds. "We'll make simple three-dimensional models using a variety of 3-D programs on either a Mac or a PC. I'll then take those and draw textures for them, using a paint tool on the computer. In some cases, as with certain ships like the *Millennium Falcon*, we'll actually use photographic reference from the real models for textures."

Game play is meant to be an involving experience, to *immerse* players in an alternative universe. Dark Forces, for example, was built so that even a good gamer would require forty hours to hurdle every obstacle and transcend every level. For Shadows, the game levels would not only drag the player into the action sequences of the story line but add an opening flashback mission to the Battle of Hoth, that historic ice planet skirmish featuring flying Rebel snowspeeders opposing the Empire's hulking walkers.

After the player-driven character Rendar exits the Hothian battle in his *Outrider*, avoiding TIE fighters and a deadly asteroid field awaiting him just outside the planet's atmosphere, the levels of adventure that lie ahead for the player/character include a bounty hunter search in a starship scrap yard on the planet of Ord Mantell, a jetpack battle with Boba Fett on the moon of Gall, a swoop bike chase through the deadly twists and turns of Tatooine's Beggar's Canyon, an assault on Xizor's fortresslike lair, and the spectacular final battle in the skies above the Imperial City.

The job of the level designers was to model those and other complex environments. Instead of the physical materials that would make up a real model, an object generated in the virtual realm would be constructed from a 3-D image of wire-frame skeletons with realistic surface textures applied. "Jon Knoles would come up with the basic idea for the levels, then I'd usually sit around with him and brainstorm action and puzzle areas, then I'd model it," explains Jim Current, a level designer who began his LucasArts career with Dark Forces. "To get from the beginning of a level to its end, the player can't jump around; it's like making your way through a building. Actually, one of the biggest challenges we have is keeping an expansive science fiction environment. In Dark Forces I'd design the Imperial City, and sometimes it was hard to figure out how to limit where the player could go yet retain the feeling that you're in a giant city that goes on forever. So we made rooftops you could see but not actually get to. The player's path would be limited, but there'd be a hint of things beyond."

The main design program for Shadows was Auto-CAD, a drafting program used in architectural and mechanical engineering. "Creating a level is a graphic process; we're essentially drawing it," Current explains. "It's only been recently that we've been able to model complex environments in 3-D, so when we design an environment, we can rotate the view and see the whole thing. For example, in Dark Forces we couldn't have an angled wall, but in Shadows we can create hexagonal hallways, arches, complex 3-D shapes. The Nintendo 64 is geared especially toward 3-D rendering. Computing power has gone up; it's been a natural evolution. Instead of linear scenes in an old game like Donkey Kong, we can now render an environment in real time and have the player move through it."

Once the wire-frame dimensions of an environment have been created, surface textures can be applied by the level designers. The digital technique of texture mapping, which some artists humorously refer to as "wallpapering," basically involves wrapping a picture around a three-dimensional object. For Shadows, once a texture file had been created and put through a special conversion program to convert it into a form readable in the Auto-CAD architectural program, the textures could then be fitted into the appropriate places. The amount of texture art and animation can be monumental; for Dark Forces there were thousands of individual texture files.

As with the games' kinship with robotics and virtual reality, the technology of level de-

Using Mike Butkus's preliminary art as a springboard, LucasArts' Jon Knoles developed his own concept sketches, notably for characters such as Xizor and Dash Rendar. In this series of Dash Rendar character designs, Knoles experimented with various looks and garb for the rogue pilot.

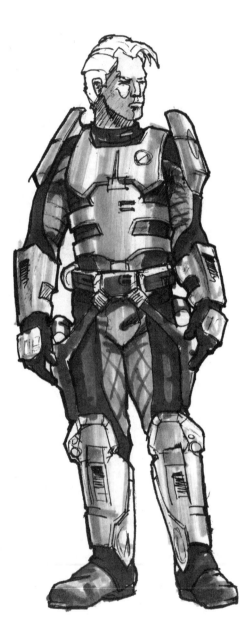

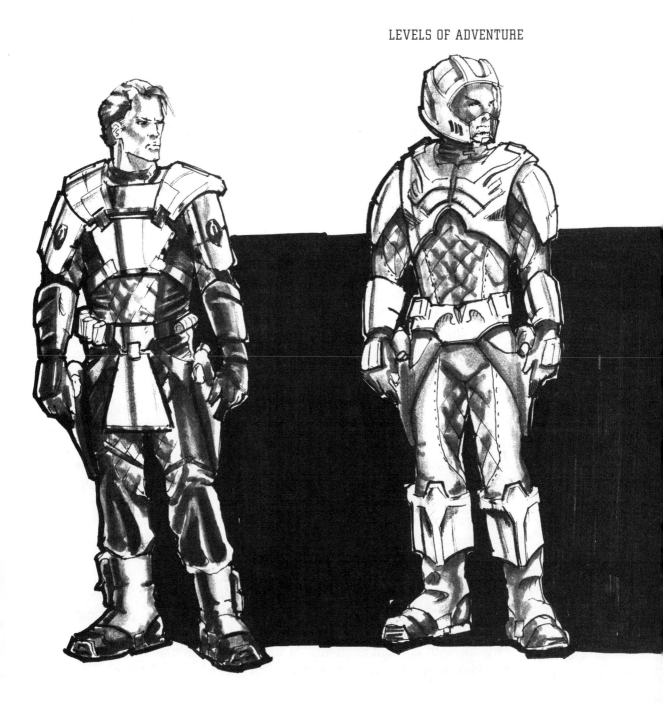

sign and texture mapping extends far beyond the domain of game play. "In the future people will be able to go to a real estate office and use this technology to design their house on a computer," notes LucasArts texture artist Chris Hockabout. "In the computer you could select the color of the walls, the texture of the floors, and what kind of tiles you want in the kitchen and give it to the contractor who'll build the house. That's more or less how level designers use the computer to apply textures to their architecture."

Texture mapping has become a common technique in the creation of feature film visual effects. At ILM the technique was used on films such as the 1991 *Hook*, during which a matte painting of Neverland Island was texture-mapped around a three-dimensional wire-frame model of the island, allowing for a camera move and the realistic perspective shift. Two years later, for *Jurassic Park*, ILM texture-mapping breakthroughs would allow for a CG (computer-generated) object to be rotated and painted in the full three dimensions, avoiding previous problems of distortion.

The texture mapping for low-resolution games environments, however, is far removed from the complexity of high-resolution, prerendered feature film effects. "Our texture mapping is nowhere near the complexity or level of detail you'd find in a film like *Jurassic Park*; it's like comparing checkers to chess," Hockabout explains. "I'm basically creating a two-dimensional plane with everything drawn on the computer made of pixels, which are dots of color. The textures I create have to repeat on all four sides, so when a texture is placed on any surface, it all comes together seamlessly.

"We're low-resolution for memory reasons, but there are programming tricks that can be done to make a game environment look a little higher-res, such as lighting and color mapping to create fog effects and enhance the particular texture's appearance.

"I work with D Paint Animator, a low-res 2-D animation program that game companies have been using for years," Hockabout continues. "Even though I'm not really using it to create animation, it has as its primary function the kind of multiple cells an animator would create. I can have a catalogue with hundreds of textures in one animation file and scroll from one page to the next. If I want to make a particular surface more distinctive, such as giving a rock surface a rougher texture, we have a high-res program with a large library of surface textures that can be lit from different angles, and I can choose one to overlay to the surface I'm working on and apply lighting to it."

Battle droid/bounty hunter IG-88 would provide Dash Rendar with a "boss monster" challenge on the Ord Mantell level.

Each Shadows level would have its own distinctive design look. The Imperial freighter carrying the Death Star plans would be designed with a dirty, metallic appearance, while the interior world of Xizor's palace would be a melange of Gothic, oriental, and other architectural styles. The levels of detail would be such that the Ord Mantell hovertrain alone (which Dash and the player ride on a bounty hunter search and destroy mission) would have forty to fifty separate textures applied. The process of assimilating the different components is referred to as "world building," according to Eric Johnston.

Dash Rendar, ready to be the player's surrogate in the dangerous world of Shadows.

91

"If we're doing a scene with a few thousand asteroids, a hundred TIE fighters, and some stars, we'll get those elements and components on a program we wrote for the SGI machine that we essentially use to tell each component how the particular world is to behave," Johnston explains. "The 3-D model of, say, a TIE fighter is really sort of a costume that the TIE fighter behavior wears. From a programming standpoint we have a whole bunch of different behaviors. One of those behaviors, which we call a TIE fighter, knows how to fly around and shoot at the protagonist. We could put a different costume on that behavior; we don't really care what costume a particular actor is wearing. We could have a human being flying around like a TIE fighter."

For project leader Mark Haigh-Hutchinson, the quantum leaps in game technology were typified by his old 8-bit Sinclair ZX-80, a circa-1980 microcomputer sitting atop the Silicon Graphics Onyx in his Lucas-Arts office. While the vintage computer had an estimated 1,000 bytes of memory, his state-of-the-art SGI computer had 256 million bytes.

"It's quite scary, actually, how technology has progressed." Haigh-Hutchinson laughs. "I look at my little Sinclair compared to the Onyx and think, This is fifteen years of progress. Where are we going to be in another fifteen years? I recently had a conversation with [ILM senior visual effects supervisor] Dennis Muren, and we came to the conclusion that real-time *Jurassic Park*–style graphics in games are seven to ten years away. In order to do that we'll need to increase our current computing power by about 128-fold. Currently we're reproducing about 120,000 polygons a second in real time, and for photorealistic creatures and such we'll need to do 20 million to 30 million a second, not to mention the storage capacity that'll be required.

"But that's historically where the computer industry has been—some people estimate computing power to double every year. Computers today are designed by other computers. People no longer go in by hand and design individual circuitry. Plus, nowadays you can get more circuitry into a smaller space, which means more power. In the past, because the technology was fairly limiting, most of the effort was concentrated on getting the game out of the machine. But I believe we're on the cusp of a change. As the technology is beginning to unfold, we're changing from technology to content. In the next few years technology will be in place that will allow people to go beyond action genres and develop games we could never have done before."

But for all the advances in real-time game machine rendering capabilities, the creation of 3-D environments, and leaps in artificial intelligence and world building, the game makers on both the hardware and software side didn't lose sight of the ultimate goal of their enterprise. "Game players are very discerning and like games for the challenge," Nintendo's Perrin Kaplan notes. "If a game looks good but doesn't have challenges, it'll bomb."

"We always kept it in mind that we were working on a game, not a research project," Haigh-Hutchinson adds. "At the end of the day people don't care too much about what goes on under the hood, as we say here. It's really the question 'Is it a fun game?' "

PART 3

JOURNEY INTO DARKNESS

From his throne room in Imperial City, Emperor Palpatine can project his holographic image across space, as in this scene where his wrathful form, projected into the communications field of Vader's Star Destroyer, orders the Dark Lord to assist Xizor in making shipping arrangements for the Death Star construction.

Shadows *Dark Horse Comic, issue 1, page 11; unedited pencils by Kilian Plunkett.*

I.
EMPIRE AND
UNDERWORLD

IN THE *STAR WARS* TRILOGY THE iron grip of the Empire is everywhere, from stormtroopers patrolling the dusty spaceport towns of Tatooine to Star Destroyers powering across the spacelanes from star system to star system. What movie-goers never saw but what did take form on the Lucasfilm drawing boards was the Empire's capital world of Coruscant. One scene—Emperor Palpatine having an audience with Darth Vader on the planet, with a vast expanse of the Imperial City visible from the throne room—had been planned in preproduction for *Return of the Jedi* but was never filmed.

Topps Trading Cards' 1994 *Galaxy* series reproduced glimpses of the Imperial home world as conjured up in the film production art of Ralph McQuarrie, Joe Johnston, and other artists. In those works we see the Imperial City as a vast expanse dominated by the pyramidal thrust of the Imperial Palace, along with other monolithic spires rising into smoky skies full of TIE fighters and Imperial shuttles.

In the *Shadows* story line a lot of the important action would be staged in the Imperial City's dark corridors of power, from the halls of Emperor Palpatine's Imperial Palace to the fortress lair of Xizor's Black Sun operations. "Coruscant is one of the major locales in the novel," author Steve Perry explains. "The planet is essentially covered by civilization; there's almost no bare ground left anywhere. It's one huge, monstrous city that covers the planet."

In the vision of Coruscant that was realized in the novel, the planet's wealthy and powerful few have access to protected corridors within the urban core, a hidden world where hawk-bats flit above the granite walls and the privileged strollers of the mighty upper class can drink in the delights of singing fig trees, jade roses, and other botanical exotica. Exalted personages such as the Emperor and Xizor also have access to their own skyhook complexes, giant orbiting satellites tethered to the surface world. On a planet

IMPERIAL PALACE

More LucasArts reference material provided Plunkett with Imperial palace concept drawings from the TIE Fighter game. The vaulting, cathedral look of the palace would be extended to the interiors for both the computer game and the comics series. (Plunkett's reference material included a photograph of the inside of a cathedral with the Jon Knoles note: "Think Gothic churches for interior shots!")

paved over with monumental plazas and superstructures, the only evidence of *natural* force is the jutting peak of Monument Park. From Menarai, the exclusive restaurant atop the mountain, one can dine at night and marvel at the blazing lights of the towering buildings below and the unending stream of space traffic above or perhaps watch a sudden burst of warm rain from the violent, ever-changing microweather systems.

And while the Imperial throne room on Coruscant had never before been fully realized, the unfolding saga had revealed numerous throne rooms strategically scattered throughout the galaxy. In *Jedi* Palpatine could dictate from a throne room on the uncompleted Death Star (the place where the mortally wounded Vader threw his old master down a

One of the earliest depictions of Imperial City can be seen in this Ralph McQuarrie movie concept painting. The Imperial Palace in the background, with its monumental scale and Gothic, cathedral-like design, would inspire the palace look in Shadows *projects such as the LucasArts game and the Dark Horse comics series.*

shaft to the core, seemingly to his death). A trilogy of novels by Timothy Zahn (*Heir to the Empire*, Bantam, 1991; *Dark Force Rising*, Bantam, 1992; *The Last Command*, Bantam, 1993) had established an Imperial throne room carved into the cavernous darkness of Mount Tantiss on the planet Wayland. On the comics side, Dark Horse's *Dark Empire* series had presented another Imperial lair on the planet Byss, a world in the central region of the galaxy.

Since the Imperial throne room would provide a dramatic setting for several scenes in the comics series, Lucasfilm provided Dark Horse artist Kilian Plunkett with a reference packet of visual and textual references. In excerpts from *The Illustrated Star Wars Universe* (a 1995 Bantam release) the Imperial throne room was described as a sunken auditorium with a prismatic skylight from which rainbow hues of light could illuminate the Emperor as he sat in regal majesty on a levitating chair. Additional visual references included schematics of the Imperial throne room on Mount Tantiss, sketches of a pyramidal Imperial Palace inspired by the original Coruscant movie production art, the vaulting arched interior of a medieval cathedral, and printouts and sketches for the LucasArts TIE Fighter game, which included a printout of TIE fighters escorting shuttles to the Imperial Palace and an image of the Emperor's chambers.

Right: LucasArts' 3-D/Background artist Bill Stoneham. Photo by Heather Sutton.
Below: LucasArts cut scene image of Imperial City, created by Bill Stoneham.

TIE fighters escort shuttles to the Imperial palace on Coruscant . . .

"When I drew an *Alien* series for Dark Horse, you'd imagine there would be quite a lot of reference material involved, but it was nothing as intense as this *Star Wars* project," Plunkett observes. "In the typical creative process an artist gets a script, which is like a screenplay, and depending on who the writer is, they will give you very tight stage direction, such as where the characters are to be in each panel, even what the lighting is like. Then you just draw it. But with *Shadows*, simply because it's appearing virtually simultaneously in so many other media, it's a little more complicated. For example, it's very easy to script something that says 'Xizor's opulent throne room' because it takes only two seconds to type. But before I can even render it, there have to be approved designs."

Xizor would be presented as a dominant force on the Imperial planet, a figure whose only rivals would be Vader and the Emperor

. . . where the Emperor awaits in his chambers. These printouts from LucasArts'
TIE Fighter game were sent by Jon Knoles to Kilian Plunkett as part of a reference
packet designed to assist the artist in conjuring up the Imperial stronghold for the
Shadows *comics.*

himself. The Dark Prince would be following in a line of storied *Star Wars* villains. In that pantheon of evil the movies had presented the evil Emperor, Darth Vader, the crime lord Jabba the Hutt, and deadly bounty hunters such as Boba Fett. In three Timothy Zahn *Star Wars* novels, set five years after the Battle of Endor, Grand Admiral Thrawn, a tall, blue-skinned master of military strategy, resurrects Imperial might and nearly destroys the Alliance's fledgling New Republic. In the LucasArts game Dark Forces there's the brutish General Mohc, who unleashes the deadly dark troopers against the forces of the Alliance.

Xizor would be created as a creature with a tragic past who could weave plots with Machiavellian cunning, snap a victim's neck with a warrior's ferocity, or seduce a female with a narcotic pheromone naturally exuded from his reptilian body. As overlord of the Black Sun, Xizor could embody all the unsavory elements of the *Star Wars* universe, making him a counterpoint to the Empire's military might and Vader's dark side mastery.

Ralph McQuarrie's painting of the interior of the Imperial Palace inspired the look of LucasArts' Xizor's fortress entranceway.

Entrance to Xizor's Fortress, LucasArts, drawn by Paul Topolos.

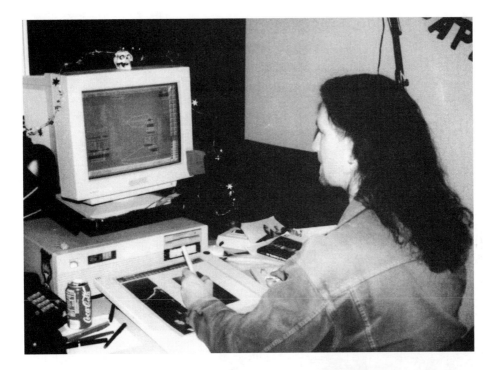

"We'd never before shown organized crime in the *Star Wars* universe from the top down," Lucasfilm's Howard Roffman observes. "The basic story line in *Shadows* was to look at the crime syndicate and reveal an organizational structure that mirrored the perceptions of our own earthbound existence. The sense is that this powerful crime syndicate has many branches and that the government and organized crime surreptitiously serve each other's interests. That was the only direction that George Lucas gave to this

Above: LucasArts texture artist Chris Hockabout helps build the Shadows *world in virtual space. Photo by Heather Sutton.*
Right: Paul Topolos, storyboard artist. Photo by Heather Sutton.

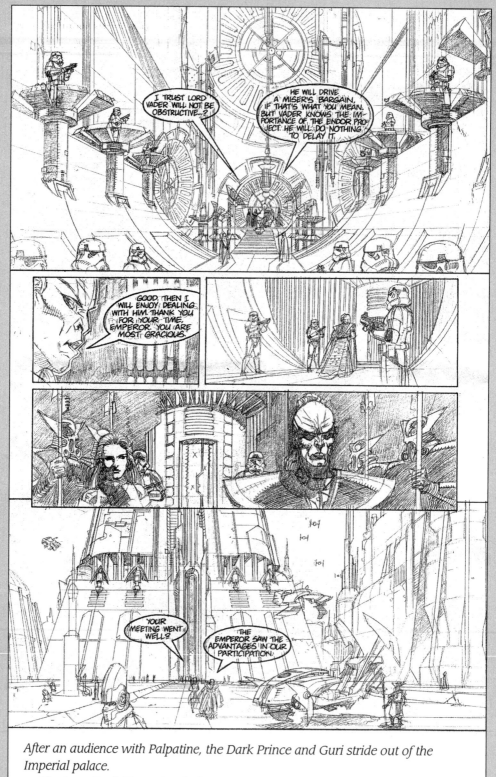

After an audience with Palpatine, the Dark Prince and Guri stride out of the Imperial palace.

  Shadows Dark Horse Comic, issue 1, page 14; unedited pencils by Kilian Plunkett.

In the great plaza outside the Imperial palace, Xizor sets in motion his assassination plans for Luke Skywalker.

Shadows *Dark Horse Comic*, issue 1, page 15; unedited pencils by Kilian Plunkett.

project. He wanted the underworld to be believable and have an antecedent in the real world."

Just as the Emperor's throne room would be the nerve center of Imperial power, Xizor's headquarters would be the heart of the Black Sun. In the novel the Dark Prince's fortified palace would tower some 102 levels above ground. And with an eye to keeping his enemies close to him, Xizor's fortress would be situated a few kilometers' walk through protected corridors to Darth Vader's own palace stronghold.

For LucasArts, Xizor's palace (dubbed the "Black Sun lair" by the gamemasters) would be designed as a medieval-looking fortress retrofitted with beams and walls of durasteel (an ultralightweight but superstrong metal found in the *Star Wars* universe). Although Ralph McQuarrie's classic Imperial City production paintings would be the major reference, texture artist Chris Hockabout would be given free rein in designing the surface elements of the Dark Prince's stronghold. Hockabout would ultimately envision a synthesis of architectural styles, with an emphasis on a mystical, eastern look.

"I suppose the theme for Xizor's palace would be 'darkly majestic,' kind of evil and sinister but with a regal air about it," Hockabout explains. "For the interior I concentrated on a lot of buttresses, arches, and some H. R. Gigeresque bioorganic stuff combined with Chinese inlaid engravings. With ancient Chinese architecture there are things like flowing lines with lighter contrasting to darker colors and interlocking lines. So I'd do a wall with that kind of inlaid Chinese border, and then below these flowing line patterns there'd be a steel archway with a bioorganic look."

In the novel Xizor's palace would also be described as a place of stately pleasures, a domain befitting a figure worth billions of credits (a credit being the basic monetary unit used throughout the galaxy). Xizor was so rich that he could spend "a warlord's ransom" having the glowtiles of a ceiling in his palace holographically set with the exact star patterns of the galaxy or expend nine million credits having a human female replica droid programmed to become Guri, his faithful assassin.

A hedonist at heart, the Dark Prince would have loved to serve spice when entertaining his wealthy and powerful guests (although it was said he never indulged himself). Xizor also took perverse pleasure in seeing his enemies suffer. In one scene from the novel, the Dark Prince is taking his ease in the palace, watching a recording of some extreme prejudice Guri had exerted against executives of business rival Ororo Transportation. Guri had just shot the chief of security and chief financial officer in the base of the skull and was turning toward the prone body of the muscular Tuyay, the chief operating officer she had just incapacitated with a powerful throat grab:

> Then she returned to where Tuyay lay, trying to breathe through his bruised throat. She squatted next to him and waited until he came to and looked up at her.
>
> "I'll tell Prince Xizor what you said." She smiled and almost carelessly shoved the blaster against Tuyay's left eyeball and pulled the trigger.
>
> Then she stood, walked to where a hidden security wallcam recorded the entire scene, and ripped the unit out of the wall.
>
> The picture went black.
>
> "Stop the recording," Xizor said.
>
> He sighed and shook his head. The recording showed him what he already knew. Guri was the deadliest weapon in his arsenal. He wondered how she would do in a one-on-one against Vader. Probably better than he would, though he was fairly certain that Vader, who had hunted down and killed Jedi adepts, could take her.
>
> Even so, it would be interesting to watch.
>
> And at nine million credits a very expensive entertainment, should she lose.
>
> "Run it again," he said.
>
> He did love to see a professional at work.

II.
THE DARK PRINCE

THE BEADY VIOLET EYES ARE shrouded by curving brows, his greenish-skinned face a sculpted mask highlighted with high cheekbones and an aquiline nose. For all its alien quality, it's a beautiful face. But it is also the gaze of a powerful soul, the slight sneering curl of the lips and the intensity of the gaze a vessel for what could be a mask of seduction, majesty, or the pure incarnation of evil.

This image, a close-cropped printout of a cut scene created in April 1995, was designed by LucasArts' Jon Knoles, inspired in part by some storyboard art by Paul Topolos. Both the image and the color of the printout were so well received by Lucasfilm, this marked the final stage in the design of Xizor, the Dark Prince.

Although other characters would be created for the *Shadows* saga—including Guri and Dash Rendar—Xizor would prove the most ambitious creation. For Lucasfilm's Howard Roffman, the Dark Prince was his favorite character, the one on whom he focused most of his initial comments on the first draft of Steve Perry's novel. "Xizor is a classic villain; he's like the Godfather with a reptilian overlay," Roffman says. "When we were thinking up the character, we definitely felt we didn't want to make him a simple human. He had to have something exotic about him. Given that the character was going to be cold, calculating, and mean-spirited, it seemed appropriate to make him reptilian."

In the early planning stages for *Shadows of the Empire* Lucasfilm press releases had promised that the new project would take fans "deep into the world of gun runners, spice traders, assassins and crime bosses like Jabba the Hutt." The then-unnamed criminal overlord was vaguely referred to as the "leader of the syndicate." Even while Dark Horse editor Ryder Windham was recommending to Lucasfilm a comics-side creative team of writer John Wagner, artist Kilian Plunkett, and series cover artist Hugh Fleming, the master crime lord was being referred to as "Jabba's boss."

The conjuring of the look, personality, and backstory of Xizor began in the November 1994 *Shadows* brainstorm session at Skywalker Ranch. In Xizor's backstory, he was a member of the Falleen, a humanoid and reptilian race. Their physiological characteristics include dusky green skin color, a reptilian ridge over the spine, the ability to breathe underwater, and a hormonal system that enables them to emit pheromones (during which the skin color changes to a warmer hue) that are intoxicating to the opposite sex of any species. "Xizor's look evolved, with Steve Perry coming up with the idea of the pheromones and the idea of his skin color changing with his mood," says Lucasfilm's Lucy Wilson.

Wilson felt that as a powerful criminal overlord the character should exude a charismatic allure powerful enough to tempt Princess Leia. Although in the novel Leia would encounter Xizor and nearly be seduced by those Falleen pheromones, Wilson felt that a more intriguing conflict could have been staged between the two strong-willed characters: "I originally wanted Leia to have a romance with Xizor. I wanted Princess Leia to be tempted, to show another aspect of her personality. My desire would have been to make Xizor be a little more emotional and not all bad. Leia is attracted to him because of the pheromones, so it's all chemical. If Leia had been intrigued and attracted to Xizor, drawn into his web, she'd also have these incredible feelings of guilt because she'd be betraying Han Solo."

Ultimately Xizor's personal history would provide plenty of fuel for the making of a classic character. The Dark Prince's power struggle with Vader would be revealed as having been prompted by equal measures of ambition and personal vengeance.

Xizor would never forget the time, some ten years before the events of *Shadows*, when an insidious biological experiment was conducted by Lord Vader at a biological weapons lab on the planet Falleen that resulted in a death sentence for his family and hundreds of thousands of other Falleens. The experiment, aimed at developing what would have been another arrow in the quiver of Imperial armaments, turned disastrous when a mutating, tissue-gobbling bacterium escaped quarantine. To save the entire planet from being devastated by the deadly, incurable bacteria, Vader ordered that sterilization lasers be used to incinerate the entire radius of the outbreak. In the burning ashes, among 200,000 annihilated Falleens, were Xizor's parents, his brother and two sisters, and three uncles. Off-world at the time of the disaster, the Dark Prince later had all records of his family's incineration eliminated from the Imperial rolls to conceal any evidence of a possible motive he might have in one day destroying Vader.

The gestation of Xizor's physical appearance lasted approximately half a year and began with early line art by Mike Butkus. "With most *Star Wars* characters we have stacks of photo reference, but we really had nothing to go on with the new *Shadows* characters; it was just coming out of our minds," Lucasfilm Licensing's art director, Troy Alders, notes. "Once we created the line art, the various licensees could have their own artists do drawings based on that. Of course, the nature of compelling characters is that people are going to want to interpret them. Creative freedom is one thing, but we don't want to confuse people. We try to keep everything as consistent as possible; that's usually our number one concern. It's fine if an artist lends his or her own style

Headgear

inhumanly
long neck

Well, it solves
the hair
problem...

XIZOR

XIZOR'S HANDS ARE CLEARLY NOT HUMAN — THE FINAL JOINT ON EACH DIGIT IS ALMOST EQUAL TO THE COMBINED LENGTH OF THE OTHER TWO + THE LITTLE FINGER IS VESTIGAL—

The initial Xizor concept involved combining a regal stature with a reptilian look. In the early concept stage, artist Kilian Plunkett contributed these sketches, experimenting with a variety of looks for the exotic character.

115

to it, but details have to be followed. That's really the core of what we do here at the licensing art department."

Conjuring up an image of the Dark Prince, one that could be replicated in diverse media, also included the creation of a twelve-inch-tall painted Xizor statue by the sculptor Susumu Sugita. "The Xizor sculpture gave us a dimensional object we could turn around and light, as opposed to just a series of two-dimensional line drawings, which we felt could provide a helpful reference to the illustrators and painters working on the various *Shadows* projects," Alders explains. "Xizor seemed an important character to do this for because of his costuming and physical complexity, as opposed to Dash, who's human, so you can figure out how to draw and paint him." (Additional sculpture work would be undertaken by Lucas-Arts as it actually did craft a sculpture of Dash Rendar and scanned the dimensional information into its computer systems to help develop Dash designs.)

Given the unique talents of the various artists, there was an inevitable organic evolution in the look of Xizor from the very beginning. One of the early design concepts, circulated in February 1995 by Lucasfilm, depicted a tall, taloned figure with a large skull that was bare except for a topknotted ponytail curling past broad shoulders that were covered by a ceremonial costume. Although the original directive, as well as production drawings, for Xizor was to feature a reptilian look, Jon Knoles felt that the initial design approach was making the

During the early Shadows *research phase, the Lucasfilm archives served up this* Return of the Jedi *concept sketch of Bib Fortuna, the chief lieutenant of Jabba the Hutt, which in turn inspired the classic Xizor pose produced by Mike Butkus.*
Return of the Jedi *production illustration by Nilo Rodis-Jamero.*

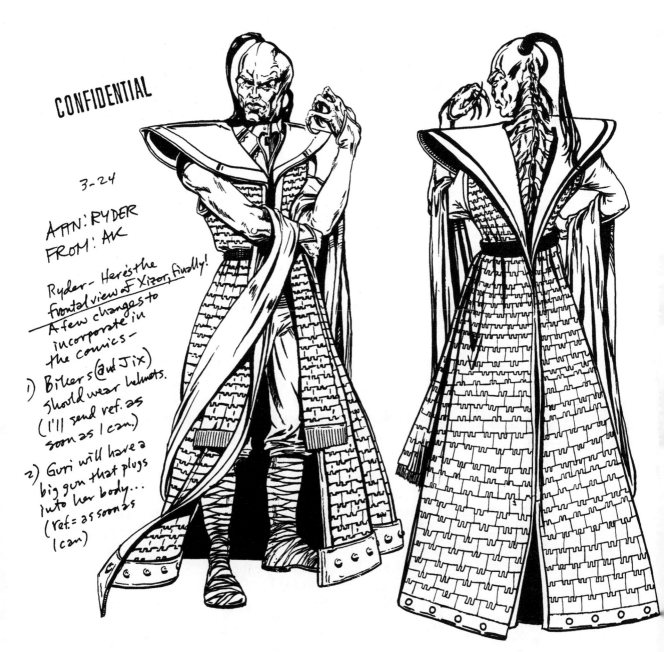

Left: Xizor, frontal view, art by Mike Butkus (with notes from continuity editor Allan Kausch to Dark Horse editor Ryder Windham). Certain details (such as the hair) would change as development continued.

Right: Initial back view illustration of Xizor by Mike Butkus.

117

Black Sun overlord a tad *too* monstrous. The accepted final look on the games side became the above-mentioned close-up image, which Knoles began circulating in May.

"I wanted to get away from the lizard look because if, as it goes in the story, Xizor's supposed to be charming enough to lure Princess Leia, we needed to give him a little more charm but still make him spooky," Knoles says. "Then there's Kilian Plunkett, who did another little twist, adding a lot of nice lines to the forehead and around the eyes for a sleek quality. Anytime you do something like this, there's another interpretation. But our overall goal was not to be too stylistic but to come up with what you'd see in a movie."

In January 1995 Plunkett had thrown a variety of character and vehicular designs into the mix, including some four pages of Xizor poses. "My big thing with Xizor was it was an opportunity to do something very oriental, because *Star Wars*, in terms of its narrative, is very much structured from samurai epics, with aging warlords and bands of warrior knights," Plunkett observes. "I went through a lot of photo references for Mongol warriors. I played with giving Xizor a furry sort of Russian hat and at one stage drew him with a cowl like a medieval knight. In the original character description Xizor was reptilian, although there was always the danger he would end up looking more like a *Star Trek* alien than a *Star Wars* character. But Xizor grew on me. What I tried to do in the drawing was change the shape of his skull so it was slightly more elongated and make the gap between his mouth and eyes longer, all to give him more of an unhuman look."

When Dark Horse began submitting Plunkett's completed pencils for the first twenty-four-page *Shadows* issue, Lucasfilm requested some subtle changes in the Xizor art. "Because I would be working closely with P. Craig Russell on the inking, I could make the pencils a little looser and we could revise them at the inking stage," Plunkett says. "So I didn't really mind the fact that Xizor was changing, because he was changing as I drew him, anyway. But requested changes are the nature of the beast on a project like this, where there are a lot of different sources of input. You really can't expect the amount of control you might have if it were purely your own thing."

In the first issue of the Dark Horse comics, Xizor is in ascendance while Vader must suffer some Imperial displeasure, particularly because Luke Skywalker, despite being defeated by Vader in the lightsaber battle of *Empire*, had still inexplicably managed to escape. The scene opens with Vader deep in space aboard his Star Destroyer and reporting by holographic transmission to the Emperor on Coruscant. Unknown to Vader, Xizor is present in the throne room witnessing the uncharacteristically terse exchange between Palpatine and his second in command. As this excerpt (complete with stage directions) from John Wagner's original script reveals:

> Emperor: You've failed me, Vader!
> Full page portrait of Vader, tall, grim, menacing, his cloak sweeping out behind him as he strides purposefully towards unseen Emperor.
> Vader: Luke Skywalker's escape was unfortunate—but not fatal! I have sown the seeds of ambition in his mind. Rest assured, he will be ours!
> Focus on Emperor here, him only, slightly histrionic.
> Emperor (JAG): Rest assured! Ahh, yes! Put my faith in you!
> Wider, both of them here, more focus on Emperor, who points finger accusingly.
> Emperor: Were I to judge by your deeds rather than your words, Vader, I would be forced to conclude you do not wish to ensnare Skywalker!
> Vader: You know that is untrue! . . . The idea to bring him to the dark side was mine! . . . Even now I am redoubling my efforts to find him. . . . I have a report of a possible sighting of the Rebel fleet.

To assist the various Shadows *artists in capturing Xizor's alien look, a three-dimensional, twelve-inch-tall sculpture based on Butkus's illustrative pose was created by sculptor Susumu Sugita. The initial sculpture is seen on the left, the final version on the right.*
Photos by Lucy Wilson (left) and Halina Krukowski (right).

    Emperor: I'm afraid that must wait. I have a more pressing matter for you to attend to. Construction of the new weapon proceeds apace. The Imperial fleet alone cannot handle our delivery requirements. To that end you will return to Coruscant to conclude shipping arrangements with Prince Xizor.

    Vader: Xizor! Do you think that is wise?

    Emperor: Xizor controls the largest merchant fleet in the galaxy. He can be useful to us.

    Vader: His ties to Black Sun are too well known. He is dangerous, and not to be trusted with a military cargo. His interests are not the Empire's.

    Emperor: Black Sun indeed! Do not concern yourself with schoolboy rumors. Better to attend to your own duties. You have your instructions.

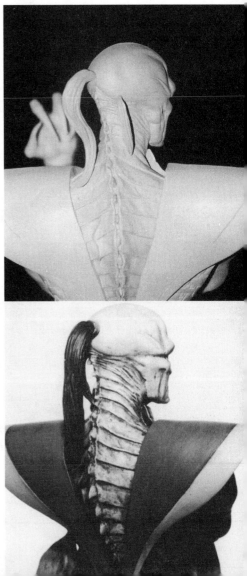

The transmission ends, leaving an unhappy Vader pondering the situation. Back in the vaulting space of the throne room, Xizor allows himself a slight smile as he addresses the Emperor: "Regrettable. The Dark Lord of the Sith has many admirable qualities but he can be a trifle rigid in his thinking. I hope his judgment is not impaired by his emotions—his hatred for me, his love for his son."

After his audience, Xizor strides out of the throne room and is silently joined by a waiting Guri. In the vast plaza that provides some open space between the Imperial Palace and the surrounding spires of buildings, Xizor discusses with Guri aspects of his plot to have bounty hunters and swoop bikers hunt down and kill Luke Skywalker. As Guri leaves, Xizor boards his shuttle. His thoughts turn to his archenemy.

"Yes, Vader!" Xizor snarls to himself. "I am dangerous—especially if you hope to deliver young Skywalker to the Emperor alive."

Unpainted and painted views of the Sugita Xizor sculpture (details).

Left: Xizor, the Dark Prince.
   Shadows *Dark Horse Comic, panel rough, issue 1, page 13; pencils by Kilian*
      Plunkett.
Right: Darth Vader, Dark Lord of the Sith.
   Preliminary illustration by Kilian Plunkett.

III.
XIZOR VERSUS VADER

PREPARATORY TO STEVE PERRY'S
writing of the *Shadows* novel, Bantam senior editor Tom Dupree provided the author with a December 5, 1994, memo of comments on the initial outline. In the six-page memo the first order of business was the planned clash of titans:

> **Xizor.** We'd like you to consider ways to make Xizor a grander, darker, more powerful character. To put it in *Godfather* terms, you have him closer to Solozzo, the weasely but smart guy who killed Luca Brazzi and engineered the assassination attempt on Don Corleone. What we have in mind is . . . closer to a corrupt Aristotle Onassis. This guy is hugely powerful, and his "legit" businesses are well known throughout the galaxy (the fact that he's tight with the Emperor is not so well known) . . . In every way, Xizor has to be able to stand toe to toe with Vader, his utter equal in stature. We'd like to see more of this awesome power, both in word and deed, and more of the sense that Xizor is constantly playing this mental chess game, trying to curry favor with the Emperor at the expense of Vader, and that he's perfectly capable of *defeating* Vader. That *Godfather* reference up there isn't completely flip: we're looking for more of that tumultuous warring-clan intrigue . . .

Vader. With this book we have a wonderful advantage that no other *Star Wars* project can boast: we get to use *Darth Vader* . . . We want more Vader point-of-view; we want to see his response to Xizor's latest move. The character is in a weird position in this story: the climactic tug of war between Darth and [Xizor] is over Luke Skywalker himself. Both of them want Luke. But only Vader wants him alive. So the reader actually hopes that Vader will win this particular tug of war (yes, we all know that Luke survived, so what you have to do is make sure the reader understands *just how close he came to dying*) . . . Xizor is probably Vader's biggest threat ever. From their experience, the movie audience sees Vader as nearly unstoppable. Now, here's a guy who could actually take him out. That has to be a critical subplot.

Vader's stature as a classic fantasy villain stems from the fortuitous events of his origin. Early on in the *Star Wars* design process George Lucas had asked artist Ralph McQuarrie to come up with illustrations for Vader and other only-dreamed-of characters. Lucas had envisioned a tall, dark figure with a cape that fluttered in the wind and a wide brim helmet like the headgear of a medieval samurai. Since the film's opening sequence would feature Vader's grand entrance, commanding his Imperial stormtroopers as they boarded the Rebel Blockade Runner, McQuarrie reasoned that the character should also have a mask to enable him to breathe in outer space. Thus was the imposing figure's face hidden behind an impenetrable facade, with such design touches as a suggestion of teeth in the mask's grillwork.

In *The Empire Strikes Back* a startled subordinate officer would catch a glimpse of the back of Vader's scarred head as the Sith Lord's dark helmet was being mechanically fitted over him. The inference that Vader wore his helmet and armor because of some physical damage he'd suffered would be explained in the novelization of *Return of the Jedi*: it was the result of the battle with Obi-Wan that Vader miracu-

Darth Vader works out his frustrations before a meeting with Xizor by slicing up this combat droid. (His agent Jix makes the mistake of being a little too disinterested and gets a bolt of the Force that snaps him to attention.)

  Shadows *Dark Horse Comic, issue 2, pages 1–3; unedited pencils by Kilian Plunkett.*

127

lously survived. By *Shadows* Vader would be regularly ensconcing himself in the healing environment of his hyperbaric medical chamber.

Vader's mysterious designation in the original *Star Wars* script as "Dark Lord of the Sith" would also be expanded on in the evolving continuity of the saga. In *Dark Lords of the Sith*, the six-part *Tales of the Jedi* series published by Dark Horse in 1994 and set four thousand years in the past, it was revealed (in the recordings of the Jedi Holocron then being prepared by Jedi Master Vodo-Siosk Baas) that the Dark Lords were a renegade band of magicians who had tapped into the dark side of the Force.

Although Xizor would be designed as Vader's ultimate adversary, the Dark *Prince* would not be a carbon copy of the Dark *Lord*. Xizor was to be a physically imposing figure with muscle mass developed and strengthened by a "myostim unit" that automatically contracted and relaxed his muscles, but he was loath to personally engage Vader in physical combat. Instead of drawing lightsabers with Vader, Xizor would take on the Dark Lord with the mental stratagems of an ultimate chessmaster. (Of course, Xizor wouldn't shirk an opportunity to mete out some physical punishment. The novel describes an assassination attempt on Xizor in the normally protected core corridors in which the Dark Prince waves off his bodyguards, toys with his attacker, and then fatally snaps the neck of his victim. Xizor afterward suspects the hand of Vader in getting the attacker into the protected area.)

In the novel Xizor also emerges as a creature who thrives on risk. Even a seemingly innocent visit to the Menarai restaurant in Imperial Park (where a table was always ready for him) could have an aura of danger if Xizor was in the mood to dine on moonglow, a pearlike fruit found only in a small patch of a single forest on a distant world. The taste of the rare delicacy was heightened by the fact that the diner faced coma and death if some ninety-seven preparatory steps were not precisely followed by a master moonglow chef.

Xizor's influence with Emperor Palpatine was based partly on his command of the Black Sun criminal syndicate. But it would be his legit-

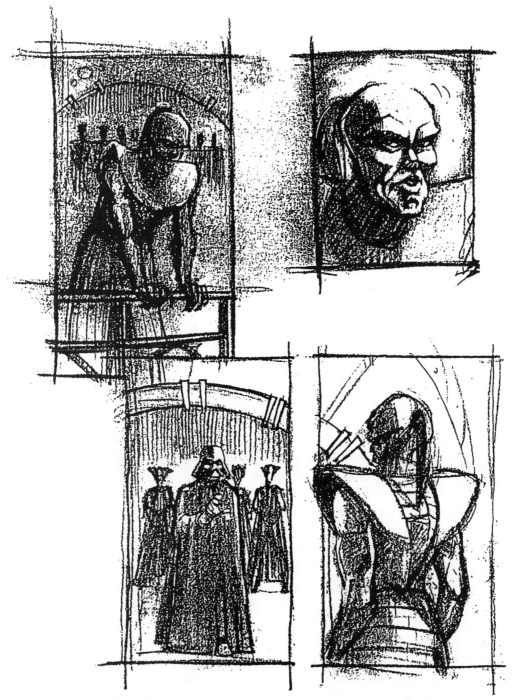

Applause storyboards were used to work out the dramatic scenes that ultimately would be fine-tuned into select poses for their toy line. These storyboards capture the drama of the momentous meeting between Xizor and Darth Vader.
   Applause concept art by Dave Williams.

imate Xizor Transport Systems business interests—and their importance in providing some three hundred cargo ships needed to get the Death Star construction project under way—that would earn him frequent access to the Imperial throne room. And it would be a bitter Darth Vader who, at the Emperor's behest, would have to negotiate personally terms with the Dark Prince.

For Xizor, such meetings would be an opportunity to feint and joust with words and ceremony. For Vader, such meetings placed him in the unaccustomed position of having to kowtow to a figure he despised. In one holographic exchange described in the novel, Xizor is in audience with the Emperor, who invites Vader to express some gratitude to the Dark Prince. Steve Perry writes: "Vader gritted his teeth. He would rather bite off his own tongue and swallow it than offer such gratitude, especially in front of the Emperor, but he had no choice."

Of course, Palpatine is aware of the tension between the two opponents. At the conclusion of the above meeting, the novel notes that Palpatine "had enjoyed . . . pitting his two servants against each other and watching to see how the play would go. He was like a man who owned a pack of semitame wolf cats. He enjoyed throwing a single bone into the pack to see which would outfight the others to claim it."

Such complex conflicts between characters have always been part of the *Star Wars* saga. As Lucas himself would say of the making of his movies, it was character and story that really drove the universe. "The characters are archetypes, but they're fairly realistic," Howard Roffman notes. "The way diplomacy or negotiations are conducted, it's not a childlike fantasy. For example, the scene that tickles me every time I see it is in *Star Wars* when Luke and Obi-Wan come to Mos Eisley to negotiate with Han Solo to have him fly them off Tatooine. It's beautifully constructed because it's so real. You have this seasoned, cynical pilot who's trying to sell himself, and he's negotiating with a wise old man who's patient and savvy, and there's this hotshot kid who flies off the handle at the slightest thing. And Han plays them off against each

Vader bows to the image of the Emperor at the end of a holographic transmission from Palpatine's throne room. Unknown to the Dark Lord, Xizor has been present all the while and has heard Vader express concerns about the Imperial alliances with the underworld.

Dialogue by John Wagner, unedited pencils by Kilian Plunkett; Shadows 1, page 13.

131

other, getting Luke all riled by saying, 'Who's going to fly it, kid?' In the hands of a lesser filmmaker that could have been a real dopey 'name your price' type of scene. But it's turned into a real negotiation based on the personalities of the people involved. It's that little spin where you kind of use the event to illustrate character and create something that's very realistic.

"And then, for the underworld figures, you look at research on organized crime and really good crime movies," Roffman adds. "Certainly the *Star Wars* movies have set a certain standard about the way people behave, particularly those who are in high positions of influence or evil. You want the interactions of powerful people in your fiction to mirror reality. In my job, I deal with a number of high-ranking, extremely powerful business people. It's taught me that while powerful people are all different and may have different kinds of strategies and tactics and idiosyncrasies, they all tend to be very serious and focused about what they do. They're generally not stupid. One thing that's a total red flag to me is if you have a fictional character who's very powerful but does stupid things. In children's fiction there's a tendency to have stupid villains. But even though *Star Wars* has had tremendous appeal to little kids, George never condescended, never said, 'Let's make our villains stupid and laughable.' The villains are very serious. And although they may make miscalculations or have foibles like anyone else, they're not stupid."

While Vader can move Imperial forces in the search for his son, Xizor has all the bounty hunters and swoop bike gangs at Black Sun's command to find and destroy the young Skywalker. Xizor also knows that any bounty hunters who can catch up with Boba Fett and his cargo of Han Solo might also find Luke Skywalker in pursuit of Fett.

Aware of Luke's vulnerability, Princess Leia would hire Dash Rendar to help keep a watchful eye on Luke. The roguish, fearless space pilot would ultimately become, like Han Solo before him, inexorably drawn into choosing sides in the galactic struggle between the Alliance and the Empire.

The regal Vader meets the scheming Xizor in this early Applause concept. The Xizor pose shown here ultimately would be used in a final figurine design that included both the Emperor and Vader.

Applause concept art by Dave Williams.

DASH RENDAR
- CHARACTER MOST
LIKELY TO HAVE
'MOM' TATTOOED
ON HIS ARM -

Although writer Steve Perry conceived Dash Rendar as a literally dashing character, the intrepid smuggler/pilot was anything but that in these early concept sketches by Kilian Plunkett.

134

IV.
REBEL FORCE

"**Dash Rendar:** Daring warrior-for-hire and freelance weapons specialist, Dash scours the galaxy looking for trouble—if the price is right. He has been employed as a bounty hunter, a demolition expert, a top ace fighter pilot . . . He is battle worn and rough in appearance."

—Early Dash character description; LucasArts Entertainment
   Company internal document (1/12/95)

ALTHOUGH CONJURING UP THAT reptilian Falleen Xizor was generally regarded as the greatest challenge in *Shadows*, bringing Dash Rendar to life also posed some tricky problems. As Bantam editor Tom Dupree, in one of his last postoutline-premanuscript notes to Steve Perry, observed: "We know [Dash is] designed to be around while the swashbuckling Han is encased in carbonite, but we don't want Dash to be a carbonite copy of Mr. Solo. Our suggestion is that rather than thinking of him simply as a mercenary, Dash is more like a swaggery *Top Gun*–style fighter pilot. A guy with real talent but a bit of a braggart and a blowhard, too. Luke doesn't like him, not only because of this in-your-face personality but also because of the natural competitiveness between these two pilots."

Like Xizor, whose family had been wiped out in the aftermath of Vader's disastrous biological weapons experiment, Dash would be haunted and motivated by his own tragic past. Rendar's family had been wealthy, owning a shipping business on Imperial Center, and Dash himself had been a year behind Han Solo in the prestigious, elite Imperial Academy. But one horrible day Dash's older brother, a freighter pilot lifting off from Coruscant's spaceport, saw his control panel blow up and his ship crash into Emperor Palpatine's private spaceport museum. Palpatine's anger was all-consuming, his punishment swift and brutal: seizure of all Rendar family assets, removal of Dash from the academy, and banishment of the Rendar family from the planet.

A bitter and angry young man, Dash would take up the nomadic life of a smuggler, prowling the spaceways in his *Outrider* with his droid copilot Leebo. If the price was right, Dash would even hire himself out to the Alliance, which valued his super piloting skills. In one memorable adventure Dash, bringing in a shipment of supplies to the Rebel's Echo Base on Hoth, was caught in the sudden Imperial attack. Always eager for a good fight, Dash joined Skywalker's Rogue Squadron in the battle against the advancing snowtroopers and AT-AT walkers. Although the Rebel base was overrun, Rendar acquitted himself nobly in the exchange, which would go down in *Star Wars* history as the Battle of Hoth.

It was a challenge nailing down the right physical characteristics to match Dash Ren-

IF DASH EVER WEARS A JACKET, IT'S SHORT, LOOSE + HAS BIG INSIDE POCKETS

Dash takes aim and fires in these early Kilian Plunkett sketches (left and opposite page).

dar's personality. Before the circulation of Michael Butkus's initial sketches of the character, Dark Horse artist Kilian Plunkett produced his own Dash designs, which depicted a wild-eyed, unshaven, disheveled figure with the beginnings of a paunch. It was a figure that if outfitted with cowboy boots and a six-shooter could have stepped out of a rugged spaghetti Western, a character sweaty from the recycled air of his *Outrider* spaceship, a guy who had suffered the blinding suns and hot winds of tough planetary terrains. As Plunkett put it in a note written above one of his character sketches: "Dash Rendar—character most likely to have 'Mom' tattooed on his arm."

"My original Dash drawings were sort of Elvis in space," Plunkett says. "In the first design I gave him a cool sort of double holster and guns strapped under his arms, like the old character the Shadow. I wanted to do a character who was in the vein of the hero-rogue but different from Han Solo, who was a slightly brainy and brawny hero, and Lando Calrissian, who was not very good with his fists but a clever and witty gambler type. I thought it'd be fun to do someone who could contrast between Han and Lando. Someone very reckless, nasty, tough, slightly running to fat and a bit of a slob who could take insane amounts of punishment and keep going. It seemed to make sense because he betrays people in the course of the narrative, such as in an issue of the comics where he leads the Rebels to Gall after Boba Fett. He takes them through all these Imperial defenses, and as soon as they get down to the level where they could get shot at by Imperial ground troops, Dash takes off and goes into hyperspace. Dash, you bastard!"

Separately, in a February 24, 1995 fax to Lucasfilm from LucasArts, Jon Knoles responded to the starting-point Dash Rendar sketches that had been prepared by Michael Butkus and voiced game side concerns on both the look and the personality of the two-fisted character: "[Dash's] clothes shouldn't be skin-tight and he shouldn't have bulging hero muscles. He should be fit, certainly, but exaggerated muscles are a bit too much. Can he have short cropped hair or combed back hair? The bushy curly look is kind of goofy for a star pilot and warrior. The face is the real trick to this guy. Mean, rough and tough or clean-cut sharp features? If he's going to be a smuggler or mercenary, we should go to town and make him the meanest looking S.O.B. in the galaxy (like Kilian's drawings). If not, let's get him as far away from that as possible and make him a determined and angry young warrior."

Jon Knoles's own character designs experimented with a number of looks. Some of the figure sketches featured bulky full-body armor and face-obscuring helmets. Other line art experimented with a range of expressions—even a mustache and Vandyke beard. Four to five months later a series of Mike Butkus and Knoles line art designs would

Dash gets cleaned up in this nearly final look by Mike Butkus (right), which would be further polished at LucasArts. "Once we were given the Butkus drawing, we tried not to veer too much," Jon Knoles says. "Lucy Wilson [of Lucasfilm Licensing] had said she wanted Dash Rendar to be young and heroic—kind of Top Gun. *Eventually we found a middle ground."*

139

still be homing in on the look of the hotshot flier. One Butkus design showed a classic comic book–style hero, eyes squinting defiantly, perfect lips showing the hint of a sneer, a holster slung low around his hips, and a blaster gripped in his right hand.

"Everybody had a different description for Dash Rendar, like 'Tom Cruise with an attitude,' or some people were saying he looked like Kevin Costner, although I don't think he looks like any of them," Lucasfilm's Troy Alders says. "Even though he's like a bad Han Solo, we kind of toned Dash down, and he came out looking more suave than what Kilian had drawn. Kilian's drawings for Dash were a little too rugged and crazy-looking. Dash is young, rugged; he has an attitude. He'll rebel against anything."

By June LucasArts printouts depicted Dash Rendar leaning forward on the saddle of a swoop bike, his long arms extended, gloved hands gripping the handlebars. His bearded face was a combination of the squinty-eyed but good-looking loner tough guy of the Butkus drawings and the unshaven, two-fisted brawler of the Plunkett designs.

Dash Rendar; cut scene portrait by Jon Knoles.

In the *Shadows* story line Princess Leia would hire the mercurial but brilliant pilot to journey to Tatooine and secretly guard Luke Skywalker. Luke had gone (at Leia's insistence) into seclusion at Obi-Wan's old home in the arid wasteland of the Dune Sea while awaiting word of Boba Fett's arrival. Of all the spots on the whole of the desert planet, this parched region of blazing heat, sandstorms, and wind-carved canyons was so desolate and inhospitable that even the Jawas and Tusken

Raiders usually steered clear of the area. (Plus there were those rumors of ghosts haunting Ben's old place—enough to scare away a superstitious nomad.) It was in that humble, rock-hewn place that Obi-Wan had contented himself with a hermit's existence until young Luke had come into his life. Obi-Wan had joined the cause of the Alliance, again taking up his lightsaber, and had sacrificed himself in his final battle against Vader, at last becoming one with the Force.

Luke had returned to the area not only to convalesce from the physical and mental wounds he had suffered in Cloud City but to further his Jedi training. It was in Ben's home that Luke would discover a strange

Dash and Leebo; LucasArts cut scene art by Jon Knoles.

Obi-Wan's house; LucasArts cut scene by Paul Topolos.

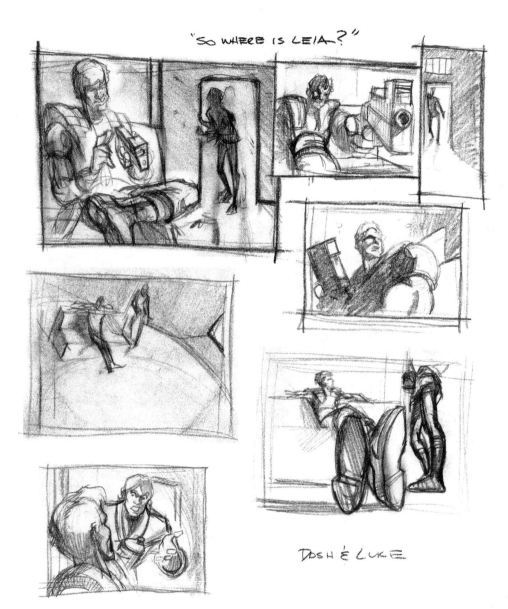

"SO WHERE IS LEIA?"

DOSH & LUKE

leather-bound book locked with a thumbprint clasp. If anyone else had attempted to open the book, it would have flashed into flames, but at a press of Luke's thumb it opened. Inside were secret plans left by Obi-Wan for constructing a new lightsaber.

The introduction of the lightsaber had been another brainstorm from Jon Knoles, who recalled that although Luke Skywalker had lost his lightsaber in battle with Vader in *Empire*, the young Jedi had inexplicably found another with which to battle Jabba the Hutt and his cohorts in *Jedi*. And a lightsaber, being a rare artifact from the bygone age of Jedi Knights, was not something easily obtained. Knoles recalled the *Jedi* scene in which Luke had surrendered to Vader, ready to meet the Dark

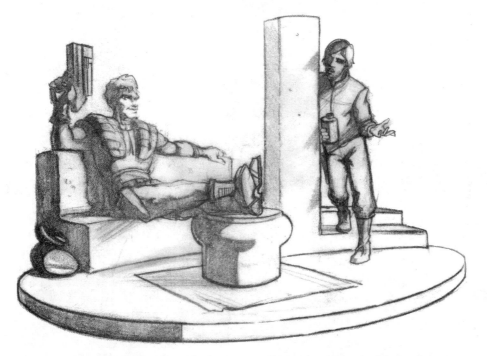

A headstrong Luke Skywalker confronts a cocky Dash Rendar in this Applause storyboard scene (opposite page) and concept pose (above).
   Applause storyboard and concept art by artist Dave Williams.

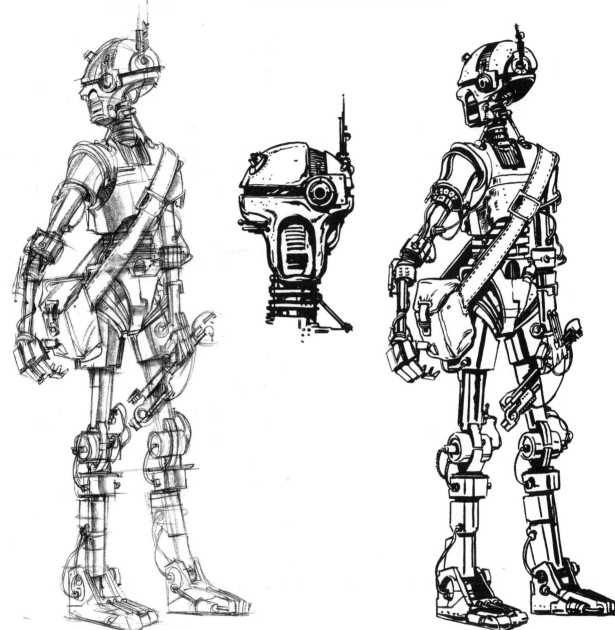

144

In the Star Wars *galaxy, droids range from menial labor automatons to sophisticated models programmed for medical service or diplomatic duties. The droid co-pilot Leebo (pictured above) evolved throughout the design process into a skeletal-looking model, tool bag slung over a shoulder and ready to meet any challenge as the Outrider's copilot. (The droid's name was inspired by the nickname for LucasArts art department technical assistant Mike "Leebo" Levine. "We just thought Leebo was a neat nickname for a droid," Jon Knoles reveals.)*

Lord as father, not foe. As Vader took possession of Luke's lightsaber, he marveled at his son's masterful advance in the ways of the Force. As the original Lawrence Kasdan and George Lucas script described it:

> "VADER: (indicating the lightsaber) I see you have constructed a new lightsaber.
> *Vader ignites the lightsaber and holds it to examine its humming, brilliant blade.*
> VADER: Your skills are complete. Indeed, you are powerful, as the Emperor has foreseen."

"So how did Luke get a new lightsaber?" Knoles rhetorically asks. "So I felt we needed to have a story element of Luke creating and assembling a new lightsaber."

"When I saw *Star Wars*, the first time I saw that lightsaber come up, I thought, Oh, boy, we've got a samurai movie here," author Steve Perry recalls. "The film is not as much traditional science fiction as it is fantasy and a combination of samurai and adventure movies."

In Japan's feudal times the sword was considered the soul of the samurai, pure spirit pounded into the steel of what was more than a mere weapon. In the hands

Luke Skywalker powers up his lightsaber in this Kilian Plunkett sketch. In the Shadows *story line Luke discovers special lightsaber construction instructions hidden in Obi-Wan's old house in Tatooine's Western Dune Sea and assembles his own saber.*

of one with the pure, selfless samurai spirit a sword was not a force of destruction but a symbol of justice, even mercy. Similarly, Obi-Wan had famously described the lightsaber of Jedi Knight tradition as an "elegant weapon for a more civilized time." To use the lightsaber properly was to be at one with the Force, that "energy field created by all living things," according to Obi-Wan.

While any fool could pull the trigger on a blaster, it took training and discipline to wield a lightsaber. In the *Star Wars* universe a lightsaber has a handgrip with a single power cell able to produce an energy flow between multifaceted jewels located within the interior of the handle. When switched on, it produces a narrow, cutting energy beam. Although a Jedi Master could construct a lightsaber in several days, in *Shadows* it takes Luke a month to construct the special lightsaber described in Obi-Wan's book.

In Perry's account Luke has to journey to Mos Eisley for power cells, controls, and other electronic and mechanical parts and has to prepare the special jewel vital for focusing the energy beam. And while Luke had used a floating Jedi training remote in the original film, by *Shadows* Luke would break in his new lightsaber by blocking and deflecting bolts of electricity fired by Artoo.

Of course, in the time frame covered in both the movie trilogy and the *Shadows* story line, lightsabers are archaic weapons, iconic objects from the legendary days of the Jedi Knights (thanks to Vader, who, in the service of Palpatine, helped usher in the age of Empire by tracking down and destroying the last Jedi Knights). *Shadows* is deep into what Obi-Wan once lamented as "the dark times." Not only does the evil Empire rule the galaxy, this is also the time of the underworld and its ruthless bounty hunters, killer droids, and violent swoop bike gangs.

Shadows *provided a rare opportunity for licensees to pair both new and classic*
Star Wars *characters, such as this image of Luke and Dash springing into action*
for an Applause "Spirit of Heroism" resin figurine concept.
   Applause concept art by Dave Williams.

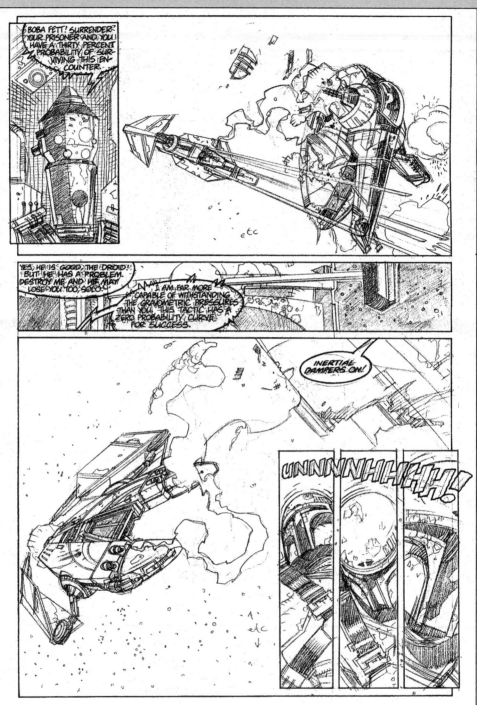

A bounty hunter battle ensues as IG-88's ship, the IG-2000, blasts out of hyperspace to attack Slave I. IG-88 is blown away, but Fett's ship sustains significant damage and must dock for repairs on the moon of Gall, home to an Imperial enclave.

Shadows Dark Horse Comic, issue 2, pages 20–22; unedited pencils by Kilian Plunkett.

Luke Skywalker is shadowed by a triumvirate of evil: Emperor Palpatine, Darth Vader, and an infamous new force in the Star Wars *universe—Xizor, overlord of the galaxywide Black Sun criminal syndicate.* Shadows of the Empire *Bantam Books novelization cover art; painting by Drew Struzan.*

Author Steve Perry's novel outline and manuscript was the foundation and creative road map for the multimedia Shadows *project. Photo by Mÿk Olsen.*

Drew Struzan is famed for his Star Wars *and* Indiana Jones *movie posters—part of a creative output that has made him one of the leading commercial illustrators in the world. Here Drew is surrounded by some of his movie poster work.*

Writer John Wagner at ease in the old rectory (built during the reign of Henry VIII), which is both home to and workplace of this influential comics creator.

Artist Kilian Plunkett, busy at his drawing board. (Note the script tacked on the wall at the left and the reference art for the new spacecraft designed for Shadows.) Photo by Ryder Windham.

For artist Hugh Fleming, a goal of cover art is to create images that capture the dynamic reality of a cinematic moment. Before his cover work on the Dark Horse Shadows series, Fleming created cover art for the Tales of the Jedi: Dark Lords of the Sith series, notably this vision from an ancient battlefield (with the look inspired by Kenneth Branagh's staging of the English-French clash at Agincourt in Henry V).

The Hildebrandts are renowned for using photographic references in their work. Here Greg (left) checks photo references while filling in the rough of Luke. Tim (right) adds fine brush strokes as Luke takes shape.
Photo by Jean Scrocco, courtesy of Star Wars Galaxy *magazine.*

Sculptor Susumu Sugita with his finished Xizor sculpture.

Composer Joel McNeely conducted the Royal Scottish National Orchestra in a 1995 recording session for Varese Sarabande. The sessions, featuring both the first recording of Bernard Herrmann's Vertigo *score and a "greatest hits" collection of Hollywood 1995 scores, represented the first collaboration between the orchestra and the record company.*

Robert Townson, producer of the Shadows of the Empire *sound track. Townson and Lucasfilm's Lucy Autrey Wilson conceived the idea for a* Shadows *sound track, a fitting touch for the proclaimed "movie without the movie" project.*
Photos by Matthew Peak.

Artist Mike Butkus, in his studio, surveys a wall plastered with his Shadows *designs.*
   Photo by Troy Alders.

Below, right: Dash Rendar action figure prototype from Hasbro/Kenner.

Two-fisted flying ace Dash Rendar underwent an extensive design phase, with looks ranging from a disheveled space loner to a Top Gun*-style flyboy. The more heroic version, embodied in the Mike Butkus illustration below, eventually won out.*

Dash Rendar

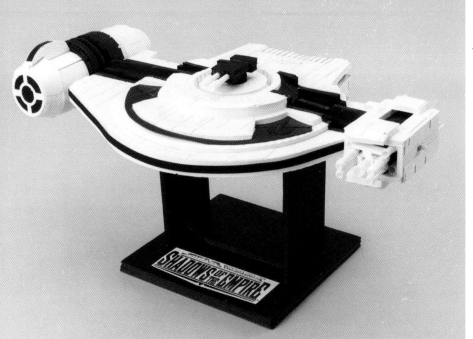

Hasbro/Kenner prototype for the Outrider.

Below, left: Xizor's Virago; *Hasbro/Kenner prototype.*

Below: This packaging mock-up was produced for the Xizor action figure from Hasbro/Kenner.

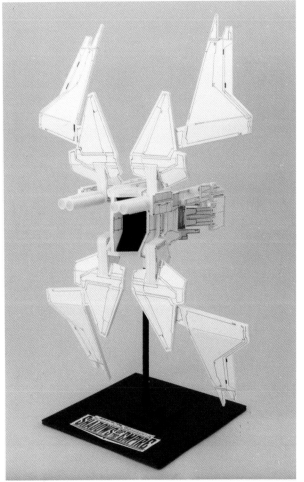

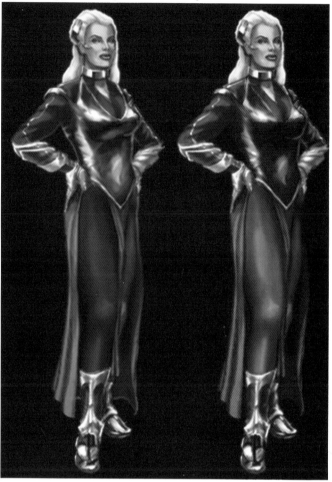

Left: Dash Rendar; as seen in the LucasArts final rendition by Jon Knoles.

Below: Lead artist/game designer Jon Knoles tried two different approaches for the colors of Guri's attire.

Below: This visage of Xizor, the Dark Prince, helped finalize the look of the inscrutable underworld overlord.
   Art by Jon Knoles, LucasArts Entertainment Company.

While taking refuge at Ben's house in the Dune Sea wasteland, Luke discovers a secret lightsaber construction book left by Obi-Wan's guiding hand. In this LucasArts cut scene, Luke, after having spent many days assembling rare materials and following the exacting instructions, powers up the energy blade of a lightsaber supreme.

During a trip to Skywalker Ranch to kick off their *Shadows* work, the Hildebrandts visited the game creators at LucasArts. Here Greg (left) and Tim (right) watch Jon Knoles send Dash's *Outrider* blasting through virtual space.
    Photo by Jeff Kausch.

Below, right: This *Outrider* computer-generated model, above view, was designed by Doug Chiang; model by Jon Knoles.

Below: LucasArts computer-generated *Virago*.
    3-D model by Garry Gaber.

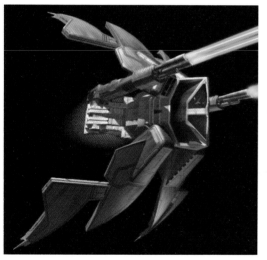

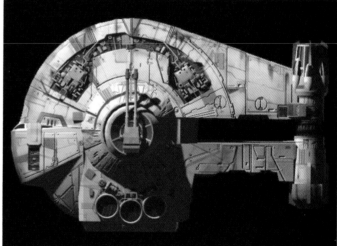

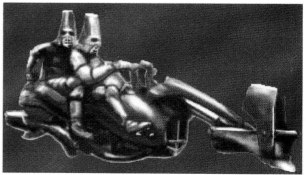

Following the ILM concept art for swoop bikers (nicknamed "coneheads"), the bikers would be rendered as computer-generated characters to be digitally composited for a brief appearance in the expanded Special Edition *Mos Eisley* movie footage.
    Art by TyRuben Ellingson, enhanced by Jon Knoles.

In the Shadows novel, comics series, and LucasArts game, Beggar's Canyon on Tatooine would be the setting for an explosive swoop bike battle. LucasArts began building its version of the Canyon with the 3-D rock formation concept art pictured above.
Art by Bill Stoneham.

This LucasArts cut scene image of Imperial City was created by Bill Stoneham.

This 3-D LucasArts production art of Mos Eisley, Tatooine's infamous spaceport city, was inspired by ILM designs of the city for an expanded Star Wars twentieth anniversary movie release. (Note the spaceship, partially buried at far left, that missed the landing pad.) Art by Bill Stoneham.

A glimpse of Ord Mantell, the planet where Han Solo once escaped from a treacherous pair of bounty hunters. In the LucasArts game an Ord Mantell starship scrap yard would be the staging ground for a particularly challenging level for player/character Dash Rendar.
Ord Mantell LucasArts production art by Bill Stoneham.

V.
BOUNTY HUNTERS, DROIDS, AND BIKERS

IN THE MYTHOLOGY OF THE OLD West the lone bounty hunter tracking his human prey is a romantic figure, right up there with the stoic sheriff, the deadeye gunslinger, and the dance hall madam with a heart of gold.

One of the many currents running through the *Star Wars* saga has been its evocation of some of the mythic themes traditionally explored in the Western genre. Such are the bounty hunters who, in their high-powered spaceships, have the frontier of space in which to track down their victims. And of all the bounty hunters roaming the galaxy, the baddest of them is Boba Fett.

Boba Fett wears the masked helmet and spacesuit and weapons armor of the legendary evil Mandalore warriors (who, as the saga tells it, were defeated by Jedi Knights during the Clone Wars that marked the ending of the days of the Old Republic). How he came into possession of his Mandalore battle armor, its plating chipped and scratched from combat, has never been told. But the armor makes Fett, an already expert tracker and marksman, an even more dangerous adversary. The suit's armament includes a miniature flame thrower encased in the right forearm, wrist lasers, and a jetpack equipped with powerful rocket thrusters.

150

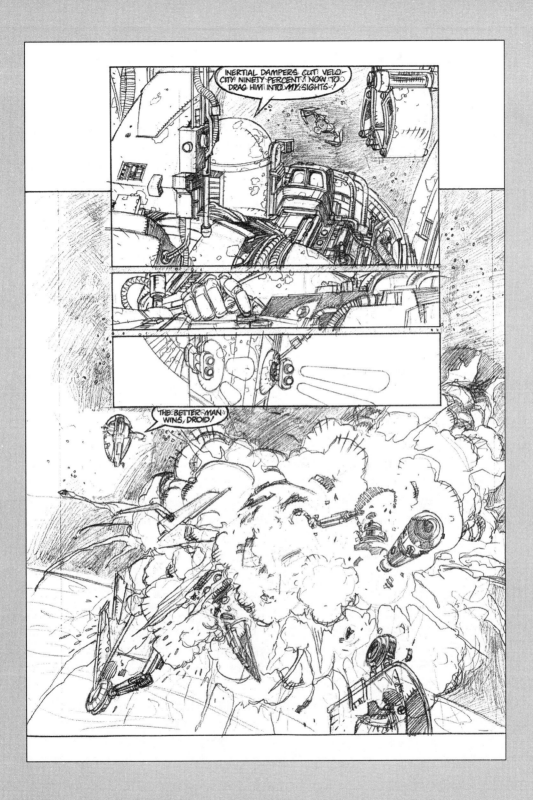

151

In *Shadows* Boba Fett would surmount every obstacle in order to deliver Han Solo to Jabba so that he would eventually find himself (in *Return of the Jedi*) enjoying his ease in the inner circle of Jabba's court. Ultimately, Fett's security would be short-lived, as a battle with Luke Skywalker and company would end with the bounty hunter falling into the maw of the Sarlacc creature.

"Although he had such a short life in the movies, Boba Fett is one of the most enduring *Star Wars* characters," Jon Knoles observes. "He's mysterious; he has all these neat weapons—why'd he have to die so quickly? It just wasn't fair!"

"There were a lot of fans who were really disappointed when, after all the buildup for the toughness of his character, Boba Fett just got swallowed up by the Sarlacc in *Jedi*," editor Ryder Windham muses.

Thanks to Dark Horse's *Dark Empire* comics series, the hunter in the Mandalore armor would be back in action, surprising Han Solo with a blaster raised and ready. ("Boba Fett! But you're dead!" Han Solo exclaims. "The Sarlacc found me somewhat indigestible, Solo," is Fett's cool response.) With Boba back in the time line, subsequent *Star Wars* projects—such as the Dark Forces game and a special Dark Horse comic planned for the character—could once again feature the fan favorite and bounty hunter supreme.

Although only a glimpse of Fett's *Slave I* would figure in the *Shadows* novel, Fett himself would be featured in the Dark Horse comics series. In John Wagner's script the reptilian Bossk, another of the bounty hunters originally put into play by Vader in *Empire*, and the droid known as IG-88 would be on Boba Fett's trail.

It would be IG-88, however, who would have the chance to star as the "boss monster" in a key game level set in a spaceship junkyard on the planet Ord Mantell. It's there that Dash Rendar, having been hired by Lando Calrissian to locate Boba Fett, has come seeking clues from other bounty hunters.

"This sequence doesn't appear in either the novel or the comics,"

Knoles explains. "Ord Mantell is a place that's briefly mentioned by Han Solo in *The Empire Strikes Back* as a place where he ran into some bounty hunters. Dash is kind of a shady character himself, so he knows where these shady characters like to hang out, so he comes to this place that's kind of a spaceship junkyard."

In the game play story line (dated April 17, 1995), Rendar's *Outrider* lands and he disembarks on the outskirts of the sea of junk, an ominous place where a sign at the outskirts states: TRESPASSERS WILL BE BLASTED. Rendar confers by wrist com with his copilot droid Leebo, who from inside the ship has followed bounty hunter trails to a salvage factory reachable by a hovertrain that runs cargo through the scrap yard to the factory door. The plan is for Rendar to get on the hovertrain, cut off the braking switch, and ride it crashing through the salvage factory doors.

In the interactive environment of a cartridge game the player becomes the hero, clinging to the top of the train as it races through man-

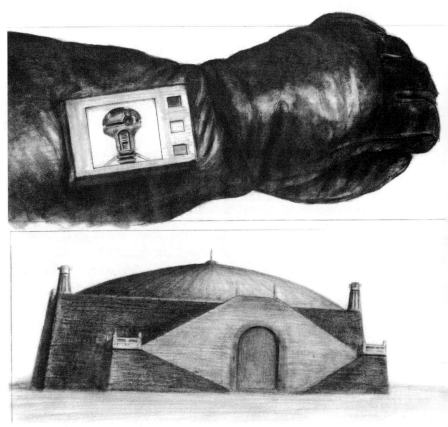

When Dash Rendar sets the Outrider *down and goes exploring, he can keep in touch with Leebo and his ship via his wrist com.*
    LucasArts cut scene by Paul Topolos.

The Ord Mantell salvage factory.
    Art by Paul Topolos.

made trenches. And everywhere there are obstacles: On the trains there are different cars, such as the flatbed car, where enemies hide behind stacks of boxes; the fuel car, where an opponent can pop up from a roof hatch; a gun turret car where guns swivel to swing and fire at the player's approach; catwalks and trestle girders above the tracks from which enemies can launch attacks; jagged mountains of space junk and low tunnels; and passing trains in other tram lanes from which bounty hunters can mount sneak attacks.

"This hovertrain sequence combines the speed and 3-D stuff of a game like X-Wing with the first-person walking ability of Dark Forces," Knoles explains. "You can actually walk onto a train, jumping from one to another. At the same time there's this incredible speed you didn't get in a game like Dark Forces. The environment is all 16-bit color, which means you get thousands of colors as opposed to hundreds. There are texture maps of the spaceship junkyard with all these old Star Destroyers, Blockade Runners, and shuttles, and the sky above is all smooth with nice gradients of clouds. We're tickled to death that with the Nintendo 64, this new generation of machine, we have this kind of detail in a real-time 3-D environment you can run around in."

Once all the obstacles and enemy attacks have been survived, the train crashes through the factory door. But, as is the way in the games world, at the end the boss monster challenge of IG-88 awaits, with the battle droid rising from the wreckage equipped with blaster rifle, sonic stunner, grenade launcher, and flamethrower. Once the player/Dash has defeated the droid, a check of the IG-88 memory banks reveals that Boba Fett is on Gall, repairing his ship.

In addition to the war/bounty hunter droids such as IG-88, protocol droids such as C-3PO, and "astromech" droids such as R2-D2, a representative of a new classification of droid was introduced in *Shadows*: Guri, the human replica droid, who author Steve Perry early on in the conjuring process envisioned as the ultimate Black Sun lieutenant, bodyguard, and assassin.

In the backstory dreamed up by Perry, Guri had been designed and

IG-88 rises from wreckage, weapons raised.

In some of the parallel Shadows story lines, characters encountered different situations or journeyed to unique environments. It was only in the LucasArts computer game, for example, that Dash Rendar went looking for bounty hunters (and leads as to the whereabouts of Boba Fett) in a starship scrap yard on the planet Ord Mantell. After crashing a hovertrain into a salvage factory, Dash meets computer game "boss monster" IG-88.

LucasArts cut scene, preliminary text by Jon Knoles, art by Paul Topolos.

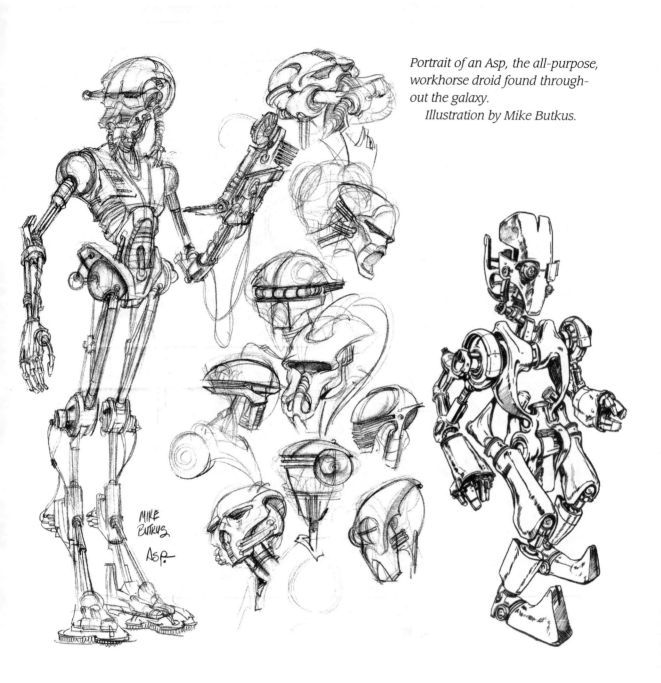

Portrait of an Asp, the all-purpose, workhorse droid found through-out the galaxy.

Illustration by Mike Butkus.

MIKE
BUTKUS
ASP.

created in a hidden outlaw enclave by one Simonelle the Ingoian. Guri's design was based on a droid stolen from the Alliance's "Project Decoy" (in which a seemingly real droid could be used to replace kidnapped Imperials) but was programmed as a ferocious assassin. For a treacherous creature such as Xizor, a programmed droid was preferable to a fallible sentient being.

Still other *Shadows* droids would serve a more utilitarian purpose, such as the weapons droid that spars with Vader in a scene from the six-issue comics series. "I suggested to John Wagner that the second issue begin with Darth Vader in the midst of some furious lightsaber battle with some combat droid, which Vader summarily carves up,"

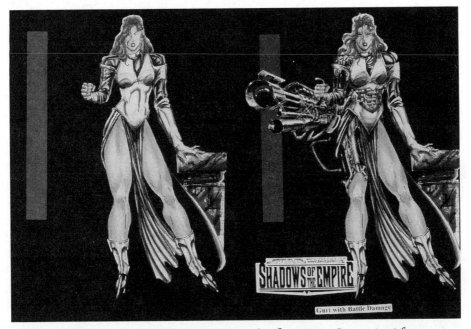

Guri with Battle Damage

A sultry Guri without and with some impressive firepower. Concept art for a never-produced figure in the Hasbro/Kenner Shadows *toy line, done by a member of the Hasbro Toy Group Design team.*

Guri approaches her master, Xizor, in the Dark Prince's stronghold in Imperial City. Fashioned in the image of a beautiful human female, Guri serves the Black Sun criminal syndicate as a lieutenant, bodyguard, and assassin.
   Shadows *Dark Horse Comic, issue 2, panel, page 4; unedited pencils by Kilian Plunkett.*

Windham says (this also inspired a similar scene in Steve Perry's novel). "I thought it would be a wonderful opportunity to see Darth Vader alive and bad and holding a lightsaber. Without putting it into so many words, we find out that it's also Vader's physical therapy to make sure his arm is fully healed after the battle with Luke at the end of *The Empire Strikes Back*. That's all I suggested, but John also incorporated something I hadn't considered, a scene I thought was both frightening and humorous: At the same time Vader is fighting this droid, he's carrying on a conversation with Jix, a swoop bike character."

The scene, as described by John Wagner in his original outline (which Dark Horse faxed to Lucasfilm a few days after New Year's 1995), had at first been staged not with Jix but with a character of Wagner's creation. In Wagner's outline Vader would be warming up for his meeting to discuss the Death Star construction project with Xizor by taking apart a weapons droid in a lightsaber sparring session. Just as he allows himself a moment of satisfaction that his injured arm has healed, a prisoner is brought into his presence:

> Intro TALAN, a primitive, a fearsome hunter, dragged in chains from the dungeons and brought before VADER. TALAN is the leader of a number of his savage race, a nomadic space tribe, held there awaiting execution. Enemies of the Empire though no friends of Rebels either.
>
> VADER offers him a deal—the lives of his compatriots, among them his wife and son—for LUKE SKYWALKER. TALAN'S son for VADER'S. "Boba Fett will deliver Solo to Jabba, and Skywalker will try to rescue his friend." A small but fast ship is at TALAN'S disposal. VADER stresses LUKE must be taken alive. If LUKE dies, TALAN'S family will be quick to join him. TALAN swears a blood oath, gashing himself. He will succeed.

Unfortunately, the reply from Lucasfilm nixed the introduction of the nomadic space savage, noting that *Shadows* provided an opportunity to integrate more of the characters from the movie trilogy into the story line. In an addendum Lucasfilm approved Wagner's outline but requested that Talan be replaced by Jix, an agent of Xizor who would infiltrate Jabba's operation. Jix would be based on an unnamed background character briefly glimpsed by Allan Kausch in the shadows of Jabba's palace in *Jedi*. Lucasfilm further suggested that Jix infiltrate Jabba's operation by joining a swoop gang. Featuring the bikers would

Before Jabba the Hutt's personal swoop bike gang goes after Luke Skywalker, they bring aboard this imposing stranger. Jix, however, is a secret agent for Darth Vader, sent to infiltrate the swoop bike gang and protect Luke at all costs.
  Concept sketch by Kilian Plunkett, left, and final Jix illustration by Mike Butkus, right.

also offer another continuity tie-in, since ILM had been in the process of preparing some computer graphic swoop bike creations for Lucas's 1997 *Star Wars: The Special Edition* theatrical release.

In a faxed response to Dark Horse, Wagner confessed to having some problems with working in Jix as an agent of Xizor. "The only way another character made sense was if Vader had sent him," Wagner noted in his transmission. "That way we get a fresh angle on things—someone whose prime function was to keep Luke alive." Noting the merit of Wagner's idea, Lucasfilm Licensing agreed to make Jix an agent of Vader.

In Wagner's script the scene introducing Vader's pawn had changed, replacing the brutality of Talan in chains with Jix's cocky swagger. Unlike the novel, in which face-to-face meetings with Xizor might make Vader grit his teeth, Wagner would give the usually imperious Vader an unusually crazed edge.

Artist Kilian Plunkett produced this early design sketch of swoop biker Big Gizz.

161

In moments Vader will be forced to meet with Xizor, and the Dark Lord of the Sith is taking out his fury on the weapons droid. As Jix insolently slouches against a wall, watching Vader's lightsaber beam slice a gash across the droid's metal casing, the Dark Lord blurts out his frustrations:

> Vader: Luke Skywalker has eluded me again! . . . One possible sighting since he and the Rebel fleet left Bespin—since then nothing!
> Now focus on Jix. He's been lounging back against the wall in casual manner. As Vader—still battling in [background]—reprimands him, Jix detaches himself lazily from the wall. He's a rough diamond who'll fit in well in a swoop gang. He's hard, he's mean, he's cunning, he's not above a little murder if the situation calls for it. He's not that impressed by anyone, even—momentarily—Vader.
> Vader: Stand to attention in my presence, Jix! You are not in one of your seedy dives now!
> Jix: Apologies.
> Jix doubles over in pain as Vader hits him with the Force.
> Vader: If you wish to prosper in my employ, learn to keep a respectful tongue!
> Jix: I . . . said sorry!
> Vader: Now you mean it! . . .
> Jix: What is it you . . . want me to do . . . L-Lord Vader?
> Vader: The bounty hunter Boba Fett has not yet delivered Solo to Jabba the Hutt on Tatooine. When he does, his friend Skywalker will no doubt attempt to rescue him . . . The Hutt is not to be trusted to carry out my bidding. I require my own agent in his camp . . . I suggest your best course is to insinuate yourself into the Hutt's swoop gang . . . By all accounts they're an undisciplined, foul-mannered band of renegades and criminals . . . You should find many like beings.

Although Jix himself would not be featured in the novel, the basic swoop gang attack on Luke (ordered by Jabba at Xizor's command) would be a staple of the three major media: the book, comics, and game. The swoop bikes and the outlaw bands who ride them had been developed in the saga in two novels (*Han Solo's Revenge* by Brian Daley, Del Rey Books, 1979; *Han Solo and the Lost Legacy* by Brian Daley, Del Rey Books, 1980) and in game books by West End Games (*Star Wars Sourcebook* by Bill Slavicsek and Curtis Smith, 1987; *Dark Force Rising Sourcebook* by Michael Allen Horne, 1993).

Similar in design to the speeder bikes seen in *Return of the Jedi*, a swoop bike has been described as an engine with a seat, with the design featuring a plowlike scoop in front with controls in the handlebars and saddle. (Because of this distinctive scoop, the bikers early on would be dubbed "scooptroopers.") Since they are fast and maneuverable, racing these bikes is a popular sport in the galaxy's Galactic Core, where domed "swoop track" arenas draw tens of thousands. (Han Solo was once a pro swoop bike racer.) But on the dark side are the outlaw gangs that use their swoop bikes to raise a little hell. In the dark uni-

The Shadows *novel, comics, and computer game all featured a swoop bike chase and battle in Tatooine's Beggar's Canyon. In this LucasArts game scene by Paul Topolos and Jon Knoles, set in a certain cantina in Mos Eisley, Dash Rendar overhears the swoop bike assassination plot against Luke Skywalker. Given the action elements required for the computer game, swoop bike chases would provide some major action sequences for LucasArts.*

163

verse these outlaw bands are major players in the underworld, adept at smuggling and physical intimidation.

Violence is the way of life in the time period of the movie trilogy, a time of civil war and brutal underworld syndicates. In *Shadows*, whether it's hand-to-hand combat, swoop bike battles, lightsaber duels, or space battles, every corner of the galaxy is a battle zone.

Swoop trooper. Concept art by Kenner.

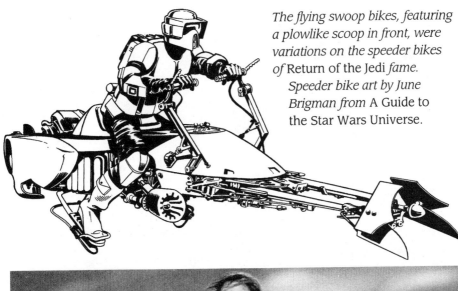

The flying swoop bikes, featuring a plowlike scoop in front, were variations on the speeder bikes of Return of the Jedi *fame.*
Speeder bike art by June Brigman from A Guide to the Star Wars Universe.

Dash Rendar at the controls of a swoop bike.
LucasArts cut scene *by Jon Knoles and Paul Topolos.*

Following this ILM concept art for swoop bikers (nicknamed "coneheads"), the bikers would be rendered as computer-generated characters to be digitally composited for a brief appearance in the expanded Special Edition Mos Eisley *movie footage.*

BATTLE ZONES

Boba Fett, stuck on Gall, enters a seedy cantina to negotiate with fellow bounty hunters Bossk and Zuckuss—always a risky proposition unless you can watch your own back, as Fett will do here.

Shadows *Dark Horse Comic, issue 2, pages 8–10; unedited pencils by Kilian Plunkett.*

I.
POWER UP!

IT WAS IN AN ASTEROID CLUSTER that the spacecraft of the reptilian bounty hunter Bossk finally cornered *Slave I*, holding the ship in his sights while a shuttle bearing members of Bossk's bounty hunter gang docked and began boarding Boba Fett's starship. In audio communication reports from *Slave I* to Bossk all seemed to be going well, with Fett reportedly under guard and the gang transporting the carbonited Han Solo to its shuttle.

As the shuttle returned and docked back at Bossk's ship, a bounty hunter assistant went to receive the returning shuttle. Bossk was contemplating how killing Boba Fett would make him the number one bounty hunter in the galaxy, when the audio communicator suddenly crackled with a familiar voice speaking from *Slave I*. As John Wagner, who staged the incident for the comics series, scripted the action:

> FETT: I have some bad news for you, Bossk.
> BOSSK: F-Fett—?
> Shocked face of the bounty hunter in background as he looks into the shuttle to see the bodies of the two dead bounty hunters along with a fairly big explosive device, a red light aglow indicating it's ready to blow . . .

> FETT: Your shuttle is on auto-pilot.
> B. HUNTER: Oh no—
> Big. The explosion.
> BIGGER. The explosion rips out a section of Bossk's ship, including the airlock, sending the ship tumbling crazily.
> **BAROOOOOOOOOOOOOOM**
> . . . Big pic showing *Slave I* streaking away at fantastic speed from Bossk's ship, still tumbling but less crazily. Accompanied by two insets, small, together, showing first the image of the ship fading—then disappearing—as it hits hyperspace . . .

The *Shadows* comic would have plenty of opportunities to display Fett's combative resourcefulness. In a cantina on Gall Boba Fett runs into more bounty hunter trouble, a scene that required some restaging.

"The script had somebody waiting to kill Boba Fett from this balcony above the bar," explains artist Kilian Plunkett, "and some dust from the floorboards lands on Fett's helmet, alerting him to the danger. He whirls with lightning-fast reflexes and blows the guy away. So I drew a little thumbnail sketch series, with little trickles of dust landing on his helmet. And Ryder pointed out that it's difficult to convey that this is dust. It might work cinematically, but it doesn't work in the comics medium because it's not visual enough. To some readers it might look like drops of water. Even if it did read, why is there dust? It requires the readers to make cognitive leaps, because it's not been established that the cantina is dusty; you haven't seen a foot creak on a floorboard anywhere else in the series. So we changed the scene to a very clear shot of the sniper pulling a gun from this balcony above Boba Fett, like a mezzanine level in an old saloon. That's really the purpose of the thumbnails, so you can go through the whole thing and see bits that don't make sense. You figure out ways of making it visually more effective and simpler at the same time."

While the Boba Fett of the comics series was having his own personal bounty hunter war, the LucasArts game would feature Fett in a special battle sequence on Gall against player/character Dash Rendar. While

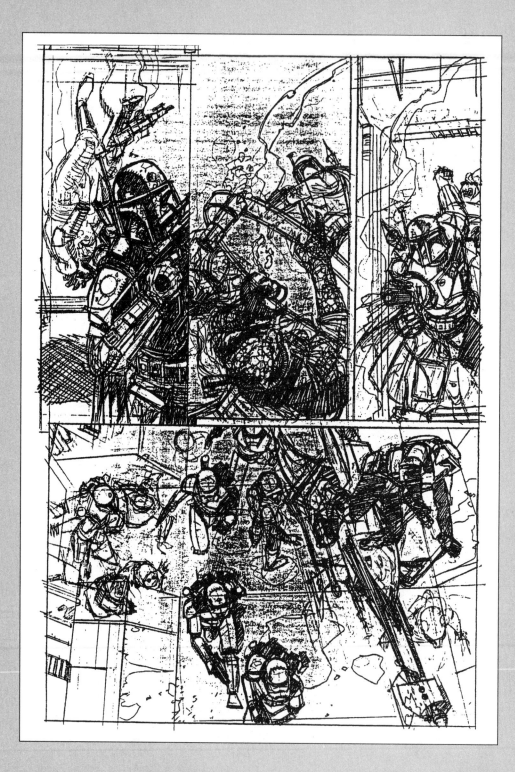

the rogue Rendar would lead the rescue attempt to Gall in the comic and novel, then leave his employers in the lurch when Imperial guns began firing, the game character would stick around Gall to engage Boba Fett in a spaceport jetpack duel, trying to prevent the bounty hunter's escape.

"When the player straps on a jetpack, it becomes a flying game, although you can still land and run around with the jetpack," Eric Johnston explains. "It's sort of an extension of the walk-around scenario. All we do is program the behavior that defines a person, that instead of walking around, when 'up' is pushed on the joystick, you can rise up in the air. The opponent will be able to do that as well because at that point you're fighting Boba Fett. When you've sufficiently beaten him up in the jetpack, Boba Fett gets into his ship and blasts off while you're flying around, still battling him with the jetpack. In the game you can't kill Boba Fett; he ends up getting away—or he gets you. So the victory on that level is surviving Boba Fett."

In addition to Fett, *Shadows* enemies throughout the game levels would include Imperial walkers (both All Terrain Scout Transports and All Terrain Armored Transports), fast and deadly TIE fighters and bounty hunter ships, Star Destroyers, and Xizor's own fleet of "Shock Raider" starfighters.

To fight back, the game player would be able to access the weapons and various "power-ups" vital to surmounting each challenge and advancing to the next level. "Typically, in this kind of game, when you shoot a stormtrooper or monster or robot, they usually leave something behind, which we call a power-up," says Knoles. "The power-up is something the player can see, run to, and pick up. It could be a 3-D icon for health points to replenish your character if he's been damaged or a shield bonus for your spaceship, or if you want a better weapon, you'll see a nice big gun."

In Shadows the Dash Rendar game character would be equipped with a blaster pistol, an armor suit, and three thermal detonators, with power-up options including additional blasters, a thermal launcher, and the jetpack. Dash's *Outrider* would also be a mobile attack force equipped with standard concussion missiles and proton torpedoes, with power-ups that provide such additional firepower as dual laser and ion cannons, autofire or player-controlled lasers, and more missiles and torpedoes.

The swoop bike chase through the craggy twists and turns of Beggar's Canyon would be one of the battle zones featured in almost all the varied media (including one of the selections of the *Shadows* soundtrack release). Although the bikers in the novel and game would be as faceless as stormtroopers, the comics script would flesh out Jabba's swoop bike gang. John Wagner describes them with relish:

> THE SWOOP GANG, criminals and ruffians, is the futuristic version of today's biker gangs. They wear similar kind of dress, all spikes, chains and leather. They're unkempt and uncouth. Their swoop bikes vary in style, being customized, with lots of fancy paint jobs. Most of them will turn out to be fodder for LUKE and DASH, but two to note are SPIKER (the BIKER), who wears so many spikes you might mistake him for a porcupine, and BIG GIZZ, the leader, who's about 6' 9", hairy and shaggy, with bones through his ears or nose (or both) and a face like JAWS from the Bond film.

To keep all the creative principles in accord on the swoop bike chase and battle sequence, continuity editor Allan Kausch wrote a June 19 memo that summarized the basic action, with Luke parrying incoming blaster shots from the attacking bikers with his new lightsaber before grabbing a swoop and leading the wild ride through Beggar's Canyon, where obstacles would include a sharply angled turn (dubbed "Dead Man's Turn") and a narrow passage in a rock formation (known as the "Eye of the Needle").

In the story line Dash Rendar, hanging out in the famed Mos Eisley cantina, has overheard the braggart bikers plotting their attack on Luke Skywalker, and he will later pilot his own swoop to the rescue during the chase in Beggar's Canyon. For the look of Tatooine's spaceport city, both the comics and games creators would be supplied with special ILM storyboards used in the preparation of the expanded Mos Eisley sequence for the *Star Wars: Special Edition*.

ILM's computer-generated additions to the original film's footage would include stormtroopers riding dewbacks (large reptiles used as beasts of burden or patrol animals) and a background cargo shuttle. "One of the cool things about this project is doing the new Mos Eisley buildings and knowing that when the *Special Edition* comes out, somebody is going to open up this comic and realize it's the same background as in the movie," Kilian Plunkett says, laughing. "John Wagner specifically scripted the scene in the comic to do exactly that, picking a background image that had been approved for the rerelease. It's kind of cheating, but I traced some of the Mos Eisley background buildings directly from the storyboards, throwing some stuff into the foreground so it'll be as close as possible to what ends up on film."

During Big Gizz's pursuit of Luke, secret agent Jix would do his best to mess up the rhythm of the biker's pursuit. But it would be the sudden appearance of Dash that would finally cause the outgunned surviving bikers to pull up and retreat. Rendar would then report to Luke the news from Bothan spymaster Koth Melan of a secret plan by the Empire (the flight of the freighter holding the new Death Star plans) and of Leia's infiltration of the Black Sun to uncover the secret behind the plot against Luke.

On the LucasArts side the ILM Mos Eisley *Special Edition* designs would help the gamemasters create a 3-D model of the dusty town. The swoop bikers themselves would also be inspired by the computer graphics biker figures created for the new Mos Eisley backgrounds and would be dubbed "coneheads" for their conical helmets. That biker approach favored the technical realities of the game, in which the limited number of polygons available was more conducive to creating conehead shapes than a realistic-looking human. The Beggar's Canyon chase would be a dizzying ride, with the player-controlled Dash capable of full interactivity with his environment, although sometimes the player would have to adapt to the dictates of "program control."

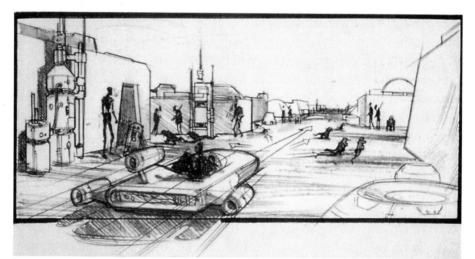

"Sometimes the POV [point of view] is from Dash's eyes, but other times an over-the-shoulder camera view allows the player to actually see the player/character on the bike," notes tech lead Eric Johnston. "Because it's a real-time 3-D game instead of a prerendered 3-D game, we can do things like pull the camera away so the player can look at what's behind him. We could give that option to the player to control, but that tends to make a game too complex to play. So we ended up leaving some of that under program control. You might be passing one section of bad guys and heading into the next, and the game would be automatically programmed so the camera would do a pan-around to show where the bad guys are coming from, setting it up a bit more like a movie."

In creating a sequence like the swoop bike chase, Jon Knoles would provide sketches and storyboards as a guide to the artists building the 3-D models. The programmers would then take the various elements— a 3-D model of Beggar's Canyon, a swoop bike and biker—and then program the action, figuring out where in the time frame to lay the traps for the player/character.

"We can determine in advance where you're going to encounter different obstacles, so you don't hit them all at once, which would make the game impossible to play," Johnston adds. "We'll figure out what feels right or wrong about the sequence, whether it needs an atmospheric effect. The swoop bike level becomes like a racecourse. On the other hand, if it's a level where you're running around on foot, we'll construct it more like a maze than a racecourse, where you explore, stop, turn around, and hit buttons that open doors or maybe activate shield generators."

In addition to the swoop bikes, the new vehicles created for *Shadows* would include Dash's *Outrider*, IG-88's *IG-2000*, Guri's *Stinger*, and Xizor's *Virago*. The ships would have to accommodate both the visual demands of static comic book art and the virtual world of game play. As usual, it would require an intensive design phase before the battleships of the dark universe could fly.

Facing page: Industrial Light & Magic, working on expanding the original Star Wars *Mos Eisley sequence for a twentieth anniversary* Special Edition *movie release, provided the* Shadows *projects with these expanded views of Tatooine's spaceport city.*

   ILM storyboard art by Erik Tiemens and TyRuben Ellingson.

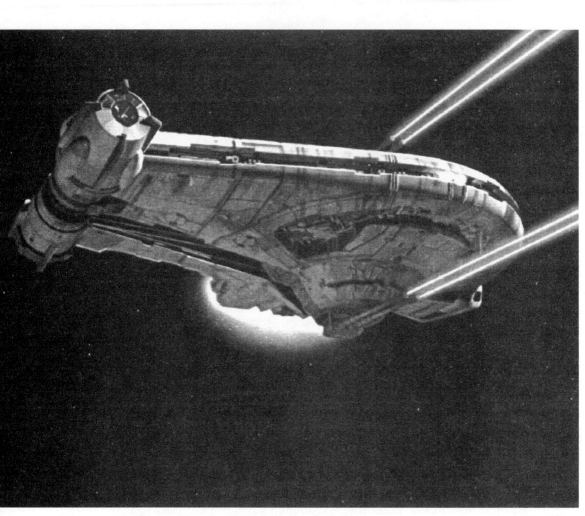

The Outrider *fires its laser cannons in this LucasArts computer-generated image. Design by Doug Chiang; model by Jon Knoles.*

II.
BATTLESHIPS

THE SPACESHIPS OF THE *STAR WARS* universe were created with what George Lucas's ILM model shop has called "boilerplate technology," and ships such as the Imperial Star Destroyers were designed to emulate the look of naval battleships with their steel sections riveted together.

With *Shadows*, a whole new generation of *Star Wars* spacecraft would be created. In an informational packet of drawings and descriptions prepared by Lucasfilm production editor Sue Rostoni, the new craft would be referenced to the traditional ships of the *Star Wars* universe: The *Outrider*, although designed along the lines of the *Falcon*, was slightly smaller than Solo's ship, while Guri's *Stinger* would be about the same size. Both Xizor's and IG-88's ships were to be similar in size to Boba Fett's *Slave I*, and the airspeeding swoops were equal in size and style to speeder bikes, although able to handle two passengers comfortably.

The creation of the spacecraft began with a variety of initial drawings that would be hammered and streamlined into final designs. Kilian Plunkett produced a version of IG-88's *IG-2000* that was inspired by the general look of an All Terrain Armored Scout Transport, featuring pin-

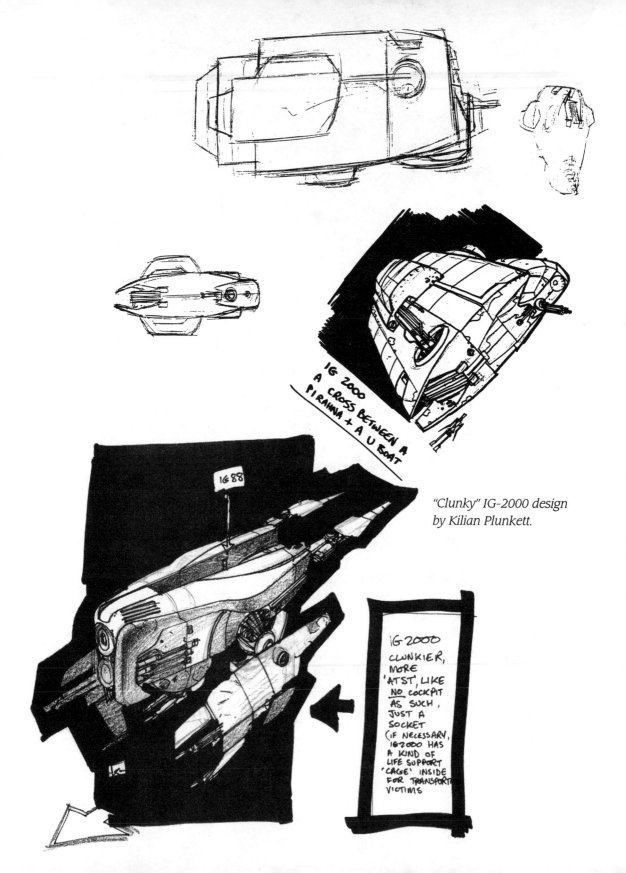

IG 2000
A CROSS BETWEEN A
PIRAHNA + A U BOAT

IG 88

*"Clunky" IG-2000 design
by Kilian Plunkett.*

IG 2000
CLUNKIER,
MORE
'ATST', LIKE
NO COCKPIT
AS SUCH,
JUST A
SOCKET
(IF NECESSARY,
IG-2000 HAS
A KIND OF
LIFE SUPPORT
'CAGE' INSIDE
FOR TRANSPORT
VICTIMS

*Rough IG-2000 sketch (top) by Doug Chiang
(with comments from Lucasfilm's Allan Kausch),
and Chiang's final sketch (above).*

cerslike wings and no cockpit but a "life support cage" by which the assassin droid could transport the victims of his bounty hunt. A more streamlined version created by Lucasfilm art director Doug Chiang, an ILM veteran since 1989, was ultimately approved instead.

Chiang would also provide designs for Dash Rendar and Xizor's ships, which would be important to the game designers, comic book artists, and even a separately published Del Rey Books *Star Wars* project, *The Essential Guide to Vessels and Vehicles*. To help Chiang get started, continuity editor Allan Kausch supplied some initial LucasArts concept sketches in a November 22, 1994, memo providing specs on the two key ships:

> #1: Dash Rendar's ship: Dash will be a Han Solo smuggler-type of character, so his ship should be comparable to the *Millennium Falcon*, though not too similar . . .
>
> #2: Xizor's ship: Xizor is the arch villain of the underworld, and the main new character of the *Shadows* project, so his ship is important. Jon Knoles pictured a large ship, but we feel that it should be a starfighter (i.e. of X-wing size), so that Xizor can slip in and out of Coruscant without attracting too much attention. Lucy [Wilson of Licensing] envisions a Stealth bomber type of design, though you have free rein to come up with something cool. Xizor is reptilian—perhaps his ship can reflect this? The only other input we've got is that it might be black, with lots of chrome: something really "bad."

During the *Shadows* project Chiang had begun work as production designer for the new chapters in the *Star Wars* movie saga. (His last major ILM art director assignment was on the look of the CG jungle animals that cavort through the 1995 feature *Jumanji*.) Mov-

Doug Chiang, production designer for the upcoming Star Wars *movie chapters, and* Shadows *design artist.*

The Millennium Falcon *has served the interests of a variety of rough-and-tumble pilots who make a living in the spacelanes, including both Lando Calrissian and Han Solo. When Lucasfilm concept art director Doug Chiang was called in to provide* Shadows *ships designs, the* Falcon *would serve as an inspiration for Dash Rendar's* Outrider.
Falcon art by June Brigman from A Guide to the Star Wars Universe.

Early design for the Outrider *by Jon Knoles.*

ing from his ILM office in San Rafael to the rustic environs of Skywalker Ranch, Chiang had already begun his preproduction illustrations and regular meetings with George Lucas (who himself was working on the scripts for the new *Star Wars* films). Then he added the *Shadows* battleship designs to his schedule.

"I guess machinery and robots are my forte," Chiang says. "I've always been fascinated by how things are put together. I started drawing when I was four years old, and by junior high school I was drawing bizarre, futuristic vehicles. Another thing that's fascinated me is creating a new environment, something totally fresh that hasn't been seen. That inclination probably came out of my frustration with certain toys I was sort of disappointed with. I'd just try to think up a better one. I've always been inspired to create my own objects, whether it's drawings, paintings, or models."

While a kid growing up in a suburb of Detroit, he drew inspiration from not only the *Star Wars* movie but from a "Making Of" television documentary of the film that was like a passkey into the secret world behind the veil of illusions. Many a summertime night Chiang spent in his parents' basement making his own 8-millimeter "science fiction epics." This basement FX shop would serve as a stage for anything from an imaginary space battle (perhaps embellished with double-exposed animated laser beam effects) to fantastic creatures brought to life (often as cardboard models animated with traditional frame-by-frame stop-motion techniques).

In his professional life design inspirations have often come from unlikely sources. During the fall of 1994, while in Vancouver scouting locations for *Jumanji*, Chiang visited an old mill where he saw some old cast-iron pulley castings that would ultimately inspire the clamshell-style design for Xizor's ship. "What I like to do is find unusual objects and kind of catalogue them for future reference," Chiang explains. "In Vancouver I had taken a whole bunch of pictures of these pulleys because I knew at some point they'd make some interesting spaceships.

These pulleys had a very organic look but were also very armorlike. It was really a unique look, and you could easily put two of these pulley shells together to form the shell of Xizor's ship. Lucasfilm definitely wanted a look that was very harsh, insectoid with aggressive-looking shapes. So I took the basic look of the actual pulley castings and modified and streamlined it.

"The idea I took was of a warship that could fold with shields, real battleworthy, yet have a mean appearance. I decided to go with this folding, sort of clamshell look so when it's flying it can configure itself into a very streamlined, fast-looking ship. But when it's going into battle in a

Rough sketches for Xizor's personal ship the Virago, *drawn by Doug Chiang.*

SCORPION-LIKE GUNS

3/4 BOTTOM VIEW
POSSIBLE XIZOR SHIP

defense mode, the shields open up and the guns pop out, so it changes shape, like different personalities reflecting the mood of the pilot."

While Xizor's *Virago* would be modeled on the reptilian personality of the underworld chieftain, Dash Rendar's ship would have a more familiar jumping-off point. "I took what I thought was unique about the *Millennium Falcon*, which is this kind of an asymmetrical cockpit that is basically a sphere with two prongs on it, and played around with different variations on that theme," Chiang says. "Normally I design a craft with some function; it can't just look good and not have a purpose. Even when I design robots, the joints need to look like they work, and it has to have a certain mass so it looks like it could stand upright. And the same with a spaceship. The proportions have to be right so it doesn't look awkward when it flies. So there's a strong element of reality in my designs that I really try to push for. I expect that my designs will be used to build something in the model shop or in computer graphics, so I don't want them pulling their hair out figuring how the thing is supposed to work."

As with the characters, there would be a backstory to go with the

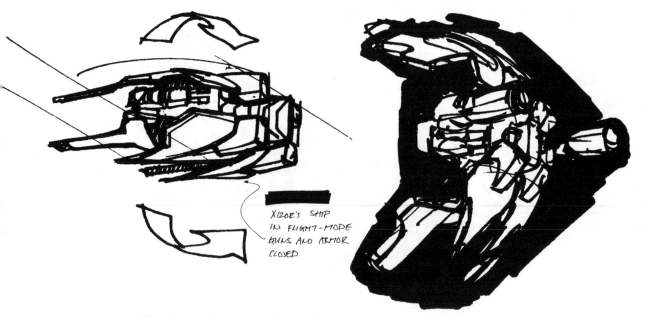

XIZOR'S SHIP
IN FLIGHT-MODE
GUNS AND ARMOR
CLOSED

The shape of some cast-iron pulley castings inspired Doug Chiang's clamshell design for the Virago. *When the ship is in battle mode, its four armored wings fold out for maximum power.*

designs that would be made available to all the *Shadows* creative principals. In the summer of 1995 Bill Smith from West End Games came up with an entire history to explain the production of both Xizor's and Dash Rendar's ships for his Del Rey *Star Wars* vehicles and vessels book.

In the background account Xizor had contracted with an entire MandalMotors design team (the same company that created the second *Slave* ship for Boba Fett, as seen in the Dark Horse comics series) to build a unique vehicle, a combination luxury vessel and attack ship. To please one of the most powerful and vindictive figures in the galaxy,

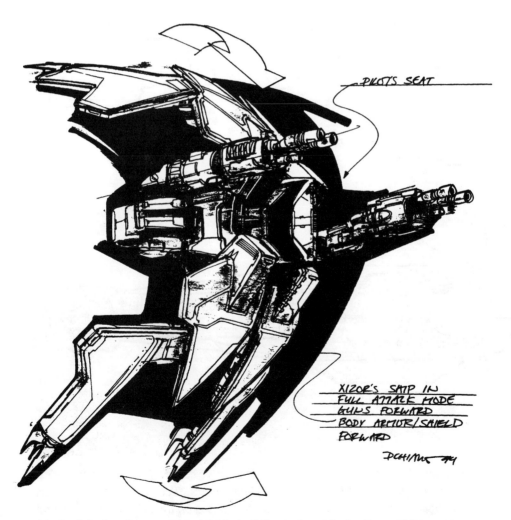

This final design features Xizor's ship in full attack mode, by Doug Chiang.

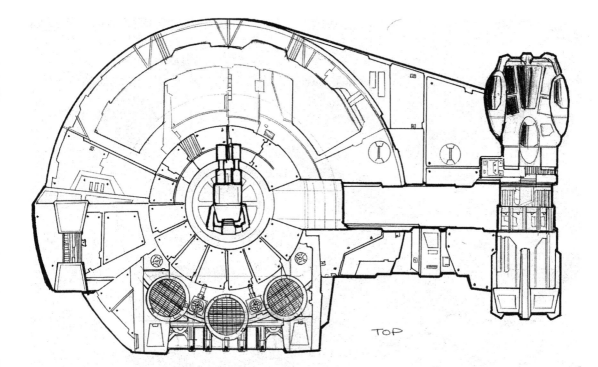

TOP

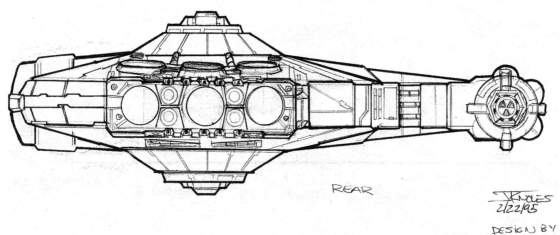

REAR

J. KNOLES
2/22/95
DESIGN BY
D. CHIANG

188

"We followed Doug Chiang's designs as close as we could when we began to design our computer graphics model," Jon Knoles notes. "Because the sketches were a one-angle view, I did a bunch of schematics based on the original sketches and sent them to Doug, and he okayed them."

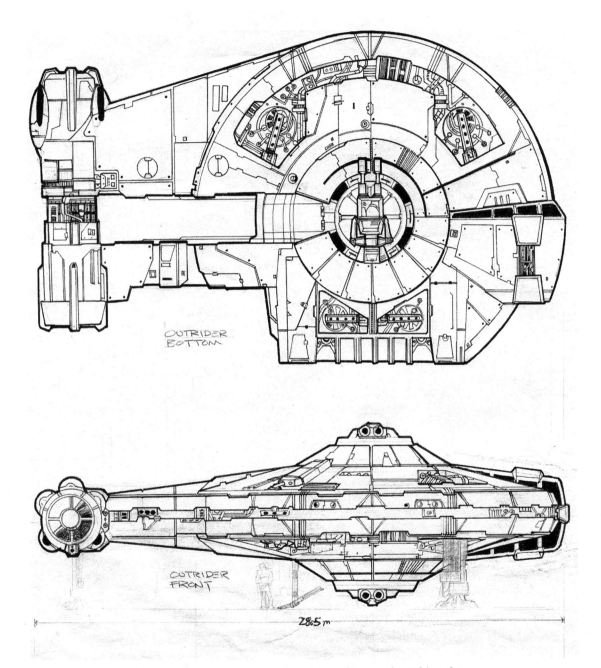

OUTRIDER
BOTTOM

OUTRIDER
FRONT

28.5 m

Final LucasArts Outrider *schematics were prepared, tweaking and working the final design preparatory to building the computer model.*
  Outrider, *top view (opposite page, top) and rear view (opposite page, bottom);*
  Outrider, *bottom view (above) and front view (below).*

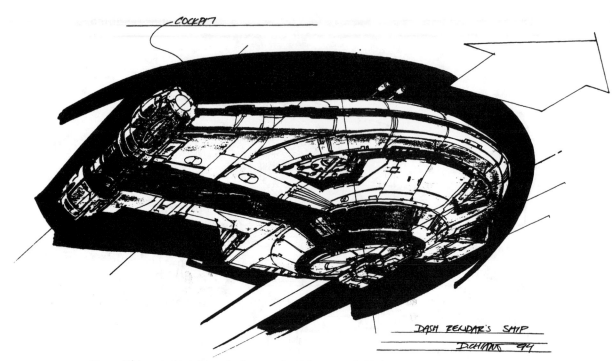

COCKPIT

DASH RENDAR'S SHIP
DCHIANG 94

Doug Chiang's Outrider *design evolved from an initial, pincerlike form to this final illustration, which locked in the image that would be duplicated throughout the various* Shadows *media.*

the design team developed a StarViper class, a heavy assault starfighter equipped with armor, weaponry, and incredible speed, powered by four separate power generators. The ship was designed as a "mobile platform" ship—with wing and thrust nacelles that could move in flight, almost like a living thing. During normal spaceflight the wings could fold flush against the engines and pilot compartment. In combat the four armored wings could expand, fully folding out to give the maneuvering thrusters maximum power. The armor plating could withstand even the laser cannon fire of an attacking X-wing, with a single forward mounted shield generator providing added protection. The rear of the ship, while not armored, would be protected by shield generators. The weapons themselves included a pair of laser cannons, each mounted on forward extending arms to rotate and fire over 180 degrees, supplemented by four proton torpedo launchers.

Dash's *Outrider* was constructed by the Corellian Engineering Corporation. The Corellia star system (home to the human species from which Han Solo was born) was famous not only for smugglers, traders, and pirates but also for the craftsmen and engineers who produced the fast, durable ships favored by the rugged Corellians who braved the dangers of deep space. The *Millennium Falcon*, with its distinctive saucer-shaped hull, was of the YT class of Corellian freighter, while the *Outrider* was a newer model of that class (modified for smuggling). The *Outrider*'s rounded hull largely served to transport its hot cargo, while Dash added souped-up hot rod engines and an extra complement of weapons for deep-space combat. The other requisite features of the prized smuggling ship included a pair of double laser cannons, hyperspace capabilities, armor plating and shield generators, and an illegal sensor stealth system. Dash has said that his *Outrider* "brought me home when any other ship would have scattered me across space."

While the books could easily launch *Shadows* ships with words, visually producing the ships would test the limits of the comics medium. "An action-adventure story like this requires a lot of technical renderings of spaceships—a superhero artist wouldn't be able to do this comic book," says editor Ryder Windham. "There aren't a lot of artists out there like Kilian Plunkett, who can do likenesses of actors and even draw droids without photo reference. He has a really precise, keen memory for detail. He doesn't even use model kits when he draws X-wings; he uses photographs from the films as a visual reference, and he doesn't copy them. He can draw them at angles completely different from the photograph. He's astonishing."

For Plunkett, the spacecraft posed the same challenges he faced with the familiar characters from the films—translating objects made for a celluloid environment to the static confines of a hand-drawn comics page. "There aren't many things in cinema more impressive than

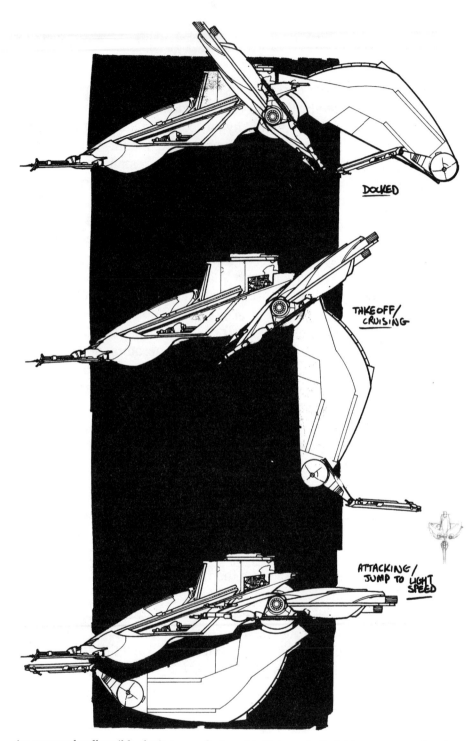

DOCKED

TAKEOFF/
CRUISING

ATTACKING/
JUMP TO LIGHT
SPEED

An unusual collapsible design was featured in this early Outrider *concept sketch by Kilian Plunkett.*

X-wings flying through space when there's a wide-angle lens on them and they sweep toward you as they come toward the camera," Plunkett notes. "But when you look at an X-wing model that's not moving, it's actually quite an awkward-looking thing. Of course, when you're drawing it in the comics, you don't have the advantage of motion. You're trying to make it look like it's moving, so you're stuck with these shapes. There are some tricks you can do to give it a dynamic look, which I used on *Shadows*, such as blurring the stars in the background. I didn't make them speed lines per se, but swooshes, a look I based on references from the Topps wide-vision *Star Wars* series trading cards. All the space scenes in this series are really high-quality freeze frames from the films, so you can look at them and see what it is about the image on the screen that makes it work. That's where I noticed that the background stars are often moving in the opposite direction to the foreground spaceship, and not just when they're jumping into hyperspace. So in the films there's motion blur to the stars, which makes it look much more dynamic, which I tried to simulate in the comics."

For LucasArts the challenge would again be the limits of games technology. In the case of their December 1995 CD-ROM release, Rebel Assault II, a version of the *Millennium Falcon* had been constructed in

In the search for Boba Fett, Lando Calrissian, piloting the Millennium Falcon, *follows Dash Rendar and the* Outrider *into dangerous territory: the fortress-like Imperial enclave on Gall.*

Shadows *Dark Horse Comic, issue 2, panel, page 12; pencils by Kilian Plunkett.*

The Outrider *in space; Doug Chiang design, model by Jon Knoles.*

the computer using 40,000 polygons (geometrically built, interconnecting series of planar surfaces that form a three-dimensional object) per frame for the ship alone. For the real-time action of the Shadows game, the *Falcon* was limited to a mere 250 polygons.

"You can't have a 40,000-polygon something in real time," Jon Knoles explains. "Our Nintendo 64 machine will do four thousand polygons per frame, and that's smokin' speed. But if you have a ship that's constructed out of one thousand polygons, you can only have four of them in a frame. For most of the ships we tried to get under a hundred polygons, but since the *Millennium Falcon* is such a complicated model,

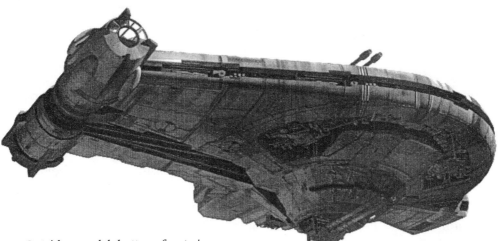

Outrider *model; bottom-front view.*

The Outrider *computer-generated model, top view, designed by Doug Chiang; model by Jon Knoles.*

The final Outrider *CG model with landing struts extended.*

we used 250 polygons. So you have the *Falcon*, add other spaceships flying around, some asteroids—and you're tapped out. If one stormtrooper is four hundred polygons, you can't have twenty of them running at you; you've wiped out your limit."

"To get around those limits we create objects with varying levels of detail," Knoles adds. "We have three versions of each model. If a Star Destroyer is far away, we can get away with one or two triangles. I think we did one Star Destroyer in twenty polygons. Then there's a middle-distance version that'll have a little more detail and finally a close-up. The other challenge is seeing that all the detail levels change smoothly when an object gets closer; you don't want it to jump when it's rendering itself in real time."

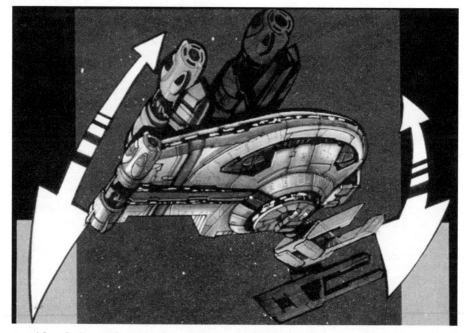

Outrider *designs (above and opposite page) for the Hasbro/Kenner* Shadows *toy line, based on Chiang's final specifications, feature "pivoting action."*

LucasArts' *Shadows* team would use five or six software tools to detail the various versions of individual spacecraft. Ultimately some ships would pose more of a challenge than others would. "TIE fighters are a breeze, and Star Destroyers are simple shapes, basically a triangle and a couple of blocks," Knoles says. "But Dash's ship is a perfect example of what not to do when designing a vehicle for a real-time 3-D game. It's a very nice ship, but like the *Falcon* it's round, and asymmetrical objects are really difficult to make."

Once constructed by LucasArts, the battleworthy ships of *Shadows* would see a lot of space combat. "In some battle sequences you'll actu-

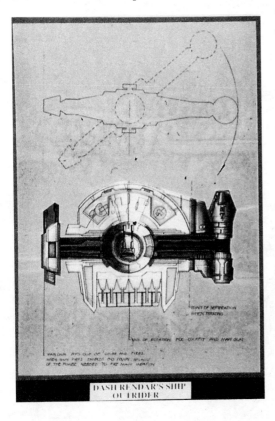

DASH RENDAR'S SHIP
OUTRIDER

ally be able to see the *Outrider* and fly it and control its guns," says Eric Johnston. "The *Outrider* is kind of like the *Millennium Falcon* in that there's a pilot and a gunner and you can have different points of view for each of those positions. You'll actually be sitting in the turret, so you won't actually see the ship, but you'll see the control console of the turret and be able to swivel around and shoot from there."

Luke Skywalker and Wedge Antilles lead the X-wing Rogue Squadron to Gall in full attack formation. (Luke inset head shot is at top left; Wedge is at bottom right.)
Shadows *Dark Horse Comic, issue 2, page 5; unedited pencils by Kilian Plunkett.*

III.
WAR GAMES

IF TATOOINE CAN BE DESCRIBED AS a world of heat and desert, its polar opposite is Hoth, a planet of cold and snow. It was on a freezing Hothian battleground that a Darth Vader–led Imperial fleet made a surprise attack against a once-secret Rebel base, dealing the Alliance one of the greatest setbacks it suffered during the Galactic Civil War. If the Star Destroyers had not made such a premature appearance from hyperspace, the base would have been easily destroyed. The Rebels had time to activate a protective shield, but it merely delayed the inevitable as Imperial ground forces, led by the fifty-foot-tall All Terrain Armored Transports and the smaller All Terrain Armored Scout Transport walkers, put the Rebels to rout.

The Battle of Hoth, as it was played out in *The Empire Strikes Back*, was a complex production for the filmmakers at Industrial Light & Magic. The sequence ran the universal playbook of effects in that predigital era, from matte paintings and the stop-motion animation of walker models across miniature sets to ILM's development and use of breakthrough technology such as the Quad, a computer-driven optical compositing printer.

The dramatic sequence had always been a fan favorite with its scenes of ground engagements on the snowy battlefield and flying Rebel snowspeeders firing their lasers or harpoon cannons at the giant, lumbering walkers. The outmanned and outgunned Rebels had fought bravely, with Luke Skywalker's own snowspeeder harpoon cable helping to trip up, topple, and destroy one of the towering walkers.

For the gamemasters at LucasArts, the chance to use the new Nintendo 64 game machine to represent the famed battle (with player/character Dash Rendar leading the attack) proved irresistible. Although Rebel Assault had included a battle with Imperial walkers on Hoth as one of the fifteen levels in that CD game, the Battle of Hoth had never been re-created in a real-time, interactive 3-D presentation—until Shadows.

LucasArts' enthusiasm for staging action between snowspeeders and walkers was the reason why the Battle of Hoth was added as a chapter to Dash Rendar's biography. Although he might have been a rogue in the other media, as a player/hero Rendar was a pilot with the right stuff and the verve to show it off. On Hoth he doesn't shirk the chance to take on the towering, laser-firing walkers but jumps into one of the snowspeeders and joins the fray. An early, internal game outline document (dated 4/17/95) describes the challenge LucasArts wanted to create for the player/character in the first game level:

AT-ST; computer-generated model by Jon Knoles.

Level 1: Destroy Imperial walkers

Objective—Give Rebels time to escape Echo Base.

After blasting several AT-ST scout walkers with laser cannons, player approaches

AT-ATs from any angle, flies through walkers' legs, using cannons to damage walker, then views change automatically to rear view. Fires harpoon gun at walker's legs. When targeting system acquires a lock (a few seconds of steady aiming), fires harpoon. Cable latches onto walker. View changes to front (or behind speeder) and player flies around walker at least three times . . . For bonus points and power-ups, player can come around and destroy walker with laser blasts to the head and neck.

In the real-time game each player would be able to fly his or her snowspeeder with seemingly unlimited freedom, zooming into the blue

Jon Knoles conjures up an Imperial walker from virtual space. LucasArts' interest in creating a real-time, interactive reenactment of the famed Battle of Hoth—and its placement of player/character Dash Rendar in the middle of the action—provided a new chapter in the biography of the new character.

Photo by Heather Sutton.

digital sky above, swooping back down and over the snowy planet surface, circling over and flying through the legs of attacking walkers. As with all the attacking forces throughout the game, whether spaceships or stormtroopers, the game designers and programmers had to provide the walkers with artificial intelligence (AI) capabilities so they could react to the actions of a player's snowspeeder.

"The walker acts naturally, moving with its head forward, but as you fly around it, the walker has an agenda to turn its head and try to track

Dash Rendar's Outrider *docked in the Rebels' Echo Base hangar on Hoth. This image would be used in a cut scene of Dash and Han Solo conversing just before the sudden Imperial attack.*

Computer-generated model by Jon Knoles.

and shoot lasers at you," Jon Knoles explains. "The intelligence needed to make the walkers react, track, and fire on the player is similar to opening the door on a level and seeing a group of stormtroopers. They didn't know you were coming, so there has to be an intelligence to tell the stormtroopers to wait until the door has opened before they turn around. AI is really basic technology. Building the walkers is almost

Dash Rendar encounters Han Solo in the Rebel hangar on Hoth. Although Han Solo would be frozen in carbonite throughout the Shadows *projects, this flashback setting allowed game players to see the classic character alive and well.*

like creating a real plastic model with movable parts, with a place to swivel so the heads can rotate, except that the programmers have given each moving part an instruction on what to do."

Project leader Mark Haigh-Hutchinson, who supervised the Hothian battle level, also had the task of programming the AI attributes for the walkers and other player opponents. "Actually, when people talk about artificial intelligence in computer games, most of the time it isn't really intelligent—I like to call it 'artificial stupidity,' " Haigh-Hutchinson says, smiling. "We don't have the computing power to do real artificial intelligence, so we're basically faking it; it's all smoke and mirrors to make things look like they're behaving intelligently. The walkers are programmed to know certain things about their environment, such as that there are enemy snowspeeders flying around their world that they want to fire at. Without getting too much into 3-D trigonometry, I know the angles the opposing snowspeeders are moving in, roughly their speed, how long it'll take my shot to go a certain distance, where speeders will be at a certain point in time. So when we're programming, we can look around and see where the snowspeeders are in relation to the walkers. The walker's got to anticipate its aiming position and the direction the snowspeeder is moving in. That's the kind of decision making it's doing.

"Each of the walkers has its own brain, so to speak," Haigh-Hutchinson adds. "A section of code is controlling its emotion and the way it behaves in its world. The computer, of course, knows more than the player does, because the computer is controlling the environment. But the nature of this type of game is that the player is also learning how his or her enemies behave and the layout of a level. So you want a certain measure of predictability, because then the player can progress and become better at the game, but you also have to balance that with elements of controlled randomness so the player doesn't get the idea the game is set in stone."

In *Shadows*, Dash would also be involved in the fateful Rebel assault on the *Suprosa*, the Imperial freighter secretly carrying a computer holding information on the Death Star construction project. The fact that the vital plans had fallen into Rebel hands later would be revealed in the *Return of the Jedi* scene set in an Alliance briefing room, where resistance leader Mon Mothma announced (in the words of Lucas's original script): "The data brought to us by the Bothan spies pinpoints the exact location of the Emperor's new battle station."

A few simple words but a whole world of dramatic possibilities for *Shadows*, where Luke Skywalker, along with Dash Rendar in his *Outrider*, and a squadron of Bothans (a species allied to the Alliance and renowned for its galaxywide spy network), would capture the freighter and its precious cargo. For the LucasArts game the action would be extended from the furious space battle described in the novel to an elaborate board and search operation. In the game play the freighter crew has escaped, a self-destruct device has been switched on, and

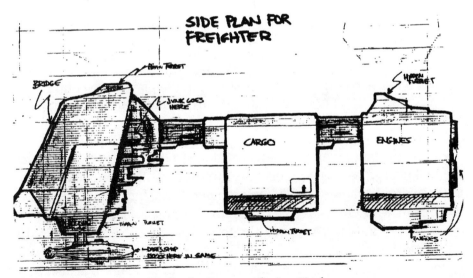

Early production schematic for the Suprosa, *by Jon Knoles.*

the player/hero has five minutes to escape with the computer before the ship explodes. An early (April 1995) LucasArts level description describes the obstacles being prepared for the player:

> Level 9: Inside Freighter
> Mission objective: Board freighter and capture Imperial Super Computer with secret construction project data . . . *Outrider* is docked under the front section of the ship. Player enters ship corridors through docking tubes. Closed, claustrophobic hallways. Hidden auto-guns pop down from hidden panels in the ceiling, some from the floor, some from walls, sometimes all three. Some stormtroopers and/or Imperial guards try to stop you. Reach the bridge and plug into control terminal to get access to doors throughout the ship. Very dark and spooky inside. Lots of turns like a haunted house.
> . . . Enter engine room. Jets of steam and flames in timed bursts spew from all walls and floor and ceiling (from obvious holes or vents which player can shoot). Encounter various maintenance droids and dangerous moving machine parts and pistons . . . Lots of secret rooms and big pick-up items hidden away to encourage exploring. Leebo warns player if time's a'wasting . . . In the tunnels leading from engine room to cargo bay, really stick it to the player in a couple of nasty trick spots with multiple targets pinning him or her down.

After surmounting all the obstacles along the way, the player reaches the main cargo bay, where the boss monster awaits: a modified maintenance droid guarding the supercomputer: "He'll have many arms and will be throwing crates at the player," the script specifies. "There will be a sweet spot in his head when the top of his head opens. This is the only time he is vulnerable to attack. He does this to see where the player is and gets aggressive after his head closes again. It is also possible to shoot the loaders over his head which drop crates on him;

causes slight damage. When boss is destroyed, the *Outrider* lands on extended platform. Level completed."

Adding to the intricacy of the scenario, in the novel and comics' story line the Death Star plans and the *Suprosa* raid are tied up in one of Xizor's wily plots. The manipulative Falleen, who has the ear of the Emperor, has convinced Palpatine to convey the Death Star construction plans to the planet Bothawui. Playing both sides, Xizor allows his Black Sun contacts to let slip to Bothan spies word of the secret cargo of vital importance to the Empire. As Xizor tells Guri in John Wagner's script for issue 3:

> XIZOR: Time and route of the freighter. You will pass the information to the Bothan spies.
> GURI: Is that wise, Prince Xizor? It is not in your interests to go against the Empire!
> Xizor: It is always best to keep a foot in both camps, Guri. In the unlikely event the Rebels win this war, they won't forget Black Sun's generous contribution to their victory!

John Wagner's original script for the *Suprosa* attack would, however, be a fairly brisk one-page summation taken from the perspective of a grim Emperor who watches the outcome on the freighter's own camera. In the follow-up scene Xizor is explaining to Palpatine how the incident can still be turned to Imperial advantage.

Steve Perry's novel, however, would play out the space battle as a dramatic turning point for Dash Rendar. In the attack Luke Skywalker in his X-wing (with Artoo along as astromech droid to interface with the ship's computers) leads Dash in his *Outrider* and the Bothan "Blue Squad" contingent of twelve Y-wings (with one pilot and gunner per ship). As the squadron attacks, they discover that the *Suprosa* is armed with hidden cannons that fire missiles that take out two of the Blue Squad ships. As Perry picks up the action:

Four of the Bothan ships looped away in pretty good formation, Dash in the *Outrider* in tandem with them.

Luke was close enough to see the missile port on top of the freighter blow a cloud of gas into space that crystallized and glittered under the local sun's light.

"He's got a missile off!" Luke yelled.

"I got it," Dash said. "I'll hammer that spike into scrap."

Luke watched Dash's ship roll and dive and his robotic guns began spewing coherent bolts of energy. He couldn't see the missile but he saw Dash continue his attack, saw the guns spraying their hardlight spears.

"Damn! Blast!" Dash said. "I've got to be hitting it! Why doesn't it stop?"

"Dash! Come on!" Luke yelled.

"Shut up, I've got it, stop, you blasted piece of junk, stop!"

"Move, Dash!"

"No, I'll get it!"

"Incoming!" Blue Six yelled. "Scatter!"

The four fighters tried to split up, separated like an opening fist.

Too late.

The missile exploded among them and when the blast cleared, all four ships, eight Bothans, were gone.

"I can't have missed," Dash said, his voice incredulous. "I can't."

Luke's anger swept over him as he put the X-wing into a sharp and twisting turn. He headed right at the freighter. Six of his squadron had been destroyed, just like that. And Dash, hotshot Dash, he'd screwed up royally. If it hadn't cost lives, Luke would have felt that the braggart got what he deserved. If he'd had any doubts that the crew of the freighter knew what they carried, they were gone now.

He was too incensed to use the Force. He ignored the energy beams stabbing at him, ignored Artoo's cacophony of whistles and bleats, ignored everything but the engine compartment of the freighter under his guns. Fired. Fired again and again. Saw the radiation absorbed by the shields, saw the blue glow brighten. Saw the force field give way under his attack. Saw the engine compartment rupture, smoke, flash red and purple as his laser beams baked and killed it.

"I couldn't have missed," Dash said. He sounded dazed.

"Stow that, Dash," Luke ordered. "It's too late to worry about that now. Get ready to bring your ship in."

None of them would know until later that Dash's *Outrider* guns had indeed intercepted the fateful missile that claimed the four Bothan Y-wings. But the Imperial missiles had been coated with new, impenetrable armor plating that had made them impervious to even a direct hit.

The computer they had fought and died for was the size of a small carrying case. Once its frightening secrets were revealed to the Alliance, they'd know the Emperor had ordered the development of a terrible new Death Star, larger and equipped with a superlaser more powerful than the one that had destroyed the planet Alderaan.

But a disconsolate Dash and a frustrated Luke (he blamed himself for the loss of the Bothan pilots) would have to gird themselves for an even more dangerous mission. Leia, who had journeyed with Chewbacca to the Imperial City to uncover the plot behind the assassination attempts on Luke, was in the clutches of Xizor, and they would have to come to her rescue.

For Xizor it was delightful to have detained the beautiful Princess in his fortresslike lair. He had let the word of Leia's whereabouts leak out. He knew Skywalker would be coming to rescue her—and the Dark Prince would be waiting.

Luke Skywalker leads the Rogue Squadron in an attack on an Imperial cruiser. Shadows Dark Horse Comic, issue 2, page 11; unedited pencils by Kilian Plunkett.

IV.
THE FINAL
BATTLE

IN THE CLIMACTIC EVENTS OF THE *Shadows* story line, Leia, who had arrived on Coruscant in the disguise of the Black Sun bounty hunter Boushh, would find herself in detention in Xizor's palace stronghold. The Princess has aroused the amorous nature of the wily Falleen, who has been exuding his usually potent pheromones in order to seduce his prisoner. Only the intervention of the loyal Chewbacca would help break the spell.

The Wookiee manages to escape and join Luke, Lando, and Dash, who have arrived via the *Millennium Falcon* and the *Outrider*. The group begins its daring rescue attempt with the help of Vidkun, an engineer who knows how to penetrate Xizor's palace through the labyrinthine passages of the underground sewer system. (Deep into the dank passageway Vidkun betrays his traitorous character by pulling a blaster and firing on Dash. It's only a slight, glancing wound, and the resourceful Rendar answers with his own blaster bolt right between the engineer's eyes.)

The journey through the dark passage into the lair of the Black Sun was a natural for interactive game play. For texture artist Chris Hockabout, his design of the sewer system was inspired by a summertime 1992, postcollege graduation trip to Czechoslovakia.

Wedge Antilles leads his Rogue Squadron against Imperial TIE fighters in the battle that opens up the Shadows comics action.

Shadows *Dark Horse Comic*, issue 1, pages 4 and 5; unedited pencils by Kilian *Plunkett.*

213

*Coruscant sewer tunnel from the
LucasArts game.
3-D concept art by Bill Stoneham.*

*Chris Hockabout's memories of a
torchlit boat tour of the sewers of
Prague inspired his texture art of
the labyrinthine sewer system
below Xizor's Palace.
Photo by Heather Sutton.*

"The original idea for the sewer system was that it was supposed to look like the kind of Gothic sewers you'd see in *Phantom of the Opera*, with these cathedral ceilings and gargoyles," Hockabout recalls. "But my main influence for the Imperial City sewers was this amazing experience I had in Prague when I took a tour of the old sewer system beneath the city. You'd go on these little boats through these old sewers, which are huge, labyrinthine passageways that look like the inside of cathedrals. They have it lit by torches and spotlights on the boat, but otherwise it's completely dark as you go through this quiet, underground sewer system. On a hot summer day in Prague it was kind of a relief to get into those nice, cool sewers."

Once inside Xizor's palace, the group rescues Leia and plants a thermonuclear bomb. Reaching level 102, the top of the Black Sun lair, Dash boards his *Outrider* (flown in by the loyal Leebo) and Luke, Lando, and Chewbacca hustle into the *Falcon* (piloted to the rescue in dizzying fashion by Artoo and See-Threepio).

The furious Xizor, escaping the destruction of his beloved Black Sun lair in his speeding *Virago*, lands on his *Falleen's Fist* skyhook. From an Olympian deck, with its 360-degree view of space, Xizor can unleash and command his personal armada against his escaping enemies. Although some additional Rebel firepower comes with the cavalrylike arrival of starfighter pilot Wedge Antilles and his Rogue Squadron (reacting to an earlier message from Leebo), it seems that only a miracle can save Luke and company from Xizor's strike force. Author Steve Perry describes the atmosphere as the heroes find themselves outnumbered fifteen to one and the noose begins to tighten around their necks:

> The attacking ships had formed a loose hemisphere in space. There were an awful lot of civilian freighter and passenger ships going to and coming from the planet and it was all Luke could do to avoid hitting one of them as he dodged

CUTSCENE 19: SHOT 1 ---SEWER LEVEL
OUTRIDER and FALCON land in remote area deep under city in huge ancient sewer

CUTSCENE 19: SHOT 2
Luke, Lando and Dash check their weapons and prepare to search for Leia.

Luke to Dash: "These tunnels lead to Xizor's fortress. Lando, Chewie and I will split up and search for Leia. Dash, see if you can find a way to cover our escape."

Dash: "Sure, I'll just set a few pulse bombs and blow this place sky high."

In the LucasArts game, Dash Rendar infiltrates Xizor's fortress through an ancient sewer system below Imperial City.

Preliminary cut scene sequences. Text by Jon Knoles, art by Paul Topolos.

Luke: "Just make sure you wait for us before you do..."

Level 11- BLACK SUN LAIR

Objective- Place pulse bombs in the main support beams of Xizor's Sky hook space elevator.

CUTSCENE 20: BLACK SUN LAIR---INTRO

Dash emerges from tunnel to gigantic arched foyer of Zizor's fortress. It looks like an old medieval castle, but retrofitted with durasteel walls and beams.

the fighters buzzing them. The civilians tried to get out of the way, which made things worse. And sooner or later, the Imperial Navy was going to wake up and probably add to the confusion. Why they hadn't already made Luke wonder.

As he watched, one of the aggressors fired at the *Falcon*. The cannon's beam struck one of those passenger ships, punched a hole through a power converter and caused a bright flash as the unit shorted out. Lot of damage, probably nobody hurt.

"Lousy shots," Lando said. "Don't care who they hit."

Luke nodded. He had thought they might weave in and out of the thick traffic and avoid being blasted but it seemed Lando was right: The bad guys didn't care who got fried.

The attackers had them boxed. There didn't seem to be any way out . . .

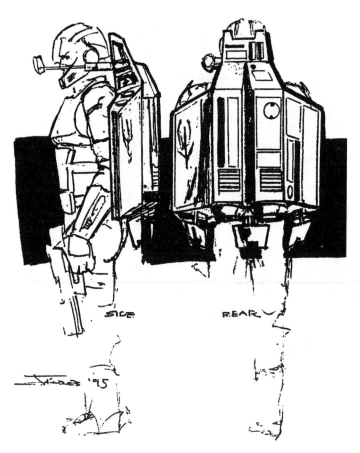

SIDE   REAR VIEW

And in the game the escape from Xizor's palace would prove equally challenging for player/character Dash Rendar. After planting a bomb, Dash would be confronted by Xizor and Guri and an attacking gladiator droid that he would have to defeat to escape by jetpack to the *Outrider* before the palace exploded.

Awaiting without would be the cataclysmic space battle. "We'll have hundreds of Xizor's ships coming at you, all shaped in the butterfly design Doug Chiang did

Early LucasArts design views of Dash Rendar with jetpack; art by Jon Knoles.

for Xizor's personal shuttle and opening up into attack position," says Jon Knoles. "In addition to the *Millennium Falcon*, the Rogue Squadron shows up, and we even add an X-wing, although it doesn't show up in the novel. So it's a big free-for-all."

For the LucasArts Shadows team the production challenge was to create hundreds of ships battling in real time in three-dimensional virtual space despite the restrictions of limited storage space.

"From a programmer's standpoint, if we have two hundred spaceships battling simultaneously, all the decisions a normal pilot would have to make need to be made by our little game computer two hundred times every thirtieth of a second," notes technical lead Eric Johnston. "It gets complicated, but there are some programmer's tricks we use to simplify the task. For example, we can have pilots in different spaceships actually share brains where they'll make similar or identical decisions, which only takes the time of one decision process. We can also group fighters into squadrons of five or six spaceships so only one leader has to make an intelligent decision and the rest can just follow information, similar to software flocking programs. Also, since there's no way we could store in memory hundreds of separate spaceship models, what we actually do is go, 'Okay, there's fifty-eight spaceships of this particular model; where are they in each location?' and then we store one and clone a copy for each separate location from where they can attack separately. So it'll look to the players like there's fifty-eight separate ships attacking them while there is actually, in the computer, one spaceship. It's all smoke and mirrors."

The tide turns when Vader, having finally gotten proof that Xizor has been behind the plot to kill his son and judging that the Dark Prince's fighters are behaving unlawfully, orders in his own Imperial strike force to attack the Dark Prince's aerial armada. In the game the final battle would represent the ultimate challenge, surpassing the difficulties of all the previous levels.

"After the player has defeated the armada, a couple Star Destroyers

Hopefully, the player has saved some jet pack fuel...

CUTSCENE 22: Shot 1---BLACK SUN ARENA---EXIT

DASH (TO WRIST COM): "Leebo, Get me out of here!"
Leebo(on wrist com) : "Right away, sir!"

CUTSCENE 22: Shot 2---BLACK SUN ARENA---EXIT
OUTRIDER and FALCON escape exploding fortress

Leebo warns Dash Rendar by wrist com that a bomb planted in Xizor's fortress is about to explode. As the Outrider *and the* Millennium Falcon *escape, player/character Dash Rendar must still battle TIE fighters and destroy the skyhook space station before the computer game's final level can be hurdled. Storyboard text by Jon Knoles, art by Paul Topolos.*

Looking down on planet as Xizor's shuttle, then Outrider and Falcon race up along beside space elevator. Fortress blowing up below.

CUTSCENE 23: Shot 1---Armada---Intro

DASH (EYES BURNING WITH RAGE): "That's Xizor's shuttle! He's trying to reach the Sky hook!"

CUTSCENE 23: Shot 2---Armada---Intro

Space above Coruscant. Look up to space, rear view of Outrider and Falcon chasing Xizor's ship.. but heroes break off as tons of Xizor's fighters arm from the skyhook base

pull in and unload lots of TIE fighters—then it becomes a real mess," Jon Knoles says, laughing. "While the TIE fighters are attacking the player, the Star Destroyers are pummeling Xizor's skyhook, which is this big space station that's connected to the planet below via this long elevator tube. But Dash gets all excited, and he wants to blow it up himself just to prove he's the greatest gung-ho dude in the galaxy, which is probably what the player's thinking at this point as well. So after a big dogfight in space the player will fly into the skyweb, the interior superstructure of this big space station which is similar to the interior of the Death Star in *Return of the Jedi*, fire a couple of proton torpedoes, and escape before it blows up at the end."

In the novel Vader engages in a telecommunication to Xizor in which he calmly explains that the Imperial Navy is attacking the Dark Prince's ships because they are engaged in criminal activity. "Nonsense" is the Dark Prince's reply. His ships are merely attempting to capture the Rebels who have just destroyed his stronghold:

> "You have two standard minutes to recall your vessels," Vader said. "And to offer yourself into my custody."
> The coldness at Xizor's core blossomed uncontrolled into an angry heat. He tried to keep his voice calm. "I will not. I will take this up with the Emperor."
> "The Emperor is not here. *I* speak for the Empire, Xizor."
> "*Prince* Xizor."
> "You may keep that title—for another two minutes."
> Xizor forced a confident smile. "What are you going to do, Vader? Destroy my skyhook? You wouldn't dare. The Emperor—"
> "I warned you to stay away from Skywalker. Recall your ships and surrender into my custody or pay the consequences. I will risk the Emperor's displeasure." He paused. "However, *you* will not be there to see it, this time."
> Xizor felt a surge of fear as the image of Vader turned ghostly and vanished. Would he do it? Would he fire on the skyhook?

To their surprise, and relief, Luke and company notice that the Imperial forces are blasting Xizor's space force. Weren't the Dark Prince and the Imperials on the same side? Luke wonders.

Regardless, the result would provide them with an escape route. As Perry describes it:

> Luke saw the giant Star Destroyer's powerful beam strobe, saw it pierce the skyhook. The planetoid shattered, blew apart, went nova, became a small star that burned brightly for an instant before it faded, leaving millions of glowing pieces behind.
>
> It was a spectacular sight for all its violence. It reminded Luke of the explosion that destroyed the Death Star.
>
> "Oh, man," Lando said softly. "They must have made somebody real mad."
>
> Luke shook his head, didn't speak.
>
> Dash said, "Heads up, boys. Follow me."
>
> Luke blinked. "Huh?"
>
> "Somebody just opened us an escape hatch."
>
> "Are you crazy? We can't fly through that wreckage!"
>
> "We don't have a choice. There are ships everywhere. What's the matter, kid? Don't think you can do it?"
>
> "If you can, my *droid* can. Go."
>
> Luke understood what Dash meant. It would be tricky, dangerous, but the space around the destroyed skyhook was relatively clear—the debris was expanding outward. If they could avoid being holed by the stuff on the way there, it was their best chance.
>
> "Yeeeehaww!" somebody in the Rogue Squadron yelled.
>
> Luke laughed. He knew just how they felt.
>
> They headed for the debris, and it looked as if it was going to be just fine. The good guys had triumphed!
>
> *"Look out, Dash!"* Lando yelled.
>
> Luke could hardly spare a glance, but he did. Just in time to see a block of shattered skyhook the size of a resiplex zero in on the *Outrider.*

"Dash—!" Luke yelled. It was too close to avoid—

There was an actinic flare of light too bright to look at. Luke turned away, saw Lando throw one arm up to block the glare.

When the light faded, the *Outrider* had vanished.

"Oh, man," Lando said. "He—he's . . . gone."

Later, at a secret Alliance base light-years from the Imperial planet, Luke and his friends could finally rest from their adventures. Although the evil Xizor had seemingly been killed, the loss of Dash Rendar in the aftermath of the skyhook's explosion left Luke with a bitter feeling. The great pilot had redeemed himself from the botched battle that took the Imperial freighter, although he would never know that nothing could have stopped those new "diamond-boron armored" Imperial missiles that destroyed the Blue Squad Y-wings.

After the final battle, Princess Leia commiserates with Luke over the death of Dash, whose Outrider *was lost in an explosion of battle debris. While the Steve Perry novel would leave Dash's survival a mystery, the LucasArts game left no doubt, with Dash and Leebo escaping through hyperspace. "It's no fun if your player gets killed in the game," Jon Knoles observes.*

Art by Paul Topolos and Jon Knoles.

But Luke and his comrades could gain some satisfaction from the perilous mission they had undertaken and survived. To rescue Leia they had gone into the heart of the Empire and into the fortress stronghold of the Black Sun. Now it was time to plan the rescue of Han, who had no doubt been delivered into the hands of Jabba the Hutt in his fortresslike palace on Tatooine.

In Steve Perry's original November 1994 outline Dash had escaped along with the *Falcon* and the Rogue Squadron moments before Vader's strike force blasted Xizor's skyhook. When the story line was changed to include the destruction of the *Outrider*, it added to the dramatic impact of the novel's finale, but that would be a problem for the game play. Since a player utilized a hero character as a virtual surrogate, hurdling the myriad of obstacles of every level (no doubt dying and being reborn many times along the way), for the player to be vaporized at what should have been the final triumphal level would be a rude, and unfair, comeuppance.

"It's no fun if your player gets killed in the game just because he gets killed in the novel," Jon Knoles notes. "We would have changed the game player to Luke Skywalker, but that would have defeated the whole purpose of utilizing this new character. So at the end of the game we have Dash *presumed* dead. We have a cut scene of Luke and Leia back on Tatooine, where they're standing with the *Millennium Falcon* and the X-wing in the background, and Luke is saying how terrible he feels about Dash's death and what a great help he was to the Rebellion and Leia is saying how he didn't die in vain and it was time to plan their rescue of Han, which sets up the events of *Return of the Jedi*."

In one of the final cut scenes in the game the *Outrider* is seen traveling through hyperspace. Dash and Leebo have cheated death once again and, in the dialogue scripted for the cut scene, make future plans:

> DASH: "Well, Leebo, we've made some great disappearances, but that was definitely the best! You think anyone will miss us?"

LEEBO: "I don't understand, sir, why you don't want Commander Skywalker to know we survived."

DASH: "Well, I wasn't hired for that stunt back there, so there's no waitin' around for a reward. Second, even with Xizor dead, someone in Black Sun will remember me and send every thug in the galaxy after us. But now that everyone thinks I'm dead—who's gonna be looking for me? Besides, just a change of identity and the whole galaxy's ripe for the picking."

While the rogue pilot blasts off for the other side of the galaxy, Darth Vader reports to the Emperor both Xizor's treachery and his destruction of the Dark Prince's skyhook. In the novel Vader is initially surprised as Palpatine dismisses Xizor as a mere criminal. Black Sun, the Emperor muses, was like a chirrua—cut off one head and another would replace it. As the Emperor explains to Vader:

"No leader of Black Sun could ever be a match for the power of the dark side."

"But what of the plot to ensnare the Rebel leaders?"

". . . The new Death Star will draw them in, and this time, you and I will be there to finish this Rebellion . . . Young Skywalker will be there, too. I have seen it."

CUTSCENE 27: SHOT 4 (EPILOGUE)
Imperial City, Emperor's Chambers

EMPEROR: "You are certain that Prince Xizor attempted to kill young Skywalker once he knew of our plan to turn him to the dark side..."

VADER: "Yes, my master. He was not to be trusted."
EMPEROR: "And you are certain that he is dead?"
VADER: "There were no survivors, my master."

EMPEROR: "No matter, Vader. I want you to go to the new Death Star and await my arrival. Soon the Rebellion will be crushed. Everything is proceeding as I have foreseen"

Vader and the Emperor discuss the outcome of the attack on Xizor's skyhook, thus setting up the action of Return of the Jedi.

Preliminary storyboards; text by Jon Knoles, art by Paul Topolos.

SHADOW PLAY

At the *San Diego Comic Con*, sculptor Susumu Sugita displayed his *Xizor* sculpture, then a work in progress.
Photo by Lucy Wilson.

I.
GATHERING
OF THE
TRIBES

THE TWENTY-SIXTH ANNUAL SAN Diego Comics Convention, held the last weekend in July 1995, was hailed by John Rogers (the president of the nonprofit corporation that put on the four-day extravaganza) as a "gathering of the tribes" from all the fields of popular culture. The con had years before earned its stature as the biggest and best gathering of comics enthusiasts in the United States, with an estimated thirty thousand fans expected to crowd the coastal town's cavernous convention center for the latest bash.

In the funky, low-key comics conventions of years past a con was a place to see the iconic "golden age" issues of pop mythology—such as Superman lifting that car over his head on the cover of *Action* 1—to conduct treasure hunts for long-lost old issues, and to learn to bargain with the kind of poker-faced assurance that might bring a knowing smile to a merchant in a Persian bazaar.

But conventions began to change with the growth of a collector's industry and as the fan gatherings became promotional venues for big-budget Hollywood action, fantasy, and comic book–theme films. Things began heating up in 1989 as fans at various conventions got the inside word on such upcoming summer blockbusters as *Batman, Star Trek V,* and *Indiana Jones and the Last Crusade.* By 1995 the multi-billion-dollar interactive games industry was weighing in as well, with fantasy subjects now available to be engaged in virtual environments.

Here and there were a few reminders of the machine age roots of mass-produced ephemera, including a booth trying to sell a few of the surviving magnesium-based printing plates once used in comics production. (At one point in the weekend, editor Ryder Windham, after exploring the crowded con space, came back to the Dark Horse area exulting in how he had passed a remote comics collector's corner where he could actually smell the inimitable aroma of old newsprint.)

Noting the multimedia, synergistic forces transforming the comics industry, the 1995 comic con unveiled its new title: "Comic Con International." The gathering would also celebrate a variety of other anniversaries and themes: the hundredth anniversary of the comic strip, dating back to an 1895 debut of the grinning street urchin whom artist Richard F. Outcault would later dub "the Yellow Kid" (although some comics historians dispute the precise date the comics medium began); the fortieth birthday of *Mad* magazine (with the magazine's "What—me worry?" mascot, Alfred E. Neuman, gracing many pages of the convention catalogue); a salute to the villains of the fantasy medium; and the designation of Friday as *"Star Wars* Day."

Actor Anthony Daniels, who had played protocol droid C-3PO in the trilogy, was in a separate convention center hall reminiscing to a full house. At a booth for Topps Publishing, the Hildebrandt brothers, Greg and Tim, were receiving long lines of autograph seekers, celebrating the announcement that the duo would be illustrating a cover of Topps' authorized *Star Wars Galaxy Magazine* as well as a card series based on the *Shadows of the Empire* story line. At the Dark Horse Comics area, dominated by a towering *Alien* creature prop, special signing sessions were under way with such *Star Wars* talent as Daniels and *Shadows* artist Kilian Plunkett. And at the Del Rey Books booth fans received copies of the classic *Star Wars* novels and caught glimpses of upcoming projects.

Strolling through the Dark Horse area was John Wagner, a tall and strapping figure dressed in an oversized Cleveland Indians baseball shirt, the grin of the logo character matching Wagner's own. He had taken a break from scripting the last few issues of the *Shadows* series, leaving the personal fiefdom of his self-proclaimed rectory in the English countryside for a visit to conventionland. Finding a spare seat in a back corner table area, he began rolling a cigarette for later, lamenting tobacco's addictive qualities. A nearby door opened, and figures costumed as the Marvel comics characters Spider-Man and the Thing sauntered out to make the rounds.

Wagner's Judge Dredd had been made into a big summer film, with Sylvester Stallone as the future supercop of Mega-City, but had hardly generated a ripple in the American zeitgeist, ringing up a dismal $30 million in box office. There was nary a Dredd promotion, poster, or cardboard cutout to be seen on the convention floor. Across the way, in the sprawling DC Comics area, a gigantic video view screen was playing images from the summer smash *Batman*

Gary Gerani (left), West Coast editor of Topps' Star Wars Galaxy Maga- zine, *shares a "Star Wars Day" moment with Lucasfilm continuity editor Allan Kausch.*

Photo by Lucy Wilson.

Forever (which had grossed some $180 million in domestic box office and seemed positioned to claim bragging rights as the summer's most successful movie) while fans crowded around and gawked at the display of one of the film's Batmobile stunt cars.

Wagner shrugged. Ah, the vagaries of pop culture. His thoughts turned to the final issues of *Shadows*, with the big space battle finale looming. "I'm dreading it," he said, smiling. "I haven't done it yet. I don't know how I'm going to get everything into the last episode. Toward the end it's gotten increasingly harder just because of the complications in the plot, all the characters going to and fro. But that's been part of the challenge of the project. Actually scripting action sequences is quite easy to do. But something like characterization is more involved, and I like to spend more time on that."

Kilian Plunkett, who would meet Wagner for the first time at the convention, was taking a break from a long signing session, and he, too, was feeling deadline pressures. "I'm finishing issue 2 and starting issue 3, and hopefully it'll get quicker now that all the reference from everyone is in." He smiled. "There's no more 'Oh, you have to erase those six pages of the *Outrider* because you've done it wrong.' There were a few things like the *Outrider* in which I had done finished pencils on an earlier design that had since been revised, which meant erasing and doing new, finished pencils.

"Now I'm getting ready to get into the swoop bike chase through Beggar's Canyon, which will be a major action sequence. That area has never been presented or illustrated before, but it's a canyon; there are rocks that jut out horizontally, so you have to fly sideways. There's the Needle, which is mentioned in the novel as this spire rock formation with a hole in the top that Luke has to fly his swoop bike through. Of course, no one else can do it; they all pile up and explode."

Although Plunkett was anticipating the final space battle, he also noted that the Han Solo rescue attempt and resulting engagement wouldn't be a lark, either. "On Gall you have the Rogue Squadron and these two Star Destroyers who just launch everything they have in terms of TIE fighters. It's a good action sequence, but there are twelve ships in Rogue Squadron, dozens of TIE fighters, the two Star Destroyers, and the planet. And they all have to be visible together at least once. There are so many spaceships in *Shadows of the Empire* that you can get completely involved in drawing blocks, triangles, and circles. I'm sure I'm going to have to go to a clinic to figure out how to draw people again." Plunkett laughed.

Graphically, it was a simpler time for *Star Wars* when the famous comic strip work of Al Williamson and Russ Manning came out during the period when the movie trilogy was in production. Dark Horse editor Peet Janes had grown up in Rhode Island reading those *Star Wars* strips in the pages of the *Newport Daily News.* Nearly two decades later he would be editing the reprinting of the strips in a special Dark Horse series titled *Classic Star Wars.*

The Force is with them. Left to right: Star Wars Galaxy Magazine *publisher Ira Friedman, Lucasfilm's Julia Russo and Howard Roffman, Topps director of publishing Greg Goldstein, Lucasfilm's Andre Lake Mayer, and* Galaxy *editor Bob Woods.*
Photo by Lucy Wilson.

"Having to work behind the scenes hasn't destroyed the magic, but it has broken the illusion of the *Star Wars* universe," Janes said, smiling as he stood in the shadow of the *Alien* monster. "But it's also invigorating to have a hand in the process of creation. It's a universe that has a life of its own now. Back when the comic strip was being published, *The Empire Strikes Back* had yet to come out, so Lucasfilm was relying on people like artist Al Williamson to put together some really great material."

It was no simple transition to adapt the black and white comic strip series, as drawn by Williamson and the late Russ Manning, to the comic book medium. Drawing and scripting an adventure strip with no more than three or four daily panels available usually required one panel just to recap the previous day's events while still maintaining a forward flow. (The color Sunday comics section was generally the place where the story and art could bust out and really roll.) For the comic book *Classic* series, some repetition from the strip's continuity was dropped and artists were hired to retouch or add art to make the separate strips flow as one seamless story.

Assembling the stories usually involved treasure hunts for the original black and white art. In the case of *Classic* Russ Manning stories the artwork would be colored by computer (as is the case with most modern comics production), but although all the color separations would be done digitally, there would be no elaborate Photoshop software effects. "We felt that Russ Manning's artwork would work best with a simple coloring approach," Janes said. "Russ Manning, in comparison to Al Williamson, was much simpler in terms of line work. His work has a very classic, four-color, comic book feel, and it really called for clean coloring, no blending or shading or any of the computer techniques they do nowadays."

Another bit of comic strip revitalization came in 1995 as the Hildebrandt brothers brought back to the daily comics section the adventures of *Terry and the Pirates*, the classic strip created by the late Milton

Caniff. The versatile brothers, whose work included a series of 1970s calendars based on J.R.R. Tolkein's *The Lord of the Rings* epic and one of the famed *Star Wars* theatrical release posters, were at the convention to sign autographs and generally celebrate their artistic return to the *Star Wars* universe.

Identical twins (Greg sported a distinguishing mustache and beard), they were both dressed all in black and had a penchant for talking simultaneously or in tandem. They had been inseparable since their childhood days growing up in Detroit until their forty-third birthdays, when they went separate ways to pursue their own careers. After a decade they had reunited, plunging into a massive, eight- to nine-month "Marvel Masterpieces" Fleer trading card series project for which they created 160 paintings of classic Marvel Comics characters. At the San Diego con they were contemplating a *Star Wars*–theme card series for Topps based on the *Shadows of the Empire* characters and events.

The brothers would bring a magic lamp full of inspiration to their *Shadows* work. A seminal experience had been their first movie, Disney's classic *Pinocchio*, which they had experienced when they were five years old. The Hildebrandts grew up not only during Disney's original golden age but in the glory days of adventure comic strips, when the likes of *Terry and the Pirates, Tarzan*, and *Flash Gordon* would transport readers to the backwaters of Asia, the heart of the jungle, or an exotic civilization on a distant planet. Radio also ruled, with programs such as *Superman* and *Captain Midnight* allowing a kid to, as Tim noted, "use your imagination because you had to invent it in your head." There were also the beloved fantasy and science fiction pulps, with men of the future whizzing about in rocket packs and flying saucers driven by those big-headed aliens.

Their parents had encouraged them to develop their imaginations, whether through their mother spinning tales of fairies flitting about in the backyard of their home in a blue-collar Detroit neighborhood, Saturday museum trips where they'd become enthralled by the mysteries of ancient Egypt and lost civilizations, or nature hikes into the thick woodlands on the edge of town. As the duo grew into their teenage years, they became fascinated with fantasy and science fiction, particularly George Pal classics such as *Destination Moon* and *War of the Worlds*, and began crafting their own homemade effects-filled films.

During the mid-1970s the twins, already successful commercial artists, decided to create *Urshurak*, their own live-action fantasy film. One day, in the middle of developing a presentation, they received a call from a small advertising agency in nearby New York City. There

The twenty-sixth annual San Diego Comics Convention, a Mecca for fantasy fans, featured a special Star Wars *day that highlighted* Shadows *projects such as a Hildebrandt brothers Topps trading card series. Here the brothers (Tim left, Greg right) sign autographs at the Topps booth.*
Photo by Lucy Wilson.

was a rush job if they wanted it, a poster for a Fox release called *Star Wars*, which was set to open in ten days. They were hesitant at first, but they are adept at quick turnarounds and love the science fiction medium, so they agreed. Working around the clock, the Hildebrandts produced and delivered their famed poster within thirty-six hours, then went back to *Urshurak*.

The brothers remember as a weird irony how many of the same elements of their own fantasy saga were reflected in *Star Wars*. But of all the screenplays and fantasy novels in all the world, somehow it was Lucas's film of that galaxy long ago and far away that had been the one to capture the popular imagination.

After three years of encouragement (including kind words from their boyhood hero George Pal) but no production capital, and with one producer telling the brothers their film required a $145 million budget (in 1980 dollars), the duo gave up their big-screen dreams and published their epic as a Bantam novel. "We were babes in the woods, two guys who lived our lives in a studio," Greg recalled of their Hollywood adventure.

The convention's special *Star Wars* day was winding down as the brothers began to contemplate jumping back into the universe of Luke Skywalker, the Rebels versus the Empire, and the mystical undercurrents of the Force. After a scheduled visit to Skywalker Ranch, some ten months of *Shadows* work would be ahead of them.

"It will be very challenging," Greg noted. "It's kind of intimidating."

"That's what's good about it, that it's intimidating," Tim added.

"Intimidating in one way, inspiring in another," Greg followed.

"Here's this huge phenomenon, this expectation you're walking into," Tim mused.

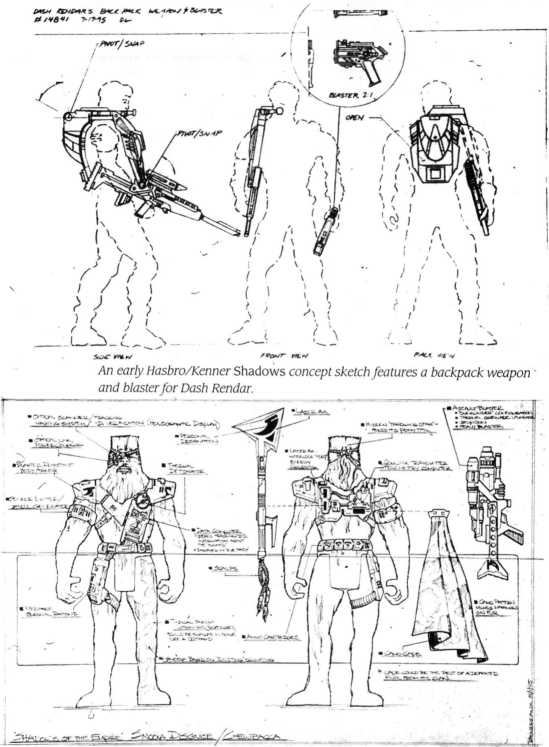

An early Hasbro/Kenner Shadows *concept sketch features a backpack weapon and blaster for Dash Rendar.*

During Shadows, *Chewbacca adopts the guise of Snoova, a famed Wookiee bounty hunter, in order to safely pass through customs at Imperial City. This Hasbro/Kenner design captured Chewie's Snoova look as conceived during the development of the* Shadows *line.*

240

II.
THE TOY
SHOP

SINCE *SHADOWS OF THE EMPIRE* was truly "the movie without the movie," no fewer than three major toy companies would be producing tie-ins to the *Shadows* universe: Kenner, Applause, and Lewis Galoob Toys, Inc.

The global licensing industry of the modern era had blasted off with the *Star Wars* phenomenon in 1977, with toys playing a big role in the overall merchandising success. Kenner, the original toy licensee, had sold in 1978 some 42,322,500 units of the movie-inspired line, generating revenues of $100 million. The Kenner toys hadn't been released until early in 1978, but the Christmas 1977 demand for *Star Wars* toys was so great that the holiday season saw the release of "Early Bird Certificate Kits," basically empty boxes that would be filled within a few months with action figures from the film. (Those empty boxes, which sold for up to $16, are today worth several hundred dollars on the collectors' market.)

Steve Sansweet, who tracked the *Star Wars* phenomenon from film artifacts to licensed products and collectibles in his 1992 book *Star Wars: From Concept to Screen to Collectible* (Chronicle Books: San Francisco), notes that the Lucas licensing empire began with daydreaming interludes during the early scriptwriting days. "When George Lucas was writing *Star Wars*, he didn't think much about the merchandising side. But he noticed that R2-D2 looked like a cookie jar and thought a mug with Chewbacca's face might be really cool. As the movie moved along in production, Lucas thought more about merchandising. In fact, Lucas even got the right to open *Star Wars* boutiques, which was interesting because there weren't that many products at the time. God knows what he would sell in *Star Wars* boutiques, but it was part of the deal."

Back in 1977, Sansweet, a journalist for the *Wall Street Journal*, had attended a special press screening of the film on the 20th Century-Fox lot and has used the word "seismic" to describe his personal reaction. "I was absolutely blown away by the film from the very beginning with the Star Destroyer going overhead. I can still remember stretching my head to look up as the Destroyer went overhead. Everybody just sort of giggled from the sheer exuberance of the scene. Afterward I really got a respect for the quality of the toys after talking to a lot of people at Lucasfilm and ILM. There's a big difference between making five *Millennium Falcon*s costing $100,000 each and making 250,000 or 500,000 highly detailed *Falcon* miniatures you can sell for $39.95.

"If you're no longer a kid and you're in the workforce, there's something about having your own money and being able to go into a toy store and you're the one making the decision about what to buy," Sansweet adds. "For a toy collector there's something about that whole thing of searching and finding that's very exciting, very rewarding. I'm still amazed at the kinds of things I find. Not too long ago I found one of the original mimeographed questionnaires that test audiences were given about a month before the opening. It's an unanswered copy, but there are questions like 'Which character did you like the best?' and 'Do you remember what the big, furry creature was called?' It's so cool."

For Sansweet, his first *Star Wars* collectible was the eleven-inch-long folded cardboard ticket he had received for the special Fox screening, emblazoned with the film's logo. At the end of the film, as he was walking out of the screening room, his head was buzzing with the thrills of the outer space adventure he'd just witnessed. Already an enthusiastic collector of space toys, he recalls walking up to the studio's senior vice president for corporate communications and, in the words of a true collector, asking: "Say, can you give me a poster for this thing?"

For its *Shadows of the Empire* line Galoob would be producing a projected spring 1996 domestic release of 100,000 units of a boxed set of "Micro Machines," miniature toys and play sets featuring six vehicles (including *Outrider*, *IG-2000*, and a swoop bike with rider) and characters both classic (Luke, Vader, the Emperor) and new (including Xizor, Dash Rendar, Guri, and Leebo).

Tony Mondini, project manager at Galoob, explains that the toy-making process begins with the Lucasfilm-approved references and design sketches. The company's engineering staff in Hong Kong then begins with the creation of handcrafted "first model" figures and vehicles. "These initial models are handmade inch-tall figures made out of casting resins, which is like a liquid plastic, and poured into molds," Mondini says. "The detail on these handmade samples is incredible. Since at that stage the color schemes for *Shadows* wasn't all nailed down, we were allowed to use our own colors for the first models. They all have a base paint sprayed on, and then they're painted by hand using tiny brushes, with things like uniform insignias put on with transfer type positioned on the model.

"Once the first models are approved, a more detailed tooling model is made, which is usually three times the actual size of the final model in order to get all the detailing and include any required changes. As a rule, Galoob is a stickler for detail, and we'll cram every bit of authentic detail in respect to size. Once they've been made ready for mass production, we can use a pantograph reducing device off those tools."

From the beginning of the *Star Wars* phenomenon, the Lucasfilm dictate has been that licensed action figure and vehicle toys adhere

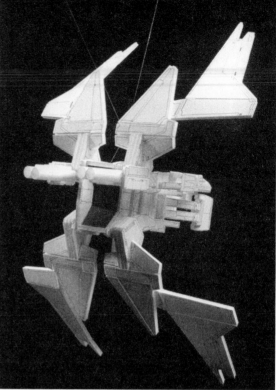

Hasbro/Kenner Virago *prototype with body armor and guns extended forward.*

Virago *prototype with body armor and guns closed.*

exactly to the look of the films. The care taken in the design and authentic details of the toys has, according to Sansweet, been an important factor in the success of the entire saga. For young fans, toys can become vehicles of the imagination.

"I think the toys gave kids the opportunity to take a piece of the movie home with them and to do their own *Star Wars* stories," Sansweet says. "It also seems to me that the Kenner toy line was instrumental in keeping the excitement going for the two-year period in between the release of the next *Star Wars* movie, when there was only anticipation. Those were also the days before video. The first *Star Wars* video didn't come out until 1982, and that was only for rental, so you couldn't have the film in the house to watch. As toys, the characters became part of kids' play life, part of the things they talked about at school or in the neighborhood."

Hasbro/Kenner prototype for the Outrider.

Kenner's original lines of articulated *Star Wars* action figures had been produced until 1984. After a lull Kenner returned to the property with a 1995 "Power of the Force" collection. "The original line was almost revolutionary in its day, but the poses and level of detailings seemed dated by today's standards," notes Kenner's *Star Wars* team leader, Tim Hall. "For the rerelease we were challenged to make the line more accessible for kids, which meant more action-oriented and aggressive, in other words, what looked most cool. The figures are still hand-sculpted—ours is a very handcrafted industry—but today there is more commitment to detailing. The materials are also more sophisticated. For example, in an early line some characters had fabric capes, but now we can produce molded vinyl capes that have more shape."

Kenner's "Powers" line would be followed by the *Shadows* action figures (including new characters such as Xizor and Dash Rendar), vehicles (from the *Outrider* to swoop bikes), and "two-pack" pairings of new and classic characters (such as Xizor and Vader). The classic character figures would also be given a new spin with Chewbacca disguised as Snoova, a Wookiee bounty hunter, and Luke Skywalker costumed in an Imperial uniform (all the better to infiltrate Imperial City).

"*Shadows* was exciting because it wasn't a movie or television property but an event," Hall observes. "It was an interesting challenge for us because unlike the trilogy, where there's so many movie stills and model props available, we only had the preliminary sketches from Mike Butkus to go with. In some cases we got to contribute, such as in the look of the swoop bike figures, which had originally been considered with the conehead look for the riders. We didn't want to do coneheads but to develop a more aggressive look. But Lucasfilm are wonderful partners, so we got to develop these menacing swoop troopers wearing helmets in a Boba Fett look. Throughout, we worked with Lucasfilm. When dealing with a legacy like *Star Wars*, we're always extra careful to make sure our toys are connected with the universe."

For those who might have outgrown child's play, such as members

Darth Vader and Xizor are featured in this concept for Applause's "Spirit of Villainy" figurine.

Concept art by Dave Williams.

Final "Villains" concept art was done for the line's signature sculpture. The creative team for this and all of Applause's designs included product manager Marc Bruderer, creative manager Robert Curet, and concept artist Dave Williams.

of the generation that experienced *Star Wars* during its initial theatrical release (and even subsequent generations raised on video viewings of the famed trilogy), there is another section of the toy market that might appeal: collector's figurines. "Collector's dolls are more display items than toys," explains Marc Bruderer, senior product manager for Applause, another *Shadows* licensee. "Ours is a very focused niche market. Our industry is basically divided into toy licensees like Kenner, which distribute mass-market to discount and toy store chains, and gift companies like Applause, which license merchandise for distribution to speciality stores like greeting card and comics shops."

Before its *Star Wars* projects Applause had created licensed toys for properties ranging from Sesame Street to Disney movie tie-ins. The company's first Lucasfilm licensing launch was *Star Wars Collector's Series*, a fall 1995 line of nine- to ten-inch dolls of Luke, Han, and company. "Prior to the release of our first *Star Wars* line we looked at what had been done over the past eighteen years of merchandise," Bruderer notes. "*Star Wars* had set all kinds of licensing precedents, and Kenner had a lot to do with that. For us to be a leader ourselves, we needed to focus on specific positioning—which was collector dolls. Our lines capture moments from the trilogy so collectors can relive the experience. Our idea was to have characters in classic but unusual poses, such as Han Solo dressed in the stormtrooper outfit he wears in the first film. We'd also have dolls in combinations, such as a pose of Luke with Yoda on his back from *The Empire Strikes Back*."

Applause's *Shadows* line would include the release of roughly nine- to ten-inch-tall vinyl dolls for Xizor and Dash Rendar. Taking a cue from the movie scene themes of Applause's Collector line, the *Shadows* figures would depict not only scenes from the story line but ones in which a new character would be paired with a classic character, such as Dash and Luke fighting swoop bikers together on Tatooine.

While toys and collector dolls might stoke some fans' fancy, there's another category that's the stuff of pure imagination: *Star Wars* role-playing games, in which participants adopt specific personae and create their own stories without the benefit of boards and toy pieces. "Any role-playing game is like 'let's pretend' with rules," notes Peter Schweighofer of West End Games, the licensee for such *Star Wars* games.

The father of role-playing games, curiously enough, was the great English writer H. G. Wells (1866–1946), whose prodigious literary output ranged from scholarly works such as *Outline of History* and *Science of Life* to seminal science fiction classics such as *The Time Machine* and *The War of the Worlds.* Less known is *Little Wars*, a war-game role-playing book he wrote "for boys and girls of all ages" based on his teenage days growing up in Bromley, Kent, England. In his youthful sojourns through the local countryside Wells fancied himself a military leader on the order of a Cromwell or Napoleon, his mind filling the surrounding countryside with phantom military clashes. In his *Experiment in Autobiography* Wells recalled how no one suspected that while on his walks "a phantom staff pranced about me and phantom orderlies galloped at my commands . . . never a suspicion of the orgies of bloodshed I once conducted . . . And kings and presidents, and the great of the earth, came to salute my saving wisdom."

The modern incarnation of role-playing games is said to have begun, circa 1974, with Dungeons and Dragons. That game's origin has an almost mythic aura to it: A group gathered in Minneapolis, Minnesota, was playing a war strategy game with toy figures and a playing board when the idea arose of role-playing characters instead of marching tiny toy figures around a board, with that gem of an idea growing into the famed TSR sword and sorcery fantasy game.

Soon after the success of D&D, other genres would be explored by other game companies, including West End Games of Honesdale, Pennsylvania, which began business in the early 1980s with war games. By 1987, West End had been granted the right to license a *Star Wars* game from Lucasfilm. The set of rules for the *Star Wars* game, as designed by West End's Greg Costikyan, typically involved four to eight participants, each of whom chose a specific character, with developments (such as the impact of a stormtrooper's blaster hit) decided by the role of the dice. Running the action would be a designated "gamemaster" who served as storyteller and ultimate referee and even portrayed any supporting characters.

As developed by West End, there are two categories of *Star Wars* role-playing games: adventures and campaigns. An adventure, which usually provides an evening's entertainment, might have a story line in which a player character, stranded in Mos Eisley with a data disk meant for the leaders of a distant Rebel base, must locate a ship and get off-world while avoiding the pursuit of ruthless stormtroopers. A campaign, by contrast, represents a more elaborate, evolving story line that may take several months for players to complete.

To help game players create their *Star Wars* story lines, West End has published more than fifty game guidebooks since 1987, which doesn't count publications such as the quarterly *Star Wars Adventure Journal*. "We've expanded the universe," states Schweighofer, editor for the *Journal* series and author of the guidebook for *Shadows of the Empire*. "We've done supplement books on plants, creatures, new aliens, technologies, different planets. We've introduced new bounty hunters and expanded familiar environments like Mos Eisley. Our source books are half-guide and half-game books and are collected even by people who don't play the games but simply love *Star Wars*."

Despite the creative freedom within a game context, West End sourcebooks and game guides can't establish characters or situations that violate the saga's overall continuity. Certain thematic areas—such as the Clone Wars era, which might figure in a future chapter of the *Star Wars* movie series—are off limits. However, company rules haven't stopped some enterprising players from putting their personal spins on the fabled saga.

"In theory, a player can do whatever he or she wants," Schweighofer says. "I've seen the battles of Hoth and Endor re-created; I've seen

The Star Wars *role-playing game books produced by West End Games have significantly expanded the universe. Pictured here is an Imperial starport tower located in the Byblos System (population: 164 billion), with its 300 active levels having the capacity to hold 115,200 bulk freighters.*
Star Wars Platt's Starport Guide; *illustration by Chris Gossett.*

elaborate dioramas of Mos Eisley that have been created. There are gamers who want to adventure during the Clone Wars. I heard of a game where Luke joined forces with Darth Vader and they destroyed the Emperor and together ruled the Empire! Then there are games of *Star Wars* versus *Star Trek*, where players try to see what would happen if the *Enterprise* battled a Star Destroyer. The problem there is the two universes aren't compatible: *Star Trek* is in our future, it's more science fiction, technically oriented, and restrained in its style, while *Star Wars* is a space fantasy, a Saturday afternoon matinee."

In the West End Games second edition of *Star Wars: The Roleplaying Game* a chapter on gamemastering provides tips on how to develop a game from devising plot and character concepts to developing maps and props as tools for the actual game play. In one section the reader is encouraged to call on a "sense of wonder" in approaching the game. The advice touches on the saga's appeal, whether it's a youth playing with *Star Wars* toy characters (perhaps imagining a sandbox as a great desert wasteland on Tatooine), an adult appreciating a figurine striking a pose on the mantelpiece, or a group of friends gathered to invent stories and act out characters from that fabled galaxy.

"*Star Wars* is a universe of mystery, magic, and epic fairy tale. It appeals to us on a very emotional level . . ." states a section in *The Roleplaying Game*. "Remember the first time you saw *Star Wars*, as your seat rumbled from the deep music and that Imperial Star Destroyer lumbered into view? Remember the first time you saw the Imperial stormtroopers come blasting into the corridor? Remember the first time you saw Darth Vader clad in his evil battle armor? Remember the first time you saw the cantina scene, with its scores of amazing aliens? Remember how you said to yourself, 'Wow! This is great!!!!'?

"This is the mood you are trying to recapture!"

Composer Joel McNeely (above) at work. According to Robert Townson (left), vice president and producer at Varese Sarabande, McNeely was responsible for coming up with the unique "sound world" of Shadows. For both McNeely and Townson a classical orchestra, with its epic range of musical possibilities, proved the perfect vehicle for exploring the Star Wars universe.

Photos by Matthew Peak.

III.
MUSIC OF THE
SHADOWS

WHEN THE SCORE FOR A FEATURE film is being planned, a temporary track of selected music is usually presented to a composer as a guide for the musical atmosphere the director wants for the final film. (Director Stanley Kubrick liked the temp track prepared for *2001: A Space Odyssey* so much that he used it *instead* of composer Alex North's original score.) When George Lucas sat down with composer John Williams to discuss the music for *Star Wars*, his temp track featured Antonín Dvořák and Richard Wagner.

As Charles Champlin quotes Williams in his book *George Lucas: The Creative Impulse* (Harry N. Abrams, Inc.: New York, 1992): "[I]t was clear that [Lucas] wanted a nineteenth-century classical sound. Lucas's reasoning, Williams says, 'was that we were going to see planets unseen, creatures we hadn't met before. Everything visual was going to be unfamiliar, and that, therefore, what should be familiar was the emotional connection that the film has through the ear to the viscera. This I have to credit George with, the idea of making the music, as the composer would say, solidly tonal and clearly melodic, acoustic rather than electronic.' "

"A classical orchestra in and of itself is one of the most powerful instruments there is because it can achieve such variety of colors and weight and emotion," explains Joel McNeely, a feature film composer whose Lucasfilm work includes the big-band themes of *Radioland Murders* and music for the TV series *The Young Indiana Jones Chronicles.* "A classical orchestra can be huge and bombastic, it can be transparent and chilling, it can be romantic and warm and lush. Films need a wide variety of emotional and action underpinnings, and the orchestra is probably the most versatile instrument for accomplishing that. Much of the good film music of the last thirty to forty years is based on nineteenth-century European classical music."

McNeely would take a classical approach in composing and conducting the Royal Scottish National Orchestra and Choir in a sound track recording based on the *Shadows of the Empire* novel. It would be the fitting touch to embellish the "movie without the movie" project. "One of the most famous pieces in the literature of classical music is 'Pictures at an Exhibition' [by Modest Mussorgsky], a piece based on a series of paintings at an art exhibition. So, if you can write a piece of music based on paintings, why not a piece of music based on a book?" McNeely asks.

The *Shadows* sound track project was conceived by Lucasfilm's Lucy Autrey Wilson and Robert Townson, a vice president and producer at Varese Sarabande Records, a label founded in 1978 that specializes in film sound tracks. Townson counts as his most successful recent releases sound tracks such as *Terminator 2, Driving Miss Daisy, Basic Instinct,* and *Unforgiven* (as well as a Jerry Goldsmith recording of that missing North score for *2001*). Townson, who already had a working relationship with Lucasfilm based on Varese Sarabande recordings for the *Young Indy* series, had earlier discussed with Wilson the possibility of a sound track based on author Timothy Zahn's trilogy of *Star Wars* novels. When Townson heard that the *Shadows* project was in the works, both he and Wilson agreed that this was the best opportunity for creating a novel-based sound track. Unlike the fusion of music and image in a theatrical score, the *Shadows* sound track would not be designed to provide background music for a reading experience but would serve as a separate musical celebration of the universe explored in the story.

"This kind of project gives more freedom to a film composer, actually," Townson says. "In a film you might have an action scene, so there'll need to be faster cutting and editing and the music needs to keep up with that to the hundredth of a second, even if it might not be in the best interest of the piece evolving from a musical point of view. For a *Shadows of the Empire* sound track the most important rule was just to write great music, to evoke the scenes and characters without the obstacles that a film can present. For the readers it's also very exciting because in a film everything is put before them, while in a book they're being asked to visualize characters and scenes for themselves. This sound track gives them another piece of the puzzle to take an extra step into this world and be a bit more of a participant. The more I thought about it, the more I loved the idea of commissioning an original score for a book."

The process of creating a sound track release, a recording based on the music an audience hears when it is watching a theatrical release, is a long creative journey. For a producer such as Townson the goal is to take the music from a film and readopt it into a purely listening experience. Each piece of music, or "cue," in the movie score is considered in arriving at a final selection to be arranged and conducted by a composer. In preparing the recording for separate release, generally cues of less than a minute are passed over in favor of more cohesive musical passages such as the overture or character themes.

"A good example of the character theme, or 'leitmotif,' approach is John Williams's *Star Wars* score," Townson explains. "You have the main theme, which is essentially evoking Luke Skywalker, and then you have Yoda's theme or Darth Vader's theme. The concept for *Shadows of the Empire* was to interpret and score the major characters and events in the book as though there was a film. We open with the main theme by John Williams to let people know they're in the *Star Wars* universe, and then we take our own symphonic journey through the characters and events that take place in the book. So, as with John's theme for Darth Vader, we'll have a theme for Xizor. Where John wrote theme music depicting Hoth and Dagobah and the other planets in the trilogy, for the first time we'll have music for Coruscant and Imperial City. Where there was the epic cue for the asteroid field scene in *The Empire Strikes Back*, we'll have the swoop bike chase in Beggar's Canyon and, of course, the cataclysmic finale taking place around the destruction of Xizor's palace. When I realized all the musical possibilities, I knew exactly who I wanted to compose this score."

Townson approached Joel McNeely, who was immediately caught up in the *Shadows* vision and would bring to the work a classical style Townson praised as being "infused with great depth and emotion that keep his music from turning into a wall of sound." For McNeely the art of writing a musical score was analogous to the work of the classical composers of old.

"In my opinion the concert music that's being created in the twentieth century that's most applicable to our time is film music," McNeely says. "For instance, a court composer like Johann Sebastian Bach would be commissioned by the king to write music for different occasions. Film music, I think, is the modern-day equivalent of that. We're writing very complicated orchestral music on demand for a specific event."

McNeely's training ranges from high school years spent at the Interlochen Arts Academy in the north woods of Michigan to master's work at the Eastman School of Music in Rochester, New York. Although he developed a jazz touch—playing saxophone in big bands led by the likes of Frank Sinatra and Tony Bennett—his first love is both classical music and writing for films. His interest in the field of musical scores was piqued by a trip to a real recording session. "My father was a television writer, and when I was about twelve years old he took me to a TV show recording session the composer Elmer Bernstein was having at Universal Studios," he recalls.

By the time McNeely began his professional career, the style of movie music had swung from the many jazz-based scores of 1960s and early 1970s features back to the classically based film music that had dominated Hollywood's golden age. "The orchestral tradition that started in the thirties was resurrected when John Williams did the score for *Jaws*," McNeely observes. "That film was really the first big orchestral score that had been done in a while. He sort of brought back the tradition."

But while a nineteenth-century classical composer might have had up to a year to create a major piece, a modern film composer is at the service of ever-accelerating production schedules. And even the film composers of old were granted two or three months to write a score, while a modern composer usually has a one-month deadline, McNeely laments.

The creative process of producing a film score, which can entail writing a solid seventy minutes' worth of original music, begins with a view to the raw film footage. As the film is being edited into a final cut, the composer sits down with the director and producer to work out in exacting detail where a musical cue will enter and exit, the emotional message to be conveyed, and even the type of instrumentation needed to achieve the musical goals. A music editor then types out precise descriptions of the actual scenes, which, along with the film images themselves, are used to write the score. When the final music is prepared, the composer will hire an orchestra for a recording session. In those studio sessions the composer will conduct from a podium with an eye on the screened images of the film, keeping the music in exact sync.

Shadows, of course, would not be limited by the demands of keeping up with a moving picture. While inspirational references such as Ralph McQuarrie's original concept paintings of Coruscant and Imperial City were provided to McNeely, the composer was free to concentrate on the personal musical visions he would conjure up from the source material of the novel. "I saw so many musical possibilities in this that I didn't want to hamper Joel with a temp track or anything he would have to stick to," Townson explains. "I had my ideas of what were the dominant things in the book to characterize musically. We had a meeting, and we both felt similarly about what needed to be composed. We had discussions about the basics of mood and grandeur. At that point it got down to Joel sitting at his piano and starting to compose a grand symphonic work."

"When I'm starting to compose for a particular subject, I'll sometimes hear in my head a particular instrument or an overall impression," McNeely says. "For example, when I first read the book, my initial impression of Xizor was—ethnic. Something Middle Eastern, slightly primitive in style, but with a real seductive side, a lot of drums. I'll get the impression of a palette of musical colors and work from that, refining until a real clear concept and theme develop. Although the score is cut from some of the same cloth as John Williams's music for the trilogy, it isn't reminiscent of a score John Williams might write; there's no point to that. Because I didn't have the motion picture considerations to deal with, I could really make the music uniquely original to me, both thematically and stylistically."

Some twelve final selections of *Shadows* highlights would be composed and prepared for recording. As with any symphonic production, the organization of the final orchestra would be based on the dictates of the score. "One of Joel's responsibilities with his *Shadows of the Empire* orchestra was to come up with a sound world that would be exclusive unto itself," Townson notes. "You have your base orchestra where you have so many violins and trumpets and so on. But to achieve what's necessary for your particular score you can supplement, enlarge the percussion section, add woodwinds, or whatever."

McNeely saw the advantage, for example, of using a choir to augment the moods of many of the *Shadows* movements. "There's a scene in the book where Darth Vader is standing on his balcony overlooking Imperial City at dusk, and he's kind of communicating through the Force to Luke Skywalker," he says. "He's melancholy because he's setting out to capture his son. For that scene I use the choir as a very quiet, reflective element about a man having a moment of introspection at a pivotal point in his life. I also use the choir as a power element for the climactic destruction of Xizor's palace as the orchestra plays with great fury and bombast."

The *Shadows* recording session was held in Scotland in the early spring of 1996 with the one-hundred-some-piece Royal Scottish National Orchestra and Choir. For the orchestra, known exclusively for its classical performances and recordings, it would be one of the first forays into sound track recording. As a warm-up, McNeely had journeyed to Scotland in September 1995 to conduct the orchestra in two separate Varese Sarabande recordings: a "greatest hits" record of Hollywood scores for 1995 and the recording of Bernard Herrmann's complete score for Alfred Hitchcock's classic thriller *Vertigo.*

While such developments were consistent with McNeely and Townson's contention that modern film music is an extension of classical music, there was the obvious question: Since so many modern blockbuster films feature full symphonic scores, why isn't classical music more popular in the United States, particularly among young people?

"I've wondered that myself," McNeely says. "I don't think American society really infuses its children with music of any kind other than the music consumed on radio or MTV. Since we haven't exposed people on a societal level to classical music, it's perceived as kind of esoteric, not mainstream. But in Europe you'll see hip fifteen- to sixteen-year-old kids at orchestral or chamber music concerts because they've grown up listening to it and they like it; it's much more the mainstream music. I think here in America classical music is something the average person feels he or she has to be educated to listen to. Opera has the same problem even though for centuries it was designed for the masses and was an inexpensive form of entertainment, the equivalent of the modern-day movie. But in the last century both opera and classical music have become the domain of the super-rich. It shouldn't be that way."

This Xizor concept illustration by Tim and Greg Hildebrandt, produced for Star Wars Galaxy *magazine, was the first image created by the brothers on the road to completing a set of 100 paintings for Topps'* Shadows of the Empire *card series.*

IV.
DARK DESIGNS

"Remember, a Jedi's strength flows from the Force. But beware. Anger, fear, aggression. The dark side are they. Once you start down the dark path, forever will it dominate your destiny."

—Yoda to Luke Skywalker in *Return of the Jedi*

THE FINAL ARTISTIC TOUCHES FOR the narrative portions of *Shadows of the Empire* would be cover art paintings prepared by Hugh Fleming for the Dark Horse series covers and by Drew Struzan for the Bantam book novel. For the Topps trading card set, one of the final *Shadows* crossover projects to be released, Greg and Tim Hildebrandt would also be producing a set of one-hundred paintings. The brothers' work for the 1994 "Marvel Masterpieces" release from Fleer had required 160 paintings (and had enjoyed an estimated 12 million card press run). The experience of producing paintings that would be reduced to a card medium roughly 3½ inches tall and 2½ inches wide dictated a special approach to the composition. "We absolutely have to take into account the reduction of the paintings to card size so we don't paint it too tight," Greg notes. "If you put too much detail in, when it's reduced, all that detail will be lost or it'll look too cluttered. We're after a stronger, quicker impact."

When introduced to the mysteries of *Shadows*, the duo had some instant creative reactions. "The whole project was so wild," Tim exclaims. "It's such a unique idea to create this reality between the two films. I also loved the villain, Xizor. It struck us that with his costume he had almost a samurai look. An interesting aspect of him was this pheromone he emits which turns women on. Also, there's a scene where Darth Vader is sitting naked in his medical chamber and he actually smiles!"

"That's one of the highlights, it seems to me," Greg adds. "And since Vader was unmasked in *Jedi*, there's nothing to hide now."

"I got this image instantly," Tim interjects, "of this overhead light coming down. There's kind of a horror to the scene, but it's also supertragic."

The creative strategy for the card series was to base seventy images on the novel, with the final thirty paintings being inspired by the comic series and the LucasArts game. The first stage began with the brothers reading the novel and using colored markers to underline possible characters, environments, and situations for their paintings. Feedback from Topps project editor Bob Woods, their business representative Jean Scrocco, and others would help winnow the image possibilities to a final selection. In the unusually long four-month thumbnail sketch stage that followed, the duo would work out their designs. As with all their projects, the brothers would take great care in considering all the elements of an image and use live models to provide a photographic reference.

"The first thing in a picture is composition, but what goes along with that is lighting," Tim says. "In composing a picture, where the light source comes from determines quite often what the composition is going to be."

"We treat these things like movie lighting," Greg adds. "You begin to set up the dramatic scenes, kind of exposing the lighting in your head. Is it a low light casting heavy shadows upward? If you're going to back-

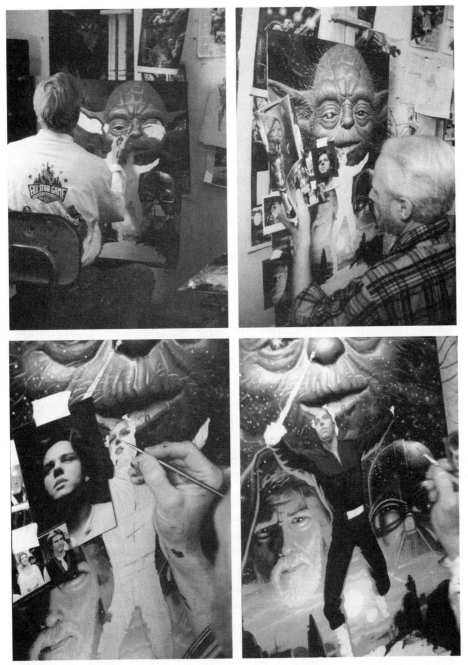

The Hildebrandt brothers, Greg and Tim, returned to the Star Wars *universe with this Topps painting of Luke Skywalker and the influential figures in his life: Obi-Wan Kenobi, Yoda, and Darth Vader. The painting was done as a cover for* Star Wars Galaxy *magazine.*

Photo by Jean Scrocco.

light an image, do you want to over- or underexpose it? Once we have a rough composition, we meet with the Topps people, and once that's approved, we get models, make costumes for them, pose and photograph them. We then use the photographs as a guide and begin to draw a very detailed picture. When we're ready to paint, we work in acrylic, which we like because it dries fast. You can keep going over it and making layer after layer. Sometimes we paint on paper which can be directly wrapped onto a separation drum which scans the art directly into the computer and does the color separations digitally. But for *Shadows* we painted on boards, so they had to shoot transparencies first. Then they'd make the separations, print proofs for our approval, and then go to print."

The Hildebrandt brothers' paintings, in addition to providing an entire new medium for the multimedia project, would establish the overall visual conception of the *Shadows* universe. The paintings of Fleming and Struzan would also reflect the spirit of the story line, but with the added challenge of inviting readers to dive into the comics series or curl up with the novel.

Fleming had already earned raves for his cover art for Dark Horse's *Tales of the Jedi: Dark Lords of the Sith* series, particularly for the second issue of the six-part *Dark Lords of the Sith* story line. It depicted an ancient battlefield with a one-eyed shocktrooper fighting on behalf of the Krath, the occult sect that embraced the dark side of the Force, screaming defiance and standing above a fallen opponent. Explosions and tracer fire erupt around him, and warships fly overhead in a sky so thick with the smoke of battle that the sun is only a glowing smudge.

"One of my goals in painting is to make an image look as realistic and cinematic as possible," Fleming explains. "If the subject is *Star Wars* or Indiana Jones, I'll first think about a particular scene from one of those films that applies to what I'm painting and try to re-create the atmosphere from the movie. You want people to look at the cover and almost think they're seeing something out of a film. So I think like a cinematographer when I'm doing these paintings. I'm conscious of color and lighting schemes. I think, If I was shooting a particular scene as a movie, would it be shot on a set or at an outdoor location? And if it was outside, what kind of fill light would be used? For example, for the cover of that second *Sith* issue I was conscious of the color of the sky and was thinking of the look of the big battle scene in Kenneth Branagh's *Henry V.* The sky over the battlefield wouldn't be bright blue but dirty, with all this muck floating in the air and obscuring the sun. Like I say, you've got to think like a cinematographer when you paint these pictures and convey the illusion that you're kind of watching a movie."

When Fleming does a comic book cover, the interior art is often not complete and he must make do with the original script or a few faxed pages of particular scenes suggested by an editor. Once either Fleming or the editor decides on the cover concept, the requisite thumbnail sketch phase follows. In working out the basic composition, Fleming will build an image of his subject with both posed models and photographic references. "You don't want these kinds of characters to look ordinary. Most of the time you want the heroes to be square-jawed and the women to be impossibly beautiful. I keep a photographic reference file with stills of the faces of models and movie stars and use that as inspiration for the faces. I'll then bring in friends and acquaintances to pose for the body. I'll light the bodies of the models to match the lighting on the still I've selected for the face. Then I put the image all together."

To begin, Fleming smears his painting board with gesso, a modeling paste that provides a thick undercoat that allows for various textured effects. After penciling in the image, he picks up his brush and begins to apply acrylics. He loves the tactile feel of brush and canvas and is loath to contemplate the art of illustration being transformed into a computerized medium.

"Most painters who work as illustrators are traditionalists; their heroes are not digital artists but Rockwell and Wyeth and the rest," Flem-

A rough cover concept for the Shadows *comic book series, by Hugh Fleming.*
Once approved, Fleming could begin the actual painting phase.

ing observes. "They're skittish about trading in their brush, palette, and traditional materials. Also, when you paint with a brush, sometimes the fibers of the brush will splay off on the board in a direction you didn't account for. There's a randomness. Of course, there are people doing digital matte paintings in movies, constructing and lighting entire sets in the computer. But everything in the computer world has to be created. It's too easy for a lot of people to use the programs to make a 3-D model of something and forget to take into account the way light bounces around, the little reflections, the wear and tear on objects."

Although largely self-taught, Fleming has been influenced by Drew Struzan, one of the leading movie poster artists in the world. Drew, whose Lucasfilm work has ranged from *Star Wars* book covers to the famed poster art for both the Indiana Jones and *Star Wars* trilogies, was a natural to paint the cover of the Steve Perry novel.

Drew's initial *Shadows of the Empire* cover design featured Luke Skywalker in the prominent role. His early pencil sketch for the full book jacket had featured a montage-style layout with the front cover (the right side of the sketch) featuring a triangular arrangement with a serious-looking Luke looming at the apex, flanked below by Darth Vader and the Emperor, with Xizor bottom front with arms and clutching hands ominously outstretched. On the back cover, floating in space, were the head and shoulders of Princess Leia and C-3PO. A huge planet united the images, with a TIE fighter and the *Millennium Falcon* blasting out of the planet's atmosphere.

In follow-up April 1995 correspondence, Lucasfilm requested some changes in the composition. Lucasfilm's Lucy Autrey Wilson sent along a fresh batch of reference material and some final notes for the overall design: "We wanted to show [Luke] in transition between the clothes one sees him in in *ESB* and the all black outfit he shows up in in *ROJ*. Please dress him in the same black long-sleeved top, pants, and boots . . . but make his sleeveless vest/tunic a khaki color (not black) and give him a utility belt with various tools/etc. hanging off of it . . . For Xizor, who's wearing chain mail, make his costume the color of gun-metal and his skin a faintly greenish/beige. His eyes are violet." It was requested that the back cover drop C-3PO and the TIE fighter, replacing them with Boba Fett and a swoop bike and rider.

By June another Drew cover art submission was approved by Lucasfilm with a few final changes requested, including a little fine-tuning for the Dark Prince's image: "Please redo Xizor's left hand . . . His fingers should be like bony human fingers with claws . . . Please redo Xizor's ponytail . . . It must be thin, straight, and shoulder-length. Please reduce the size of the band at the base of the ponytail."

For Drew it was the typical process that came with portraying popular characters. "When I do a *Star Wars* book cover or any other artwork for George Lucas and Lucasfilm, they don't give me a lot of information; they give me what they think is necessary," Struzan explains. "The fact is, I've done this so long that they really trust me to sense the spirit of what they're trying to accomplish, which is what you're trying to do with the art, anyway. I kind of make the characters iconic, beautiful, interesting, desirable. An emotional connection is what I try to create. It's not that I render a specific planet or something as much as I'm creating an atmosphere. If you want the specifics, you'll read the book. The cover art is supposed to give you an emotional feeling of what's inside."

In Drew's final *Shadows* painting a planet and moon fill the canvas, with a brilliant burst of sun casting light on the characters. There's a pensive Leia, Boba Fett with his gun raised, a swoop biker heading for the stars. The wrinkled, hooded visage of Emperor Palpatine glares out above Luke, who appears startled as he spins in a low crouch, and the samurai blade of pure energy from his lightsaber shoots out and mingles with the sun's rays. Vader stands impassively behind him, the polished, black surface of the Sith Lord's mask and helmet catching points of light, while an elegantly robed Xizor raises a taloned hand and casts a sphinxlike gaze.

"The specific design for the *Shadows* cover was willfully kind of formal; it's symmetrically designed," Drew explains. "The way the background planet is designed and cropped gives it a feeling of grandeur and scope. I then painted it kind of mysterious, dark, with strange colors. A feeling of foreboding. The concept for the cover is that it's supposed to be from the dark side for a change, featuring the three villains and having Luke look a little intimidated, a little frightened."

Lucasfilm's walk on the dark side had been a success, according to Lucy Wilson. "I'd love to do this again," she concludes. "But you have to have a big enough story and time enough to develop it and work with everybody in a collaborative process. We had an advantage because since we set the story in the *Star Wars* trilogy, so many things were already defined."

Shadows of the Empire had ultimately opened up new creative territory in the ever-expanding *Star Wars* universe, adding new characters, places, and vehicles to be accounted for in the Lucasfilm Canon. In the process the story line had stayed true to the spirit of the epic, which, with its mythic overtones and chronicle of a galactic battle for truth and justice, had not lost its capacity to inspire a sense of wonder, perhaps even hope for the future.

"I think *Star Wars* has been successful because it touches what humanity ought to be struggling for, the side of love, honesty, and community," Drew Struzan muses. "There's a war in humanity between good and bad; that's what the original *Star Wars* was about. Youth and struggle, the Empire against the Rebels, the battle between the light and dark sides of the Force. It's the classic story of the struggles of humanity characterized by the good guys winning. We need to know, to have hope, that there will come a time of justice and peace. Some of us still want to say that there's hope for the world if you'll just try. You can conquer the bad not by becoming bad but by becoming good. Wasn't that Luke's struggle? Don't give over to the dark side, Luke. When he went into that cave on Dagobah with his weapon, which Yoda had told him not to do, he met Darth Vader, but he killed himself."

SHADOWS GUIDE

Luke Skywalker with C-3PO and R2-D2; illustration by Kilian Plunkett.

Chewbacca and Dash Rendar; illustrations by Mike Butkus.

CHARACTERS, LOCATIONS, AND VEHICLES

IN *SHADOWS OF THE EMPIRE* THE universe expands with new heroes and villains, droids, spacecraft, and planets and even a previously unknown humanoid species (the reptilian Falleen from whose stock Xizor sprung). With the story line set within the original movie trilogy, most of the original characters would be along for the adventure: Luke and Leia, Chewbacca, See-Threepio and Artoo-Detoo, Boba Fett, Darth Vader, and Emperor Palpatine (with only a sighting or two of poor Han Solo, frozen in a carbonite slab and en route to Tatooine as a trophy for Jabba the Hutt).

The following illustrations of final vehicle designs and the glossary of key characters, places, and things described in the novel will help fans orient themselves and chart a course through the *Shadows* universe.

Artoo-Detoo (R2-D2)

Artoo-Detoo is Luke Skywalker's trusty astromech droid (specializing in starship maintenance and repair, one of the five basic automaton classifications). Artoo is along for some of the pivotal events in *Shadows*, including the Bothan Blue Squad mission that captures the Imperial computer holding the Imperial Death Star plans.

Asp

This is an all-purpose droid found throughout the galaxy.

Avaro Sookcool

Sookcool is a Rodian, a species from the planet Rodia whose members are characterized physically by tapirlike snouts and green skin. Rodians love hunting, and this makes them perfect bounty hunters. Given their inbred disdain for the law, it's no surprise that Sookcool owns a casino in a gambling complex on his home planet that's controlled by the Black Sun crime syndicate. Even though he's the uncle of the late Greedo—the slow-draw bounty hunter blown away by Han Solo in the Mos Eisley cantina—Sookcool still agrees to help Leia and Lando Calrissian make contact with the Black Sun.

Bajic Sector

In this star system cluster are located the Vergesso Asteroids, home to both a secret Rebel base and Ororo Transportation (a competitor of Xizor's profitable shipping business). Xizor, who has the ear of Emperor Palpatine, elicits the Imperial command that sends Lord Vader off to ostensibly destroy the Rebel base, with the resulting conflagration consuming Xizor's desired target of Ororo.

Beggar's Canyon

As a child Luke Skywalker honed his flying skills racing skyhoppers at full throttle through this twisting canyon, which had been formed by the confluence of three mighty rivers that had flowed a million years before. In *Shadows* Luke flies a swoop through the canyon in a deadly chase and battle with swoop bikers out to assassinate the young Jedi.

Benedict Vidkun

This henpecked engineer, with his sallow complexion and emaciated form, hardly seemed the type to risk his neck for the likes of Luke Skywalker and company, who have come to Coruscant to rescue Leia from her prison in Xizor's palace. But Vidkun not only provides maps revealing a passage into the palace through a labyrinthine passage of sewer conduits but helps Luke, Lando, Dash, and Chewbacca navigate the sewer passageways. The engineer does show his treacherous nature when, safely through the sewer, he pulls a blaster and shoots Dash. It was a shaky shot, a hip wound for Dash but the end of Vidkun as Rendar returns fire with a bull's-eye blast of his own.

Bentu Pall Tarlen

On Coruscant graft and corruption rule. In that spirit, Tarlen, head of the Imperial Center Construction Contracts Division, keeps Xizor informed about the latest bids for construction projects on the planet, allowing the Dark Prince to underbid competing interests.

Black Sun

The largest criminal organization in the galaxy is commanded from the shadows by Xizor. The syndicate's tentacles reach everywhere, from the army garrisons and naval intelligence offices on Imperial Center to gambling operations on the planet Rodia. Black Sun's underworld spynet is equal to the espionage resources of the Empire itself (although the spy network of the Rebellion-aligned Bothans is reportedly slightly better). The Black Sun has tens of thousands of minions. Nine lieutenants known by the title "Vigos" coordinate criminal activities in the separate stellar systems.

Blue Squad

Blue Squad was the moniker squadron leader Luke Skywalker gave the twenty-four Bothans who manned Y-wings in two-man teams for an attack on the *Suprosa*, the Imperial freighter carrying the secret plans for the second Death Star. But the unescorted freighter, bound for the Bothan home world of Bothawui, was equipped with cannons and shields. Although the force captured the secret plans, the furious space battle that ensued cost the lives of twelve of the Blue Squad Bothans.

Bothan Spynet

In a galaxy teeming with Imperial and Black Sun spynets, it is the Bothan spies who have the intelligence-gathering edge. From their own Imperial and Black Sun sources the Bothans learned not only of a secret Imperial project (which would eventually be revealed as the second Death Star) but of the fateful freighter carrying the secret plans for the mysterious project.

Boushh

This bounty hunter, a contract worker for the Black Sun, made the mistake of withholding credits on a job for the syndicate and paid the ultimate price. Guri, Xizor's own assassin, provided Princess Leia with Boushh's helmet and clothes, with which she disguised herself for her entry into the Imperial Center. Leia would later use the disguise to infiltrate the palace of Jabba the Hutt in *Return of the Jedi.*

Chewbacca

Before he was frozen alive in carbonite, Han Solo's last request to Chewbacca was to watch after Leia. Much to the annoyance of the Princess, the faithful Wookiee does exactly that, joining Leia in her attempt to intercept Boba Fett before he delivers Han Solo to Jabba the Hutt. When Fett's *Slave I* is spotted on the moon of Gall, Chewie accompanies Leia and Lando Calrissian on what will be a failed rescue attempt. Chewie also follows Leia to Coruscant on a dangerous mission to find out who is behind the assassination plot against Luke. Chewie joins her in Xizor's fortresslike palace, escapes, and helps lead the rescue effort through the sewer tunnels under the Dark Prince's lair.

Coruscant

During the period of the Galactic Civil War and the Imperial reign of

Emperor Palpatine, the Empire's headquarter planet of Coruscant was renamed the Imperial Center, although Xizor and many in the Rebel Alliance still prefer to call the Empire's capital world by its old name.

Darth Vader

The embodiment of Imperial power and the dark side of the Force, Vader was once Anakin Skywalker, a Jedi disciple of Obi-Wan Kenobi. Then the seductive lure of the dark side began to poison his spirit. When Obi-Wan tried to rescue him from the evil embrace, the two battled and Skywalker fell into a molten pit. Alive, but with his damaged body imprisoned in life-supporting armor, Skywalker would be reborn as Lord Vader, practitioner of the dark side of the Force and master of the occult secrets of the Sith.

In *Shadows of the Empire* Vader periodically spends time in his hyperbaric medical chamber, which provides a supermedicated and oxygenated field that allows him to breathe free of his helmet and body armor. Between his healing sessions Vader oversees a galaxywide effort to find Luke Skywalker and bring his son to his side. His dream of turning his flesh and blood to the dark side is imperiled by Xizor's secret plot to assassinate the young Jedi.

Dash Rendar

Dash Rendar had a promising career at the Imperial Academy until the fateful freighter accident by his brother, which destroyed Emperor Palpatine's private museum and led to the Empire seizing all Rendar family property and banishing the Rendars from Coruscant. Dash took up the mercenary life, piloting his state-of-the-art craft *Outrider* with the aid of his droid copilot LE-BO2D9 (Leebo).

Despite Dash's roguish ways, his dazzling skills as a pilot have led to many contracts with the Alliance. (During one such mission, flying in supplies to the secret Rebel encampment on Hoth, he distinguished himself in joining the fight against a sudden Imperial attack.)

In *Shadows*, Dash is in on most of the significant action, even accom-

Darth Vader; illustration by Kilian Plunkett.

panying Luke Skywalker and the Bothan Blue Squad in the battle that claims the new Death Star plans for the Alliance. Dash blames himself for the lives lost in that mission but will eventually redeem himself, assisting Luke and company in a daring rescue of Leia from Xizor's dark fortress. Rendar, escaping in his *Outrider*, engages in a furious aerial battle involving Xizor's fighters, TIE fighters, and Rogue Squadron ships over the Imperial Center. The battle ends with Dash and his *Outrider* seemingly blown up in the conflagration that destroys Prince Xizor's skyhook.

Elite Stormtroopers

These armored stormtroopers, with their full-face helmets, are stationed around the Imperial Center.

Emperor Palpatine

Once an unassuming senator in the waning days of the Old Republic, Palpatine was elected president in the hope that he would lead the galaxy out of the festering malaise of corruption and injustice then permeating the system. Instead, Palpatine made himself Emperor and mysteriously mastered the dark side of the Force.

In an attempt to trap the Alliance forces, he allowed Xizor's Black Sun underlings to leak to the Rebels information that the freighter *Suprosa* would be carrying vital Imperial secrets. Throughout this and other major events in *Shadows of the Empire*, Palpatine watches as Xizor and Vader jockey for his favor.

Evet Scy'rrep

Evet is a storied space bandit who in the course of his career held up fifteen luxury starliners, escaping with millions in credits and jewels. When eventually apprehended and asked why he robbed luxury ships, Scy'rrep's famous answer was, "Because that's where the credits are." An old holoprojector program on the famous bandit stoked the imagination of Luke Skywalker when he was a boy on Tatooine dreaming of adventures beyond the stars.

Falleen Exotics

The green-skinned race to which Xizor belongs, this is a genus both humanoid and reptilian. Falleen characteristics include an ability not only to breathe underwater for extraordinary lengths of time but to exude powerful pheromones that make a Falleen nearly irresistible to the opposite sex.

Falleen's Fist

This is the name given to Prince Xizor's skyhook retreat and command center, located high above the Imperial Center. In the final battle of *Shadows*, Vader ordered a Star Destroyer to blow up *Falleen's Fist.*

Gall

Out in the Outer Rim Systems, circling the gas giant Zahr, is the moon of Gall. In addition to violent atmospheric and planetary storms, Gall is home to an Imperial Enclave of naval powers, including several Star Destroyers and a complement force of TIE fighters. Princess Leia leads an ultimately unsuccessful rescue attempt to Gall after Boba Fett's *Slave I*, with its precious cargo of Han Solo in carbonite, is spotted on the moon.

Guri

Guri is Prince Xizor's trusted aide, to all appearances a beautiful human female but in fact a replica droid. Guri is the *only* replica droid thus trained as an assassin, and she demonstrated her abilities as a one-woman death squad when she killed, with both bare hands and blasters, Xizor's business rivals at Ororo Transportation.

IG-2000

The battleship piloted by feared war droid IG-88, one of the bounty hunters hired by Darth Vader to track down the *Millennium Falcon* and

Guri and Koth Melan; illustrations by Mike Butkus.

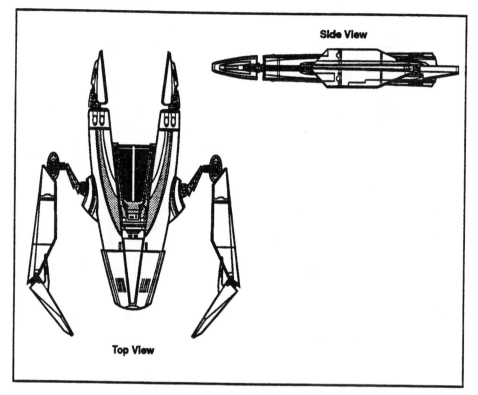

IG-2000, *top and side views. Illustration by Troy Vigil.*

its crew after the battle of Hoth. In *Shadows*, IG-88 would pilot this ship into battle against Boba Fett's *Slave I*.

Imperial Center (Coruscant)

During the reign of Emperor Palpatine (and during the time of *Shadows*) the planet Coruscant was renamed the Imperial Center.

Jabba the Hutt

Throughout the events of *Shadows* Jabba's dark presence is felt as he awaits in his Tatooine citadel the delivery of the double-crossing Han Solo.

Kile

Kile is another of the moons that, along with Gall, orbit the planet Zahr. It's on Kile that the Alliance's crack Rogue Squadron lands its X-wing starfighters and sets up a temporary base from which it launches the unsuccessful attempt to raid Gall and release Han Solo from Boba Fett.

Koth Melan

The overseer of the vast Bothan spynet, Melan, operating from his home world of Bothawui, is an unassuming physical presence: short, long-haired, and bearded, dressed in forest green overtunic, pants, and boots. Melan accompanied Dash Rendar in the *Outrider* during the raid on the *Suprosa* and was instrumental in turning the plans for the second Death Star over to the Rebel Alliance. But in the aftermath of that engagement, at a Bothan safe house on the planet Kothlis, Melan would be killed when a neutral team of bounty hunters kidnapped Luke Skywalker.

Lando Calrissian

A rogue soldier of fortune who lost his *Millennium Falcon* to Han Solo in a game of sabacc but won the governorship of Bespin's floating Cloud City in a separate sabacc round, Calrissian betrayed Solo, Luke, Leia, and company when they sought sanctuary during the events of *The Empire Strikes Back.* Unknown to Solo, Vader had forced Lando to betray his old comrade, promising that the Empire would leave Cloud City free of any future Imperial entanglements.

By the conclusion of *Empire* Lando had begun to redeem himself, helping Princess Leia escape in the *Millennium Falcon* and rescuing the wounded Luke Skywalker, who was spotted hanging on to an antennalike exhaust port on the underside of the floating Cloud City. In

Shadows, Lando is part of the failed Solo rescue mission on Gall, later accompanies Leia as she infiltrates the Black Sun to find out who is behind the plot to kill Luke Skywalker, is part of the rescue mission that infiltrates Xizor's dark fortress, and is a participant in the final battle in the sky above Imperial Center.

Leebo (LE-BO2D9)

Dash Rendar's trusty droid and the copilot of the *Outrider*, Leebo is usually seen with a leather tool bag draped across his skeletal form. Since he has seen some rough action in space, the droid's form is composed of new parts and older, dented metal parts.

Leia Organa, Princess

In *Shadows*, Leia risks her life to infiltrate the Black Sun criminal syndicate. After Guri provides her with the helmet and clothing of the late Black Sun bounty hunter Boushh, she uses the disguise to journey to the Imperial Center, where she is ultimately taken to Xizor's palace to meet the Dark Prince. In Xizor's fortress lair, with the underworld master exuding his intoxicating pheromones, Leia nearly falls under his spell. During the adventure, her Jedi powers begin to manifest themselves and she starts to become accustomed to the power of the Force. By the conclusion of *Shadows*, Leia and Luke are plotting the rescue of Han Solo from Jabba the Hutt.

Luke Skywalker

A sudden rush of events engulfs the young Jedi at the conclusion of *The Empire Strikes Back*: Luke is defeated by Vader, who reveals that he is Luke's father. After nearly falling to his death (but making a saving grab at that antennalike device on the underside of Cloud City), Luke is miraculously rescued. As *Shadows* opens, Luke is conflicted, seeking to advance his Jedi training but also feeling the first stirring of the dark side's siren call. As he soon discovers, he is the target of Vader's Imperial search party *and* Xizor's bounty hunter assassins.

Luke leads the Bothan Blue Squad in the battle against the freighter carrying the secret plans for the new Death Star. During a subsequent secure operation at a safe house on the planet Kothlis, Luke is kidnapped by bounty hunters led by a female named Skahtul. She reveals to Luke that there are two rewards for him—one for him dead, the other for him alive—and that she is willing to turn him over to the highest bidder. Using Jedi mind powers and a little help from his friends, Skywalker escapes from the planet with Lando and Threepio in the *Millennium Falcon.* Through the Force, Luke realizes Leia's peril in Xizor's palace at Imperial Center. He, Lando, Chewie, and Dash head into the epicenter of Imperial power for the dangerous rescue attempt.

Ororo Transportation

When this shipping company, a competitor of the Dark Prince's Xizor Transport Systems, attempts to overturn XTS's domination of the spice trade in the Bajic Sector, the full fury of the Dark Prince is unleashed: agent Guri personally kills leading Ororo executives with her bare hands and blasters, while Xizor persuades the Emperor to send Vader on a mission that, ostensibly aimed at destroying a secret Rebel shipyard, in fact destroys Ororo operations.

Outrider

This is the name of Dash Rendar's ship, which, although patterned after the *Millennium Falcon*, is not a hot rod ship but a shining new, state-of-the-art multiweapon-equipped craft.

Rogue Squadron

This famed squadron of Alliance X-wing starfighters, led by expert pilot Wedge Antilles, spearheads the failed rescue attempt of Han Solo on

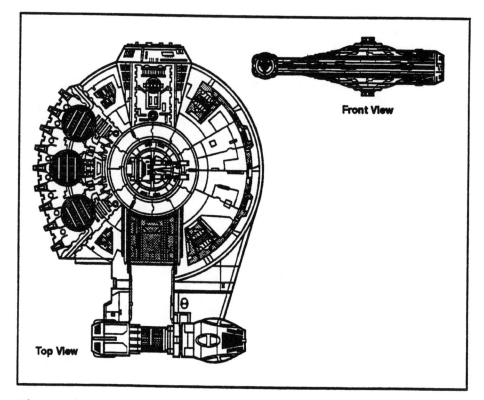

The Outrider, *top and front view. Illustration by Troy Vigil.*

Gall. During the finale of *Shadows* a call from Dash's droid Leebo summons the squadron for the final firefight above Xizor's skyhook on Imperial Center.

See-Threepio (C-3PO)

In *Shadows* Threepio is a constant companion of the team of Leia, Lando, and Chewbacca. He is with them during the failed rescue attempt on Gall and is aboard the *Millennium Falcon* when it lands on Imperial Center for the risky rescue attempt of Leia in Xizor's palace.

While Xizor's lair is being infiltrated, Threepio and Artoo stay behind to guard the ship. When it's spotted, Threepio, receiving Luke's instructions via comlink, powers (with Artoo's help) the *Falcon* up to a safe level of Xizor's fortress lair. In *Shadows*, Threepio reveals that he wasn't always a protocol droid: for one long month he had actually programmed converters and run a shovel loader.

Skahtul
This female Barabel (a bipedal reptilian race) is the leader of the bounty hunters who capture Luke on Kothlis.

Snoova
Snoova is a well-known Wookiee bounty hunter whose identity is assumed by Chewbacca in order to pass safely through customs on Imperial Center.

Spero
Spero, who owns a plant shop in the Southern Underground section of Imperial Center, earned the title of Master Gardener for creating a strain of yellow fungus used throughout the galaxy. An old friend of Leia's, Spero also supplies the Princess with information about Black Sun and the Dark Prince Xizor.

Stinger, the
Guri's ship, christened by her master, Prince Xizor, this sleek craft not only boasts powerful engines but is armed with gun placements both fore and amidships.

Suprosa
This unescorted but heavily armed freighter, under contract to XTS, carries to the planet Bothawui not only fertilizer but the Imperial computer holding information concerning the top-secret Death Star con-

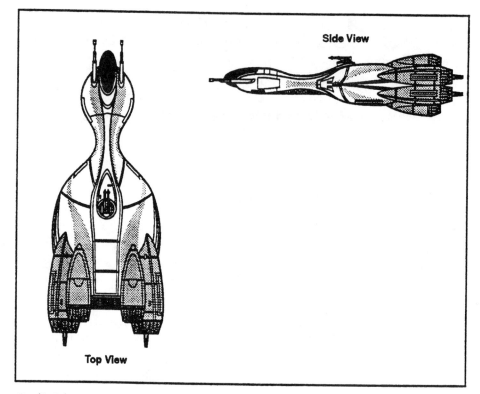

Guri's Stinger, *top and side views. Illustration by Troy Vigil.*

struction project on Endor. A squadron of Bothans led by Skywalker sustains heavy losses in an attack on the freighter but ultimately comes away with the Imperial computer.

Swoops

Turbothrusting airspeeders, they are built for power, speed, and maneuverability.

Swoop Gangs

Although swoop racing is a popular galactic sport, souped-up airspeeders

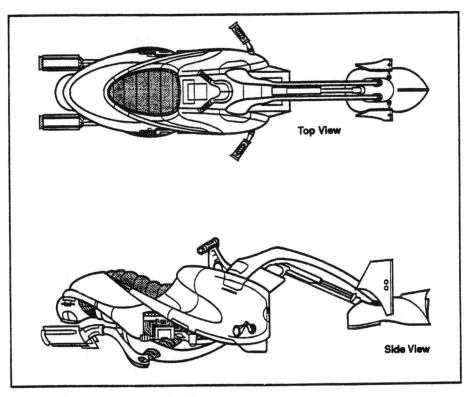

Swoop bike, side and top views. Illustration by Troy Vigil.

have also engendered an outlaw biker culture active in smuggling spices, running weapons, and other underworld activities. Crime lords such as Jabba the Hutt have their own swoop gangs that do their bidding.

Virago

Prince Xizor's personal ship, it is one of the fastest on the Imperial Center.

Xizor, Prince

Publicly he is the head of XTS shipping, privately the master of the feared underworld Black Sun syndicate. His legitimate and underworld

Spero and Xizor; illustrations by Mike Butkus.

292

interests make Xizor the third most powerful figure in the galaxy (behind Vader and the Emperor), although this is not popularly known, as the Dark Prince is content to work in the shadows.

Xizor, a member of the humanoid and reptilian species known as the Falleens, is an exotic figure with his tall, muscular body and top-knot ponytail dangling from his bald head. His wealth is said to be beyond the gross planetary product of entire worlds. From his fortresslike palace on the Imperial Center—a short walk through protected corridors to both the Imperial Palace and Vader's stronghold—Xizor can keep a firsthand watch on both the latest Imperial developments and the activity of Vader, his greatest enemy.

One of Xizor's darkest secrets is his personal vendetta against Vader, who was responsible for a disastrous Imperial biological experiment on the planet Falleen that resulted in a deadly mutant bacterium escaping quarantine. Vader's ensuing order—to use sterilization lasers to contain the runaway bacterium—incinerated some 200,000 Falleens, including Xizor's immediate family. In *Shadows*, Xizor places a bounty on Luke Skywalker, believing that with Skywalker dead and Vader discredited, he can become the ultimate confidant of Emperor Palpatine.

Xizor Transport Systems (XTS)

This galaxywide, Imperial Center–based shipping concern provides Xizor with his legitimate businessman front. XTS's status as a major contractor for Imperial business also gives the Dark Prince access to Emperor Palpatine. To maintain his companies' preeminence, Xizor ruthlessly buys influence within the Imperial bureaucracies and has ordered the murder and destruction of his competitors and their operations. It is to Xizor and XTS that the Emperor turns when it's time to arrange for work on the new Death Star (for which a mortified Vader is ordered by Palpatine to make personal arrangements with Xizor).

Zahr

This is a gas giant planet located deep in the outer Rim Systems of the

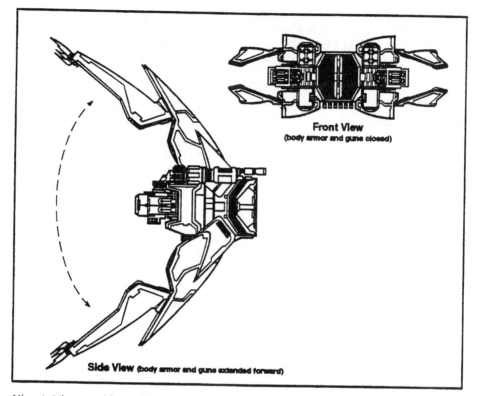

Xizor's Virago, *side and front views. Illustration by Troy Vigil.*

galaxy. Zahr's moon of Gall is not only the site of an Imperial Enclave but the place where Boba Fett lands *Slave I* for repairs after a space battle with the war droid IG-88. From Kile, another nearby moon, the Alliance's Rogue Squadron sets up a temporary base for what will prove to be an unsuccessful attempt to capture Boba Fett and rescue Han Solo.

STAR WARS REFERENCES

ALTHOUGH MUCH OF THIS BOOK was based on interviews and access to proprietary materials, the following published books were valuable reference sources:

The Art of Star Wars: Episode IV A New Hope. Del Rey Books: New York, 1994 (reissue of 1979 edition)

The Art of Star Wars: The Empire Strikes Back. Del Rey Books: New York, 1994 (reissue of 1980 edition)

The Art of Star Wars: Return of the Jedi. Del Rey Books: New York, 1994 (reissue of 1983 edition)

A Guide to the Star Wars Universe. Bill Slavicsek, Del Rey Books: New York, 1994

From Star Wars to Indiana Jones: The Best of the Lucasfilm Archives. Mark Cotta Vaz and Shinji Hata, Chronicle Books: San Francisco, 1994

Star Wars: From Concept to Screen to Collectible. Stephen J. Sansweet, Chronicle Books: San Francisco, 1992

George Lucas: The Creative Impulse. Charles Champlin, Harry N. Abrams: New York, 1992

References also included various issues of *Star Wars Galaxy Magazine*, a quarterly magazine published by Topps Publishing, and a variety of

Dark Horse *Star Wars* titles, notably the *Dark Empire* graphic novel (a reprint collection of the original six-part series published in 1995), *Dark Empire II* (a six-part series, 1994–1995), and *Tales of the Jedi: Dark Lords of the Sith* (a six-part series, 1994–1995).

CREDITS

Direction, Lucasfilm Ltd.

Howard Roffman, Vice President of Licensing

Lucy Autrey Wilson, Director of Publishing, Licensing Division

Julia Russo, Director of Merchandising, Licensing Division

Allan Kausch, Continuity Editor, Licensing Division

Sue Rostoni, Production Editor, Licensing Division

Troy Alders, Art Director, Licensing Division

Doug Chiang, Art Director, Lucasfilm Ltd.

Mike Butkus, Butkus Illustrations (concept art)

Novelization, Bantam Books

Steve Perry, Author

Tom Dupree, Editor

Drew Struzan, Cover Art

Sue Rostoni, Lucasfilm, Editor

Comic Book Series, Dark Horse Comics

John Wagner, Script

Kilian Plunkett, Pencils

P. Craig Russell, Inks

Hugh Fleming, Cover Art

Dave Cooper, Lettering

Cary Porter, Coloring

Ryder Windham, Editor

Peet Janes, Editor

Allan Kausch, Lucasfilm, Editor

The Secrets of Star Wars: Shadows of the Empire, **Del Rey Books**

Mark Cotta Vaz, Author
Steve Saffel, Editor
Allan Kausch, Lucasfilm, Editor
Alex Klapwald, Production Manager
Alex Jay/Studio J, Designer

Interactive Game, LucasArts Entertainment Company

Steve Dauterman, Director of Production
Jon Knoles, Lead Artist/Game Designer
Eric Johnston, Technical Lead
Mark Haigh-Hutchinson, Project Leader/Senior Programmer
Mark Blattel, Chief Math Wrangler
Tom Harper, Chief Polygon Wrangler
Andrew Holdun, 3-D Modeler
Ingar Shu, Level Designer
Chris Hockabout, Texture Artist
Matthew Tateishi, Level Designer
Jim Current, Level Designer
Brett Tosti, Production Associate
Bill Stoneham, 3-D/Background Artist
Paul Topolos, Story Board Artist
Peter McConnell, Composer and Sound Designer
Garry Gaber, 3-D Artist
Amos Glick, Motion Capture Actor
Paul Zinnes, 3-D Artist
Eric Ingerson, 3-D Animator
Larry the O, Sound Designer
Darren Johnson, Lead Tester

Card Series, Topps Trading Cards

Greg and Tim Hildebrandt, Artists
Ira Friedman, Publisher
Bob Woods, Project Editor
Stacy Mollema, Lucasfilm, Project Coordinator

Soundtrack, Varese Sarabande Records

Joel McNeely, Composer and Conductor

The Royal Scottish National Orchestra and Choir, Performing Orchestra

Robert Townson, Conception and Production

Sue Rostoni, Lucasfilm, Editor

AUTHOR'S BIOGRAPHY

Mark Cotta Vaz, a senior writer for *Cinefex* ("the journal of cinematic illusions"), has written four previous books: *Spirit in the Land: Beyond Time and Space with America's Channelers* (Signet/NAL: New York, 1988), *Tales of the Dark Knight: Batman's First Fifty Years* (Ballantine Books: New York, 1989), *From* Star Wars *to* Indiana Jones: *The Best of the Lucasfilm Archives* (with Shinji Hata, Chronicle Books: San Francisco, 1994), and *Industrial Light & Magic: Into the Digital Realm* (Ballantine Books: New York, 1996). His interest in popular culture has led to a term on the board of directors of the Cartoon Art Museum in San Francisco, for which he curated several exhibits, notably the 1992 show "Visions of the Floating World," one of the most comprehensive exhibits ever of original Japanese comics art. Vaz was born and still lives in the San Francisco Bay area.